Wet

Wet

Joylynn M. Jossel

Urban Books
www.urbanbooks.net

This is a work of fiction. Any references or similarities to actual events, real people, living or dead, or to real locales are intended to give the novel a sense of reality. Any similarity in other names, characters, places, and incidents is entirely coincidental.

URBAN SOUL is published by

Urban Books
10 Brennan Place
Deer Park, NY 11729

ISBN-13: 978-1-59983-014-8
ISBN-10: 1-59983-014-0

First Printing: April 2007

10 9 8 7 6 5 4 3 2

Printed in the United States of America

This book is dedicated to my husband,
Nick "Bang" Ross:
You were my sole—my solitary—inspiration
for this book on those scenes
where I needed a little inspiration ;-)

Thicker Than Water

*Is the blood between two brothers
thicker than the love for a woman?*

Prologue

What's Done Is Done
(The Affair)

"I can't believe I just fucked another man's wife," Wade said to himself as he showered, using his hands to rub the soap against his firm, dark brown physique. He thought that if he scrubbed hard enough, he could wash away the sin he had just committed. Wade ran his hands over his bald head and down his face, then buried his face into his hands. He shook his head and let out a deep sigh. He put his head directly under the water and allowed it to slap down on his clean, shaved face. He deserved to be slapped for what he had just done.

Just then, Dinah entered the bathroom, still naked from the passionate love she and Wade had just made—in her husband's bed no less. Wade bit down on his thick bottom lip, damn near drawing blood, as his dick stiffened at the sight of Dinah's sexy silhouette. He wiped away the steam from the glass shower door to get a clear look at each and every curve of her voluptuous body.

"Might I join you, love?" Dinah said in a faint whisper, moistening her thin, puckering lips with her tongue.

Wade stared in awe at her five-foot-seven-inch frame. It housed all one hundred fifty-five pounds of her thick, but solid, womanly body. Looking at Dinah for the hundredth time still felt like the first time for Wade. Her coal-black shoulder-length mane was in disarray, but in a sexy way, a way that reminded Wade of how they had just gotten buck wild. He quivered as his dick tingled. Dinah's D-cup breasts hosted a pair of chocolate nipples that seemed to stare back at Wade. He imagined them glistening with sudsy water and began to stroke his throbbing manhood at just the mere thought. He had never seen Dinah's breasts drenching wet before. He had seen them damp from the sweat their two bodies had created by smacking up against each other, but he had never seen them glistening with trickles of water dripping off them.

In fact, this was only Wade's second time he'd ever seen Dinah's breasts at all. Although he had known her for over sixteen years, he had been with her intimately only once before, but that was before she had gotten married.

Dinah stood before Wade like a well-poised dime piece. Her pussy was well trimmed as a result of the regular monthly waxing she received from Sasha at the Charles Penzone Grand Salon. It was a perfectly shaped Bermuda triangle. Her confidence, which was sometimes mistaken as conceit, was the sexiest part about her. She was happy in her skin. Dinah didn't act silly and shy about her body or try to hide the extra thickness around her thighs and midsection. She wasn't fat, just bigger than most women preferred to be. While other women were starving themselves on liquid diets or stuffing themselves on the Atkins diet, trying to become size sixes and eights, Dinah maintained her size-twelve figure most of the time. During the summer bunny months of June, July, and August, she was sure to be a firm size ten, but as for the remaining months of the year, she was a comfortable and attractive size twelve and proud of it. And around November and December, when she had indulged in one dessert too many during the holidays, there was no shame in her game when she had to frequent Lane Bryant a couple times for those size fourteens.

"Well?" Dinah said, walking right up to the shower door, her bare feet softly padding against the gray marble floor. She took her finger and traced a water droplet down the shower door, looking into Wade's dark brown eyes the entire time.

How the fuck did it come to this? Wade thought as he looked back into Dinah's slanted eyes—eyes that made most people think she had Asian blood somewhere in her bloodline. *She's my best friend. She's my married best friend.*

Staring into Dinah's eyes, hearing them beg for entrance into the shower with him, Wade pushed the shower door open for her to accompany him.

"I take that as a yes." Dinah smiled.

How much worse could things get anyway? Wade thought as he watched Dinah step partway into the shower to test the water temperature. She lifted her left leg and stuck it under the spray before succumbing her entire body to the water. With all of the steam filling the bathroom, she figured the water must be pretty hot. She fluttered her toes, of which the nails were painted in a fiery red, a polish

Wade had had the pleasure of applying earlier, right after he had tongued them down.

Watching Dinah's movements actually made Wade precum. The shit seemed to be happening in slow motion in Wade's mind. *Fuck it! It can't get any worse,* he told himself again. *What's done is done.* His eyes burned through Dinah's thick flesh.

"Umm, perfect," she said, referring to the temperature of the water. She was now all the way inside the shower and stood directly under the stream of water, allowing it to run down the front of her body. Wade closed the shower door behind her.

Not wasting any time, Wade stepped behind Dinah, pulled her against him, and entered her from the back. He was rock hard and there was no need to play around, besides, her husband would be home soon. The thought of him walking through the door and catching him cumming inside his wife only intensified the moment for Wade. Pumping in and out of Dinah, he pulled her head back and began sucking her neck. With his eyes wide open, he looked down and watched her titties bounce to each of his thrusts.

Still inside Dinah's warmth, Wade reached up and adjusted the showerhead so that the water pounded down onto her juicy breasts. Wade imagined that the water running down and between them was his cum. He pumped harder as her wet, glossy titties mesmerized him. Wade was definitely a breast man. He wanted to just bite down on them, and that is exactly what he did.

Wade pulled himself out of Dinah and quickly turned her around. He began nursing on her breasts, going from one breast to the other.

"Wade," she moaned. "But it felt so good. I want you back inside of me."

"Now it's going to feel even better," he promised as he took one hand and lifted her leg, and then took the other and placed himself inside her. He began to thrust deep, but slowly, in and out. He cupped her breasts in his other hand and began to bite down softly on her nipples. He then sucked them hard, and the harder he sucked, the harder he fucked. He had her rammed up against the shower wall, fucking her hard. Fast and hard. Faster and harder.

"Slow down before you cum," Dinah said. "I want you to cum in my mouth, not my pussy."

"I won't cum yet," Wade promised. "It feels too good up in here to end it right now."

"Okay, baby." Dinah threw her head back and took every inch of him inside of her. She closed her eyes and let Wade do the damn thing, pushing every button, slamming against her walls. *My husband never fucked me like this*, Dinah thought. "He never made me feel this good . . . ever!"

"Huh?" Wade asked.

For a minute Dinah thought that she might have spoken everything she was thinking. But, fortunately, it was just that last part she had allowed her subconscious to voice out loud.

"I said just fuck me, Wade," Dinah said, her voice filled with ecstasy. "You can cum if you want to, all you want to, and where you want to. Just don't stop making me feel good. I've never felt this good before. I swear."

Wade's head was getting bigger by the minute— both heads. Dinah's sexy commands only aroused him more. His dick throbbed with sensation, and his head throbbed with the fact that he was giving it to Dinah just right. He had never even fucked Slim this good before. He hadn't remembered receiving this much excitement and pleasure during the lovemaking between him and Slim. It wasn't because Slim was his on-again, off-again girlfriend, and sometimes fiancée, of eight years and that he had gotten tired of fucking her. It was because Slim never told him how good he was making her feel. Dinah stroked his ego as if it were a soft six-week-old puppy.

When they first started having intercourse, the sex between Slim and Wade was out of this world. The fact that Wade was Slim's first made it just that much better. Maybe things had simmered down because Slim hadn't had much experience and never took the initiative to experiment. She was still a good regular lay, though. If only she knew just how much of a big part sound effects play in lovemaking. That would have made it all the mo' better. Slim moaned and groaned during sex, which turned Wade on. He had made her toes curl on many occasions, generating a few oohs and ahhs, but she wasn't nearly as talkative as Dinah. Wade liked for a woman to talk dirty, to at least assure him that he was hittin' it right. Dinah was an ego booster for sure.

"Oh shit, Dinah." Wade groaned as she tightened herself up around his muscle, grooving to her own melody up and down his dick.

He placed his hands on Dinah's ass and lifted her into the air. Wrapping her legs around his waist, Dinah continued sliding her pussy up and down him.

"I love you, Wade," Dinah said as she stared into his eyes and began to kiss him on the mouth. She had never kissed him on the mouth before, not like this—not this passionately. It was almost as if a kiss this passionate only confirmed their indiscretion; sealed it with a kiss, so to speak. Wade sucked on her tongue, giving her some tongue love right back. "I really do love you," she reiterated, just in case he hadn't believed her the first time, or heard her over his moans of ecstasy.

Of course she loved him. They had been confidants since the tenth grade. He loved her too. But at this moment, their love was something much more than it had ever been before. It was something much more than they had ever imagined it being.

"I love you, too, Dinah," Wade said, looking into her eyes and slowing his tempo. "I want to be with you forever. Damn, why can't I be with you forever?"

Dinah closed her eyes and sighed with a faint smile. How was it that another man, a man other than her husband, was making her feel this way? So good? Like she was the only woman in the world worthy of being loved? Why hadn't she just gotten together with him when she had the chance? How did things turn out the way they did? He was the man she should be married to.

Dinah could feel her body starting to slip from Wade's grip as she weakened and lost herself in thought.

"Hold on to me, baby," Dinah said. "Don't let me go." She tightened her closed eyelids and held on to Wade like it was a matter of life and death. "Please don't let me go."

"I'll never let you go," Wade responded. "Never." Staring down at the base of her neck, unable to determine whether the moistness that covered her body was from the water or the sweat they had worked up in the steam, Wade began giving it to Dinah as if this was the last nut he'd ever crack.

Dinah began to moan as Wade thrust himself as deep as he could possibly go inside of her. The quick, deep strokes penetrating Dinah simply blew her mind.

"Oh, baby!" Dinah yelled. "That's right, baby. That's the spot. Um-hmm, right there. Oh, Wade. Oh shit, Wade. Yeah. Yeah. Fuck me, damn you! Fuck me!"

Wade knew Dinah was cumming. He could feel her pussy muscles gripping his dick. He could feel her fingers pressing into his back like she just wanted to rip away his skin. He stood still, allowing her to ride his dick until she had been pleased. Until her limp body trembled.

"Put it in your mouth," Wade said, pulling out of her after her trembling ceased.

Without an ounce of hesitation, Dinah fell to her knees and wrapped her lips around his thick, manly muscle. Tasting herself turned her on as she performed oral sex on Wade. She didn't care about the water ruining her fresh perm. All she cared about was making Wade feel as good as he had made her feel.

"Oh, Dinah. That feels so good," Wade said, grabbing hold of her wet hair. He clenched her hair tightly between his fingers and started pumping her head up and down on his dick, slowly milking the cow.

As Dinah devoured Wade, she began to massage his balls. This drove him crazy, and he started to get weak in the knees. Wade placed his hands on each side of the shower wall to balance his weight. He then closed his eyes and was in heaven as Dinah sucked his dick like no other woman could have, like no other woman ever had.

"I'm about to cum," Wade moaned. "Oh shit, baby, I'm about to cum."

Just then, Wade erupted into Dinah's mouth. She swallowed what she could but let the overflow run down her chin. She grabbed hold of his dick and jacked it off all over her neck and breasts. Talk about wearing a pearl necklace proudly. She then began using her hands to rub it in.

"Goddamn!" Wade said as he watched her.

Wade pulled Dinah up by her hands and aided the water in cleansing away his cream. He then grabbed the soap and created a lather as he began to wash Dinah's body with his hands. Silently, she allowed him to cleanse her. Once he had rinsed all the soap from her body, he took Dinah's face into his hands and spoke softly and sincerely.

"You know we can't ever do this again, don't you?" Wade asked.

Dinah knew those words were coming, but she hadn't really had time to get ready for them. With no response prepared, she looked down as her eyes began to water.

"Don't cry, baby," Wade said, pulling her against his chest.

"But I love you," Dinah managed to say through a cracking voice. "I want to be with you again and again and again, Wade. It's always been you. I've tried to hide it by marrying a man who I wish was you. But I can't do it anymore. I can't wear this mask any longer. It's time that we are true to ourselves."

"I know," Wade whispered. "But we can't," he protested. "Things are too complex now. It's too late, Dinah. You are not mine. You belong to another

man. You belong to him." Wade lifted Dinah's face
to his own. They stared into each other's eyes as he
continued. "You are another man's wife—and not
just any man. You're my brother's wife."

Chapter I

"You Say She's Just a Friend"
(a couple years prior to the affair)

Slim sat at the bar, watching the action going on at the pool table behind her through the oblong mirror that was lined with liquor bottles. A couple of Wade's buddies—Cory, who was a taxicab driver, and Mike, who was an old college buddy—and Wade's identical twin brother, Tye, lingered around, downing beers and heckling as Wade and Dinah played each other in a game of pool. This was the Friday night norm for this clan of high school and college friends. Watching her man laugh, drink, and play games with another chick was really starting to take its toll on Slim. Every time she thought that she had accepted and could deal with the fact that her boyfriend's best buddy was a woman, the next life of the catty bitch deep down inside her surfaced.

How Slim could let any woman intimidate her was incomprehensible. She had to know that when

God handed out beauty and class, he gave her seconds. Take Halle Berry, Gabrielle Union, and Beyoncé and then combine them into one woman, and that woman still wouldn't have anything on Slim.

Given the nickname Slim in high school because of her very thin frame, Zoey Cambridge was a five-foot-three-inch head turner with big brown saucer eyes that glistened. Her set of perfectly thick and long black eyelashes couldn't be patented to be sold in drug store cosmetics departments. They were one of a kind. Women even eyed her down, wishing they had even a mustard seed of her beauty. More so than her pretty face, it was the way Slim carried herself that made her so beautiful. She never wore clothes that were too revealing, but she didn't dress like a nun either. Slim's Donna Karan, Ralph Lauren, and Liz Claiborne wardrobe complemented her elegant style. Although she was a solid size six, she always bought size eights just to make sure that her clothing wasn't tight-fitting.

Noticing his woman sitting at the bar with her back to him, drinking her third wine spritzer, Wade thought it might be a good idea to let Slim know he hadn't forgotten about her. Well, actually, he had forgotten, but he didn't want her to know that. He wasn't used to her popping up and joining them at their Friday after-work happy-hour ritual. He had been doing this for years now with his buddies, but for the past couple of months or so, Slim had started showing up. Her mother must have been giving her the "how to keep the fun in a relationship by doing some of the things your man likes to do" talk, also known as "the compromise" talk. It was either that or her best friend, Broy's, "don't let no other bitch be around your man like that" talk.

In all actuality, Slim decided to start showing up only when she thought her women's intuition was trying to tell her something. She was certain that if Wade and Dinah hadn't already fucked before, they were gonna. So she was bound and determined to be on the scene as much as possible to cock-block, and popping up unannounced was only one way of doing it.

Wade had never invited her to his little Friday night happy-hour get-togethers, not once. After all, he knew that a smoke-filled neighborhood hole-in-the-wall wasn't really the type of atmosphere Slim enjoyed. She preferred a more upscale downtown-Columbus restaurant/bar, like the Brown Stone. She wasn't bourgeois, nor did she prefer to be around bourgeois people; she just enjoyed a guaranteed nice adult crowd minus even the slightest hint of drama.

"Hey, Slim," Wade shouted to her over Usher's song "Confessions." "You sure you don't want to play next?"

Slim glared at Wade through the mirror with her burning brown eyes. She swept her bangs to the side, even though they settled right back into place. She had had bangs for only a week. She hadn't gotten used to them yet. For years she had worn her shoulder-length hair straight with a part down the middle. But Broy, a gay guy she had worked with for the past five years, told her that she was long overdue for a hairstyle change. Thinking that perhaps a change in her appearance would add even more spice to her and Wade's relationship, and perhaps keep his mind off Dinah, Slim had her stylist not only give her bangs, but also dye her hair dark brown with light shades of honey. Broy had once suggested to her that her straight black hair was not becoming to her fair skin. He teased her by telling her she looked like the mother from *The Munsters*.

At first, contemplating whether or not to acknowledge Wade's query, Slim slowly turned her petite frame around on the barstool. What came out of her mouth surprised Wade, as well as herself and everyone else in the room who knew her to be a soft-spoken debutante.

"You know gotdamn well I can't shoot no gotdamn pool," Slim snapped. Obviously she had downed one too many drinks and was starting to let the alcohol speak for her.

Everyone just looked at Wade, who was covered from head to toe in a slimy sheet of embarrassment. Just then, Tye walked up to the bar and stood next to Slim, then shouted to his brother, "I told you, man, about fuckin' with these high-yellow chicks. They evil. Got split personalities and will change on your ass in a matter of minutes, just like pit bulls and shit, man." The cackling from the clan could be heard over Usher's voice.

Slim looked at Tye, who was the spitting image of her boyfriend, the man she deemed the most handsome man in all of Columbus, Ohio, but saw nothing but ugly in Tye every time he opened his ghetto mouth.

"Fuck you, Tye," Slim said between her teeth. Her slick tongue was on a roll now. She might as well go all out. It wasn't often she could let loose with her vocabulary and blame it all on the alcohol.

"Fuck me?" Tye said, looking around to make

sure Slim was actually talking to him. "Fuck me? Baby girl, I'd have to charge you." Tye winked at her, then proceeded to order a drink from the bartender.

"Well, you can file that under NEVER," Slim spat in a slur.

Tye just shook his head and laughed as he waited on his drink and then made his way back over to the pool area. He loved messing with Slim, always trying to push her buttons, not because he disliked her, but because it was fun teasing his brother's girlfriend. Besides, he loved the side of Slim that he knew existed deep down inside of what he considered to be her stuck-up ass. The normal quiet side of her bored the shit out of him. He always saw it as a challenge to bring out the bad in a good girl. Plus, from his past experience with women, the good girls were always wishing for that bad boy to bring out the bad in them, and he had had the pleasure of making quite a few good girls' wishes come true.

Dinah, on the other hand, had always tried to cater to Slim's feelings, at least in the beginning. Even though she knew that her and Wade's relationship was strictly platonic, Dinah knew that it must have been hard for Slim to get used to and accept the idea. It would probably be hard for any woman to completely grasp and be 100 percent comfortable with it. But she knew that it was difficult for Slim. Wade had shared with Dinah the numerous arguments and conversations that he and Slim had had over his close relationship with her.

Finally, Dinah realized that no matter how much she accommodated Slim, Slim was bound and determined not to fully accept her as Wade's friend and nothing more. That's when she decided that—behind Wade's back, of course—she'd have a little fun with Slim by tapping on her eggshell skin every now and then, taunting her about her and Wade's friendship, doing and saying little things that she knew would aggravate Slim. But considering that Wade hadn't as much as gone over to Slim and asked her if she wanted a drink for the past two hours, Dinah gave Wade "the look." It was the look that said, "Enough pool playing with me—go over there and check on your girl."

"She'll be all right," Wade replied to Dinah's unspoken comment as he continued to shoot pool.

Slim whisked back around on her barstool, and once again watched Wade through the mirror and sighed. She had told herself that just as soon as she found the time, she was going to pay someone to teach her how to play pool. She had been saying that for years, though. Too bad she never actually got around to doing it. She would have loved to have gone over there and just regulated that pool table, even whipping Dinah's ass in a game or two. She sucked down the last of her wine spritzer, then sat her glass down on the bar.

"You fine?" the bartender asked.

"No," Slim answered. "I'll take another drink."

"One more wine spritzer coming up."

"No. I think this night calls for a shot of tequila."

"You got it," the bartender said, picking up her glass and walking away.

Slim looked into the mirror and glared at Wade and Dinah, who appeared to be totally enjoying their game of pool. "Make that a double," she yelled to the bartender.

Wade and Dinah were the absolute epitome of the

perfect friendship. It was like he was Jack Tripper and she was Janet. Looking at the two of them now, no one could have ever imagined that they would ever end up involved in the twisted relationship they would soon find themselves in.

"Are you going to be okay in there?" Wade asked Slim through the master suite's bathroom door in her roomy free-standing condo.

She didn't respond to his question, but the sound of her hurling into the toilet was answer enough. It was that double shot of tequila that put her stomach over the edge, leading her to pray to the porcelain goddess. Wade knocked on the door a couple more times, with no response from Slim; then he walked over and sat down on her queen-sized bed.

Finally, the toilet flushed and Slim walked over to the sink and brushed her teeth. A few minutes later she exited the bathroom, looking as pale as a ghost.

"Come lie down, baby," Wade said, getting off the bed and rushing to her aid.

He walked her over to the canopy bed, which was draped in a dark navy blue material intertwined with light blue sheer pieces. Pulling down the satin blue-and-silver comforter and the matching sheets, Wade tucked Slim comfortably into her bed. "You really slammed 'em down tonight, huh?" he stated.

With a look of shame on her face, Slim nodded in agreement. How could she have drunk herself sick? Not even in college had she ever needed a designated driver. Hell, she had always been the designated driver. Lucky for her, though, Wade was there to see to it that she got home.

"Now just get some rest and you'll feel a lot better

in the morning," Wade said, rubbing her forehead, then planting an almost fatherly kiss on her head. "Do you need anything before I go?"

"Before you go?" Slim questioned with a confused look on her face. "Where are you going? Aren't you going to stay here with me tonight?"

"Honey, I can't. Dinah's waiting outside for me. I brought you home in your car and she followed me so that she could take me back to the bar to get mine."

"That's stupid," Slim said, rising up in the bed as if she was experiencing an amazingly quick recovery. "Why didn't you just drive me home in your car anyway? Then you could have just stayed here, spent the night with me, taken care of me, then taken me to pick up my car in the morning, once I felt better."

Wade shrugged his shoulders. "I didn't think of all that. I was just so worried about you. I mean, when you stood up from that barstool and puked right there all over your new designer shoes, I just wanted to get you home safe and sound. Dinah just offered to help and I accepted. It made sense then. I guess it doesn't matter now."

"It does matter!" Slim snapped, her anger partly from hearing the replay of the humiliating night's events. "Because now here I am, sick as a dog, can't even move or get out of bed, and where is my man? Is he here with me? No, he's off with some woman."

"Here we go again," Wade said with a deep sigh.

"What do you mean, here we go again? I'm sorry, Wade, am I tiring you? Are my feelings a burden?"

"Oh, Slim, honey. I'm not off with some woman. It's Dinah," Wade said with a chuckle. "I love you, babe. You know that. We've been together for umpteen years, and Dinah has always been my friend, even before I met you."

"Is telling me that Dinah has been a part of your life longer than me supposed to make me feel better? Because believe me, Wade, when I tell you that it's not!" Wade began laughing. "Oh, and now this is funny to you too? Oh, I get it." Slim flopped straight back onto the pillows and pulled the covers up to her neck. "I'm just a joke to you now, huh?"

"You're not a joke, Slimee Slim," Wade said, his chuckle fading. "It's just that you sound like one of those girls in the movie *White Chicks* when you get all mad and jealous."

Slim thought about how she had sounded while on her tangent. "I guess I do, don't I?" she said as she, too, began to slightly chuckle.

"Yes, you do," Wade replied, nodding his head. "I'm gonna have a BF," he said, mocking the movie.

"A bitch fit," Slim played along as the two began laughing. "I can't help it," she coughed, grabbing her stomach. "I'm just so frickin' pissed," she said, once again imitating one of the characters in the movie.

Wade began to laugh hard at that point because Slim really did sound just like a white chick. Slim picked up a pillow and threw it at him. He caught it and threw it right back at her. Wade then walked over and sat down next to her on the bed.

In a serious tone, Wade asked sincerely, "Have I ever given you a reason to be 'so frickin' pissed' when it comes to Dinah?" Slim shook her head in the negative. "Have I ever given you a reason when it comes to any woman?" Slim shook her head. "Even when we had our breakups and weren't to-gether, did you ever hear of me getting with any other woman?" Again she shook her head. "Then why is it that you can't see that you are the only woman for me, Slim? The rest of the world sees it. Why can't you? I'll never do anything to jeopardize this right here." Wade pointed to his chest and then to Slim's. "And don't forget that, you hear?" Slim stayed silent. "You hear?"

"I hear," Slim said, smiling, feeling much better about the situation now.

"Now, do you need anything before I go?" Wade asked again as he rose off the bed.

"No, I'll be fine," she assured him.

"Call me if you need me." Wade picked up her hand, kissed it, and then let it go softly.

"Can't you come back after you get your car?" Slim whined. "But then again, your car is on the other side of town where you live, and I know you probably don't feel like driving all the way back over here, do you?"

"But I will if you really want me to," Wade said, hoping deep down inside that she really didn't want him to.

"No, you go ahead and get yourself some rest too. I'll be all right."

"Okay, sweetie. Love ya," Wade said as he headed out of the bedroom.

"Call me in the morning," Slim shouted as Wade vanished out of her sight.

Wade exited Slim's condo, locking up behind him with his key to her place. He walked out to Dinah's black convertible Sebring, where she had been waiting with the car running.

"Sorry it took so long," Wade said, getting in on the passenger side.

"Don't worry about it," she said, waving her hand. "Is your girl straight?"

"Yeah, she's good."

"Alrighty, then. You ready to head back to the bar so I can whip yo' ass in another game of pool?"

"Let's do it," Wade said, hitting the dashboard and then pointing. "Only I'll be doing the ass whipping."

Dinah put the pedal to the metal, and the two headed to join the rest of the crew that was still hanging out at the bar, waiting on them to return . . . minus Slim.

Chapter II

Brotherly Love

Wade, Dinah, Tye, Cory, and Mike sat in a crowded sports bar shooting the breeze and downing pitchers of beer. They had all just finished a strenuous workout at California Fitness, as they often did once or twice a week. Mike was the more serious exercise fanatic, and it showed in his muscle-bound build. He was actually the one who had convinced the others to join the gym, none of them getting nearly as much of their monthly fee's worth as Mike, who went to the gym five days a week—with or without them. But when they did all go, they got their money's worth for that day anyway, doing numerous sets on the weight machines as well as free weights, and several miles on the treadmill. Dinah kept up with the guys as if she were one of them.

"Yo, bartender," Tye called out, running his hand

over his bald head, "can you get me and my dudes
here another pitcher of MGD, please?"

"Dudes plus lady," Dinah corrected him.

"Oh, girl, no offense. You know you just one of
the dudes." Wade grabbed Dinah in a headlock and
proceeded to give her a knuckle sandwich. Actually
all of them considered her to be just one of the
guys.

"Boy, get off of me," Dinah said, pushing him
away. Tye then turned his attention to Wade.

"Yo, bruh, where's Shelby?" Tye joked in reference to Slim. After seeing the movie *The Best Man*,
it had been an inside joke amongst the friends that
the character Shelby in the movie reminded them
of Slim.

"She's in her cousin's wedding, so her and Broy
are out looking for a dress, shoes, or something. I
don't know, man," Wade answered, finishing off the
last swallow of beer from his mug.

"See, that right there. I don't get it," Tye said,
lighting a cigarette. Smoking wasn't a huge habit
for him. He only smoked when he was in a bar
drinking a beer; even then, he'd have to borrow a
drag from someone. Fortunately for Tye—but unfortunately for the rest of the gang—earlier that
night the bartender had slipped him a cigarette.

"Aw, come on, man," Cory complained. "Don't
nobody wanna smell that shit. Kill yourself but
don't take us with you." He began to shoo away the
smoke from Tye's cigarette.

Wade gave Tye an evil look. Tye had been promising Wade for some time now that he would give
up smoking. Losing their father to a stroke when
they were only ten years old and then losing their
mother to diabetes the year after they graduated

college, all they had now was each other. Wade often had nightmares that he would lose his brother next. He worried that Tye would give himself lung cancer and die. He had begged him to give up smoking; he'd even stolen his packs of cigarettes on occasion, which was another reason why Tye didn't buy them.

"Next week, man, I promise," Tye said, replying to his twin brother's evil glare. "I can stop if I want to. I don't do it all the time."

"There is no certain amount that you can die from," Wade argued.

"Next week, man," Tye said, taking a puff. "Next week."

"Yeah, you said that last week," Wade snapped. He poured himself a glass of beer from the pitcher the waiter had just set down on the table.

"Anyway, like I was saying," Tye said, taking the conversation back to Slim, "I don't understand how it is that she goes and kicks it with Broy, who just happens to be a man, but yet she gets all bent out of shape when you wanna hang with your partner, who's a girl."

"Yeah, but the dude is gay," Wade said in Slim's defense.

"So you mean to tell me that if Dinah was a lesbian, she'd be cool?"

Wade shrugged his shoulders. "Man, I don't know. It don't even matter. Dinah's my peoples, regardless, and Slim is my woman. That ain't gon' change, so she'll just have to deal with it."

Dinah smiled. It was always comforting to know that everything about her friendship with Wade was two-sided. She knew that some of Wade's and Slim's breakups were because of her; it made her feel bad, but at the same time it made her admire their friendship even more. Wade always tried to convince Slim that he wasn't choosing Dinah's friendship over their relationship, that he was just choosing not to have to deal with the distrust and nagging and that if their relationship was going to be based on such, then he'd rather be by himself. Dinah knew that even if Wade and Slim were to ever break up permanently, the same dilemma would exist with the next broad. But she didn't worry because she knew that she and Wade had been friends for so long and had shared so much that there wasn't a person in the world Wade would choose over her; that was with the exception of his brother.

Although Wade had been born only five minutes before Tye, one would think that Wade had been born five years before Tye. The twins were identical, down to the birth marks that rested between the small of their backs and the cracks of their asses. But one evening, while scrubbing them down during a bath, their mother had discovered that Wade's mark dented in slightly at the top to take on the shape of a heart, while Tye's was simply oval-shaped. Even though the two brothers were identical in their features, in personality and character it was evident that Wade and Tye were different individuals.

Sophisticated, chic, and clean-cut, Wade had always been the overachiever. In school, he had not only aced his own exams, but on occasion he had also even aced a few of Tye's after playing the ole switcheroo on a teacher or two. Up until the boys were in the eighth grade, their mother had forced them to dress alike. She thought it was "sooo cute." But in high school, Tye flat out refused to run

around with Wade while looking like a pack of
Twinkies. Besides, wearing different clothing would
be the only way people could tell them apart, once
they figured out who was wearing what for the day. It
had always been impossible to tell them apart; they
had even fooled their mother a time or two, but just
as soon as one of them opened his mouth, the mystery of who was who was immediately solved.

Tye, the smooth operator, playa-playa, was the
loud and outgoing one. He had been secretly slated
as the "asshole" twin. Wade was a much nicer and
more caring person than Tye, yet Tye's gregarious
spirit is what attracted people to him. While they
were growing up, people never saw one without the
other. Wade had friends because Tye had friends.
Wade never made it a point to go out and meet new
people, so each of their friends had started out as
Tye's friend first. But to befriend one, you had to
befriend the other because the twins were one in
the same.

They had attended Ohio State University together
and shared a dorm. After graduation, they moved
into a luxury apartment together at the complex
where Tye was the manager, which is where he currently worked and where the two brothers still
resided. Because of his people skills, whenever Tye
hosted the annual tenant-appreciation BBQ/swim
party, it was like Mardi Gras—exciting, fun, and
sexy. Sexy because Tye made it a point to personally
invite all of the single female tenants, who in turn
came dressed like they were trying to make the
cover of the *Sports Illustrated* swimsuit issue.

Wade was soft spoken and kept to himself, never
taking the initiative to introduce himself to people or
mingle and associate with them. If Dinah hadn't liter-

ally run into him one day in the school hallway when she was running to class, breaking his nose—with blood squirting everywhere, including on her— the two of them might not have ever become friends. But she felt so bad about his injury, all due to her, that she made it a point to find out where he lived and go check on him every day after school. Once he was able to return to school, they ended up having lunch together every day and attending the school football games that Tye played in as the running back, just like they had been friends for their entire lives. The type of relationship the two had was clear, and they were never mistaken as a couple. Even people who didn't know them would ask them if they were sister and brother. She and Wade were inseparable, joking that it was due to the blood splatter from Wade's busted nose, and called themselves blood brother and sister. So of course, Dinah became like their third twin but was never as close a friend with Tye as she was with Wade. Tye simply came along with the package. But still, if she was at lunch with Wade, then Tye was definitely sitting at the table, and if she was at a basketball game with Wade, then you'd best believe Tye was sitting on the other side of Wade, cheering on the team along with them.

Being an only child, Dinah felt Wade and Tye were like the brothers she never had. Because of their strong unity and bond, which she deeply admired, she felt honored that they even allowed her to play a role in their lives. By the time Dinah had met the twins, their father had already passed, but their mother was still living.

"You know Samuel and I were best friends for ten years before we ever started seeing each other as a couple," Mrs. Preston would tell Wade and Dinah, who would look at each other and giggle. They knew all too well where the conversation was heading. "We went to the prom together, but each with our own dates."

"Oh, don't get up, Mama," Wade would say to her as she gripped the arms of the floral-patterned chair she always sat in in an attempt to push herself up. "I'll get it." Wade would look at Dinah and wink as he'd head over to the basket in front of the fireplace that held the family photo albums.

"The red one with the pink hearts on it, son," Mrs. Preston would say to Wade.

"I know, Mama. I've got it." He knew very well which photo album he needed to retrieve. It was the one his mother referred to every time she had to convince him that he needed to prepare himself for the shift in his and Dinah's relationship that would occur someday. "Here you go." Wade handed his mother the photo album.

As she would flip through it to find the exact page she was looking for, Wade would always look over at Dinah and roll his eyes up in his head.

"Something in your eye, son?" Mrs. Preston would say without even looking up from the photo album. "Need me to blow it out for you?"

"No, Mama, I'm okay," Wade would say, looking over at Dinah with a perplexed look on his face, never able to figure out just how his mother knew of the facial expressions he was shooting at Dinah without her looking up.

"I don't know," Dinah would say while shrugging her shoulders.

"See, right there," Mrs. Preston would point to the page in the photo album before turning it around toward Wade and Dinah. "There's our prom pictures. See, two separate dates we had."

Both Wade and Dinah would stare at the pictures like they hadn't seen them a hundred times already, but Wade loved seeing just how sharp his pops looked in his all-white tux with a pink cummerbund and bow tie to match his date's pink dress. And he loved seeing his mother in what had to be the most beautiful picture she had ever taken.

Had Mrs. Preston been alive and in her prime today, Slim would look like the ugly duckling compared to her. Her dark chocolate shoulders oozed out of her strapless, creamy, satin, off-white prom gown that she wore, with matching long gloves. Her long legs planted themselves into satin dyed pumps. The French roll she wore, with parted pieces of hair left out that were two feet down her back, wasn't due to the weave half the women who try to wear that hairstyle nowadays have to use. Mrs. Preston was the epitome of the saying "black is beautiful."

"Mrs. Preston, you're so beautiful," Dinah would always say in awe, no matter how many times she had seen that photo. "I can't believe you and Mr. Preston were only friends. How on earth did he resist you?"

"Child, everything is in God's timing, but I'm giving you two a heads-up so that you'll be prepared."

"Come on now. Mama," Wade would blush in embarrassment. "Dinah and I aren't you and Daddy. I'm sure there must have been some type of chemistry going on between you and Daddy. But trust me, Dinah and I are really just friends, Mama."

"I was friends with your father through many a girlfriend as he was my friend through many a boyfriend. You could have never told us that we would someday end up being boyfriend and girl-friend with each other, let alone married and having kids." Mrs. Preston laughed. "Oh, just wait and you'll see. I acted the same way the two of you are acting when my mama tried to tell me that no matter if your daddy and I went to the highest mountain and proclaimed our friendship that he was gon' be her son-in-law one day regardless. She said she could just look at us and tell. Well, you two got that same look."

"What look?" Wade would ask.

"That same look my mama saw in your father and me," she would answer. "That look." She'd take the photo album away from Wade and Dinah, almost out of frustration that they weren't taking her seriously. "You'll see. Mark my words. You'll see."

Tye definitely got his personality from their mother. She spoke her mind regardless of what was on it. Wade, on the other hand, figured he'd get more out of life by listening; besides, since Tye insisted on doing all the talking anyway, why not let him? Tye's gift of gab had benefited them on more than one occasion, such as the time he went from door to door pretending to be collecting for some school fund-raiser when the two really needed the money for a new game system their mother refused to buy them.

Tye worked his smooth mouthpiece while Wade stood behind him and put on the charm with his clean-cut innocent smile. After a week of hitting up the neighborhood, they had their new Nintendo game system. But once word finally got back to Mama about the scam, they found themselves doing household chores and raking leaves for every neighbor they had conned out of money; not to mention, Mrs. Preston took the game system from them and donated it to charity.

"I don't know how I let you talk me into that mess," Wade had said as he held the bag that Tye was dropping leaves into.

"Quit cryin'" was always Tye's favorite line to say to a complaining Wade. "You wasn't saying that when you was playing Space Invaders."

"I ain't never doing nothing crazy like that with you again," Wade swore, wiping the sweat from his brow.

Wade might have told himself that then, but a few weeks later the two had another game system, this time compliments of a neighborhood that Mrs. Preston would never find out they had hit up. As a matter of fact, they were so sneaky that she never even realized they had another game system, thanks to their hiding it.

When Tye told Wade that he was going to repeat the collection scam once again, Wade couldn't let his brother go off and do it on his own. That's just how the two were. If one was going to get into trouble, then so was the other. They had learned early on as children that if one got punishment because they did everything together and were so close-knit, then the other felt like he might as well be punished too. And although Wade's conscience would bother him more so than Tye's, whenever Tye had managed to convince Wade to accompany him in something simple, he'd do it all the same. It was just an unspoken love between the brothers. They'd do anything for each other . . . even die.

Chapter III

Crossing the Line

"So, you sure you don't want to join us?" Dinah asked Slim as the two stood in Wade and Tye's living room. She couldn't actually care less about Slim's joining them at the poetry reading at Salaam's, but it made for a conversation piece during an uncomfortable moment of silence as she waited for Wade to come out of his bedroom, ready to go.

"It's kind of last minute to be inviting me now, don't you think?" Slim replied sarcastically.

Dinah knew Slim was going to get fly with her. She always did whenever Wade wasn't around to witness it. Of course, if Wade knew what a bitch Slim actually was to Dinah, then her playing the role as the victim in the triangle wouldn't be as believable. But Dinah never let it get to her. She figured that two could play that game; whenever Slim fired at her, she always fired back.

"Yeah, but a little spontaneity never hurt anyone,"

Dinah taunted. "As a matter of fact," Dinah said, licking her lips as she walked in closer to Slim, "I know for a fact that your man loves a woman with a little spontaneity."

"Watch it, Dinah," Slim warned, wiping away the phony cordiality act and getting right into Dinah's face.

"Don't you think you're the one who should watch it?" Dinah asked with a smirk. "But then again, all you do is watch us. Tell me, Slim, just exactly who are you jealous of anyway? Me or Wade?"

"Fuck you, Dinah," Slim spat in a harsh whisper.

"Now, see, if Wade knew you wanted to fuck me, then I'm sure we could have worked something out. We could have cleared the air a long time ago and then we could all get along just fine."

"Although you could pass for a man, I'm sure, the fact still remains that you are a woman and I don't do chicks."

Before Dinah could retaliate, Wade came out of the bedroom of their one-floor, two-bedroom luxury apartment. A mischievous grin swept across Slim's face. She loved fucking with Dinah behind Wade's back, and he was none the wiser about her tactics. Dinah was sure, too, that her slick comebacks here and there played a huge role in Slim's jealousy, which always managed to strike up an argument between her and Wade every now and again. But Slim didn't dare inform Wade of Dinah's other side; if that was the case, she'd have to reveal her claws that she didn't mind whipping out in what she considered self-defense on occasion—Dinah had started it all by being her man's best friend in the first place.

"Wade, honey, you all set?" Slim said, snapping back into the good little girlfriend mode as she straightened his dark pink and gray tie that rested down the front of his pink shirt. It was a classy complement to his white slacks and gray leather Bill Blass shoes.

"Yep," he said, kissing Slim on the lips. Even though he was going for just a peck on the lips, Slim pulled his head close to her and slipped her tongue in his mouth. "Damn, where did that come from?"

"Ummm, I don't know," Slim said, wiping her Mary Kay almond glaze lip gloss from Wade's lips. "Someone once told me that a little spontaneity never hurt anyone."

"Well, I like where you get your advice from," Wade said as he hugged her. Dinah smiled with confidence and patted herself on the back as Slim looked over Wade's shoulder at her. Wade then turned his attention to Dinah and said, "Oh yeah, Tye and the guys are meeting us up there. They stopped over at the Lobby for a quick drink first."

"No problem," Dinah said.

"Babe, you sure you don't want to go?" Wade asked her one last time. Despite what Slim had led Dinah to believe, Wade had invited her to go out with them prior to Dinah's invitation.

"No, I already told you, since Broy helped me pick out a dress for my cousin's wedding, I have to help him pick out something for his friend's wedding." Wade and Dinah looked at each other strangely, then looked back to Slim. "Oh, God, please don't ask." She shooed with her hand and headed for the door. "Anyway, call me after the poetry reading. It's only six-thirty; maybe I can connect with you later on this evening if I'm not too beat up from casing the mall. It's Saturday, so most of the stores will stay open until ten. Hopefully we'll be finished way before then."

"Sounds good," Wade said as Slim made her way over to the door. "I'll call you later."

"Ta-ta," Slim said as she exited out the door.

Wade grabbed his keys so he could lock up. "Let me just set the alarm and we're good to go."

"You wanna just follow me since you don't know exactly where Salaam's is at?" Dinah called to Wade, who was in the kitchen setting the alarm.

"Why don't you just drive and I'll ride with you?" he said, coming out of the kitchen and leading her to the front door.

"You got the big ol' truck and don't never want to drive it," Dinah said, referring to Wade's four-year-old Escalade that he had bought for damn near the price of a sedan off of the Internet. In addition to all of his other characteristics, he was an economizer— not cheap, just careful with the hard-earned money he grossed from being one of the top independent life insurance salesmen in the region. "Besides, then I'll have to drive all the way back to your house to bring you home."

"Oh, quit cryin'," Wade said, mocking Tye's famous line. They both laughed. "Besides, Tye can bring me home since we both live here, you know."

"All right, damn, come on," Dinah said, taking her keys out of her purse. "Let's do the damn thang."

Dinah drove to the poetry spot where she and Wade met up with Tye and the boys. Cory had just received a $10,000 check from his Ohio lottery winnings and paid for everybody's food and drinks, buying round after round of shots. They found every reason in the world to toast and had never put away that much alcohol in their lives. They hung around the club until closing, letting as much liquor wear off as they possibly could.

"You cool to drive, Tye man?" Wade asked as they all headed to their cars. "I don't want you killing me in no car accident."

"Whatchoo talkin' 'bout?" Tye slurred. "I ain't driving and yo' ass wouldn't be riding with me no how." He then pointed to Dinah, unable to pronounce her name at the given moment. "You ridin' with her."

"Man, I figured I'd just ride with you," Wade said.

"I didn't drive, yo. My car is parked over Mike's, and we ain't going straight to his house. We got a couple honeys we 'bout to hook up with."

"Yeah, twins," Mike joined in, walking up to Tye and giving him a high five.

"And you know how twins get down," Tye joked.

Wade just smiled and shook his head. "Man, you crazy." He then looked over at Cory.

"Don't look at me, man," Cory said. "My woman already been blowing up my cell phone."

"Yeah," Mike jumped in, "and you know that chump don't weigh but a buck-o-five. His girl's left hand weighs that much alone, so we don't want her knocking him upside his head. We'll have to go get this cat from a domestic violence shelter for men and shit like we did the last time."

"Oh, fuck you, man," Cory shot back with an attitude. "I went to my mama's house just to let her cool off for a minute."

"Man, you mean you was hiding in your mama's basement." Mike laughed.

Everyone couldn't help but laugh because they knew that Mike was pretty much on point with his prediction. Cory was about the size of one of those crows from the movie *The Wiz* while his jealous girl-friend was the size of Big Shirley from *Martin*. Because she was so self-conscious about her weight, she never wanted to hang out with them. She sat home on pins and needles, worried that Cory was going to cheat on her while he was out. After she couldn't take the thoughts of infidelity anymore is when she'd start blowing up his cell phone.

As the laughter faded, Wade then looked over at Dinah with a look of last resort in his eyes. She quickly crossed her arms and stomped her foot.

"Come on, Wade, damn," she said, rolling her eyes and stomping over to her car.

"Thanks, sweetie," Wade teased in a cooing sound as he followed behind her.

Dinah stopped in her tracks, turned around, stuck her middle finger up, and then stomped back off to her car.

"I love you too." He smiled as they got into her car. "Anyone ever tell you that you're so cute when you're mad?" Dinah tried to stay mad and hide her smile, but it managed to creep out as she pulled off and they headed to his house.

"Will you hurry up and unlock the damn door?" Dinah said as Wade fumbled with his keys while she stood behind him doing the pee pee dance. "I gotta pee. I know I ain't gon' make it home, considering I have to drive all the way back to the other side of town."

"Oh, come on, Dionne, *that's what friends are for.*" Wade laughed at his joke, referencing the once popular song by the lovely artist Dionne Warwick.

"Who told you that when you're drunk you were funny?" she asked just as he managed to get the door unlocked.

"Uhhh . . . nobody."

"Good, because you're not." Wade opened the door and moved out of the way to let Dinah pass. "Cute," she said, stopping in front of him and looking into his drunken eyes, with her eyes only two drinks from being in that same state, "but not funny."

"Cute, huh?" Wade asked as he stood there staring back into Dinah's eyes. He rubbed her chin with his thumb.

"Yeah," she said softly, "cute." After staring at Wade for a couple more seconds, she quickly kept it movin' down the hall and into the guest bathroom that was situated across the hall from Wade's bedroom.

What the fuck just happened out there? she thought to herself as she pulled up her white flaring skirt and sat down on the toilet. It felt like a wave of electricity had volted between and through her and her friend of umpteen years. *Get it together, Dinah. You're imagining things. It was nothing.*

Dinah flushed the toilet and then washed her hands. She straightened out her crisp white button-up blouse and then stood in the mirror and took a deep breath before opening the bathroom door. When she did, Wade was standing right there to greet her . . . butt naked, dick hangin'.

"Wait! Wade, stop it," Dinah said, out of breath, placing her hands on his bare chest and pushing him off her. "This is not going down. No way."

Dinah got up from the pistachio-colored microfiber-upholstered couch, something Slim had ordered from the SOHO collection, out of a catalogue, for Wade and Tye a couple years ago for their birthdays. She picked her blouse up, slipped it on, and began buttoning it back up.

Wade sat on the couch with his elbows on his knees and buried his hands in his face. "Damn," he said with a sigh, shaking his head. "How the fuck did we let it get to this point?"

"I don't know, Wade. I don't know," Dinah said nervously. "Must be the alcohol. I don't know, but this is crazy."

Wade looked up at Dinah who was flattening out her shirt, which fell just beneath her belly button. He stared at her for a moment. Here he was, butt-ass naked with the woman who had been his best friend for as long as he could remember. This was the girl he had told all of his secrets to and never worried about her telling anyone else. He had joked with her. He had downed beers with her. He had laughed with her. He had even cried with her. Then it all came to him like a ton of bricks. She was a part of everything about him. Except for his brother, Wade had never shared so much of himself with another human being in his life, not even with Slim. He loved her. And not just because she was his friend. He loved her, tonight, because she was Dinah.

"You're right," he said, standing up and walking over to Dinah. "This is crazy." He grabbed Dinah by the face and began kissing her. "It's crazy for us to act like we ain't feelin' each other like the way we are feelin' each other now." He kissed her again. "But you're wrong about something else." Dinah looked at Wade with questions in her eyes. "It's not the alcohol." He kissed her again.

"Wade," Dinah said in between his tongue going in and out of her mouth. "Wade." He ignored her calls to him and continued kissing her. Finally, she

gave in to the brand-new feeling she had for him
and started kissing him back. "Damn you, Wade,"
Dinah cursed as she grabbed him by his bald head
and indulged in the game of suck-face. "Motherfucker, look what you're making me do." Angry at
Wade for making her feel like more than a woman
and for allowing her to make him feel like more
than a man as she felt his hardness against her,
Dinah continued to curse him while giving in to
her feelings. "You son of a bitch," she said, shoving
her tongue down his throat.

Wade began to unbutton Dinah's shirt, but when
he started having trouble with a button, he just
snatched her shirt open and yanked it off of her
and threw it onto the floor, all the while kissing her
passionately. He then unfastened her bra and
pulled away just long enough to watch her breasts
spill out. They were the most beautiful breasts he
had ever seen, perfectly round. He had never noticed what beautiful, perfect big breasts Dinah pos-
sessed. He kissed her again and then removed his
tongue from her mouth and hungrily tasted each
of her erect nipples.

"Wade," she moaned as she lifted her leg and
used her hand to press his dick against her pleasure
spot.

"Oh, Dinah. Oh, Dinah," he repeated over and
over as he felt her wetness on the tip of his dick
even through her panties. When he couldn't take it
anymore, he roughly pulled her panties down, allowing her to step out of them, then placed himself
deep inside of her.

"Ohhh, Wade," she cried out in both pain and
pleasure as he allowed himself to sit idle up inside

her, just enjoying the warmth like a baby in its mother's womb. "Wait!"

Dinah quickly pulled away from Wade, leaving him standing there with a dripping wet dick. "Protection?" she questioned.

Wade thought for a moment and then headed down the hall, disappearing into his bedroom. He returned wearing one of the dozen Magnum condoms he had bought for those occasions when Slim was on her period and they still wanted to have sex.

Right before Wade got back into position to enter Dinah again, she stopped him.

"Wade, are you sure about this?" she said, backing away from him so she could observe his body language and look him clearly in the eyes. *Damn, why had I never noticed just how many words this man's eyes spoke to me?* Dinah thought. *Or is it that they just never had anything to say until tonight?* "I mean, what about Slim?" Dinah said, giving Wade one last chance to put his dick back into his pants and walk away.

Wade dropped his head and sighed. Slim had been the last thing on his mind. Matter of fact, it wasn't until Dinah had spoken her name that he remembered his girlfriend. After thinking about all the years Slim had been in his life, all the shit they had been through together, and all the times she had been there to support him, he looked up at Dinah and said, "I'm sure." He then walked over to Dinah and began sucking and kissing on Dinah's neck.

"But this is so crazy," Dinah said, moaning, rolling her head back.

Wade suddenly stopped and held Dinah by the

back of her head. "Then what you wanna do, girl?" he asked.

Dinah backed away from Wade, stared at him for a moment, licked her lips, and then replied, "Let's go crazy!"

She jumped up on him, wrapping her legs around him, which was only the beginning of the sextasy the two had in store for each other.

Carrying her into his bedroom, Wade pulled down the beige and cream comforter and threw Dinah down on his king-sized bed as if he was angry with her. He was angry that she hadn't allowed him to taste just how good her pussy was before tonight.

Obeying the command of Wade's eyes, Dinah bit down on her bottom lip and removed her skirt, staring into Wade's eyes the entire time. She then laid back on her elbows and slowly opened her legs, exposing her bare waxed pussy. Wade couldn't help but dive in with his tongue.

"That's right, Wade, fuck it with your tongue. Fuck it with your tongue," Dinah ordered as she rolled her hips, grinding her pussy all up against Wade's face. He looked like he was in a watermelon-eating contest the way he thrashed his face and tongue in and out of Dinah, nibbling on her clit and pressing over it with his tongue. Tears actually began to seep from Dinah's eyes. The pleasure she was receiving felt unreal.

Wade was so into the pleasure that he was giving Dinah that he began stroking himself to her moans, groans, twitches, and turns. Afraid he would bust through the condom by jacking off, he just decided to stick it inside in her and allow her walls to make him cum.

"About time," Dinah said as she felt his pole enter

her pond. She grabbed her ankles and opened wide as Wade began to thrust in and out of her so hard that his ass was tightening and denting in each time he flexed his muscles. "Wade, you feel so good. I don't ever want you to leave from up inside of me. Stay here forever," she begged as she let go of her ankles and wrapped her arms around Wade, grabbing his ass and stuffing him deeper inside of her. The two then began pounding against each other like wild animals as the bed banged and bounced.

Before Wade could cum, Dinah pushed him off of her and onto his back. "You got another one?" she asked as she gripped her hand around his dick in preparation to slide the condom off.

"Yeah." He nodded. Dinah proceeded to remove the condom and embrace him with her mouth. "Ahhh," he said, relaxing everything but his erect muscle. "Dinah, baby, shit," he said with pleasure.

"Mmm," she groaned as she took in over half of his dick down her throat without the slightest gag reflex.

"Oh damn," Wade said, amazed. One time Slim tried that and ended up puking all over his dick, but Dinah knew what she was doing.

Up and down, Dinah worked it out on Wade's dick. She had that grown man gripping his three-hundred-count beige linen sheets and whimpering like a bitch the way she was giving him head. She was juggling his balls around her mouth as easily as she gargled mouthwash, spitting them out and then taking his dick in again. Wade didn't know what to do with himself.

"Get another condom," Dinah ordered, and sat up. Upon command, Wade reached over and opened the drawer to the honey oak nightstand that was part of the four-piece set that decorated his bedroom. He pulled out another condom, opened it, then moved to put it on.

"No, I'll do it," Dinah said, taking it out of his hand with her teeth. She took her index finger and thumb and slowly ripped it open.

Slowly she put the condom on Wade's dick with her mouth. Wade sat up on his elbows, watching like it was a magic trick he was trying to figure out. The next thing he knew, Dinah was dropping it, like it was hot down on his dick, making it disappear into her deep, warm pussy. Losing all ability to control himself, he fell flat while Dinah rode his dick backward.

She leaned down and placed her hands on his knees to balance herself while her ass flopped up and down, smacking hard on the down stroke. Wade would get the energy to lift his neck and watch her ass drop, and as bad as he wanted to just grab it and squeeze it, he was in a zone. He couldn't even move his hands. He just watched as Dinah went up and down, finally turning her body around, without removing his dick, until she was facing him.

"I'm ready to cum," she said matter-of-factly, as if he had been the one holding her back.

Wade sat up and grabbed her ass, sliding her tight pussy against him. "Then let's do this shit," he said, and began stroking in and out of her. With a devilish grin on her face, she began rocking to his beat. After a few steady rocks, she grabbed his hands and placed them on her hips.

"Hold on," she warned. "I'm about to take you for a ride." And that's exactly what she did as she lost control and lost herself inside of him—him inside of her—as she wildly rolled her hips, putting her entire back into popping her pussy against Wade.

"Oh shit!" Wade cried out. "Dinah, damn. Oh shit. I'm about to cum. I'm about to cum."

"Cum, baby. Come on," Dinah whimpered on the verge of her climax. "Come on, come on." Her whimper got louder. "Come on, damn it! Oh shit, come on, damn it, I'm cumming! I'm cumming!"

It was as if someone had hit a fast-forward button as the two of them, in sync, went at it full throttle. And almost as if someone had hit the pause button, the two froze as each of their volcanoes erupted, pouring out warm lava. Trembling, they both sat upward, allowing the juices to release from their bodies. Seconds later, once the play button was hit, the two collapsed, Dinah lying on top of Wade, tears streaming from their eyes.

Neither Dinah nor Wade had ever thought of the other sexually, not even when they'd first met as tenth-graders in high school when their hormones were in full gear. Besides, the week after they'd met, Wade started seeing some little cheerleader Tye had introduced him to, and Dinah was too much of a woman to ever even consider stepping on the toes of another sistah. She knew there were plenty of fish in the sea, and she didn't want to catch something trying to catch another woman's man. But little did she know that the day would come when she would not only step on another woman's toes, but she would also stick her whole damn foot in her mouth.

Chapter IV
Runnin' Game

It had been a couple of months since that night after Salaam's when Wade and Dinah had crossed the friendship line, running at full speed. Surprisingly enough, their friendship hadn't been affected at all by that night of passionate sex. The two were able to act like their night together was nothing more than any other night they had spent together watching a game on television or something. There were no awkward moments of trying not to look each other in the eyes. There was no blushing, and no underlying fear that everyone around them would be able to sense their indiscretion. They didn't make up excuses why they couldn't be around each other. Dinah still hung out with Wade and the guys just like she always had. Nothing had changed . . . well, almost nothing.

"Where is everybody?" Dinah asked Tye as she

walked over to the bar where he was sitting, waiting for the rest of the gang to arrive.

"Cory's tied up in traffic," Tye answered, "and Mike can't make it today. He had to go out of town for a funeral. And my brother should be here any minute."

"I talked to him about an hour ago, and he said he was on his way," Dinah said.

"Yeah, but he just called my cell phone and said he had to stop over and have one of his customers sign some papers."

"Oh well, looks like it's just me and you for now," Dinah said, sitting down on the barstool next to him. "So what do you say? Buy a girl a drink, huh?"

Tye looked past Dinah as if he was looking for the girl he should buy a drink for. "Who?" he asked, as serious as having a heart attack.

"Me, stupid," she said, slugging him.

He looked her up and down, admiring her perfectly fitting turquoise slacks and the sleeveless white knit top with tiny turquoise buttons going down just the top, all five buttons undone, exposing Dinah's delicious-looking cleavage.

"Yeah, you are a girl, aren't you?" Tye said, licking his lips as he took a drink of the beer he had been sipping when Dinah arrived. "I forget sometimes." He winked.

"You forget that I'm a girl? Hmm, should I take offense?"

"Oh no, that's not what I meant." Tye was quick to save himself. "It's just that, you know, you hang with the fellas and all so much, shit, it's like you one of the fellas. You know that. I'm always joking with you, girl."

"I know, I just wanted to see how quick you could

save yourself." Dinah chuckled. "Anyway, how about that drink?"

"You got that coming," Tye said, nodding his head. "Go on and order. Get whatever you want."

The bartender came over to take Dinah's order. Tye watched her lips, painted with a shiny lip gloss, move in what seemed like slow motion as she gave her order to the bartender. Tye wanted to reach out and touch her creamy skin. Before he knew it, he had. Dinah turned and looked at him, but he was so engrossed in the softness of her skin that he had reached out and touched that he didn't care that she realized that he was touching her.

"Oh," he said, snapping out of his trance. "There was something on your cheek. I got it, though. It's gone now."

"Thank you," Dinah said, wishing the aftermath of Tye's touch would hurry up and go the fuck away.

She had been touched before, but never by Tye, and never that softly, gently, and sincerely. She had never been reached out to and touched just to be touched. It felt good. It felt different. Both of them were silent for a moment, dog-paddling in the pool of awkwardness they quickly found themselves in.

"Hey, a pool table's free," Tye said, pointing to the one that two men had just abandoned after finishing their last game. "Let's go claim it."

Tye grabbed his beer and headed over to play pool. When the bartender returned with Dinah's drink, she followed behind him. Tye sat his dink down on the round free-standing bar that stood a few feet next to the pool table he claimed by placing four quarters in the slot, and then laying eight more quarters on the rim.

"You and I are the first ones here," Dinah said, setting her drink down and then picking out a pool stick. "So we are going to be the first ones to play. The next person who shows up plays winner, just like always. You can break."

"Oh no. By all means, ladies first." Tye nodded.

Dinah could feel Tye's eyes burning a hole in her as she prepared to break the balls. A nervous chill took over her where she could hardly focus on, or even recollect, the object of the game. When she pulled the stick back and went to break, instead of blasting the center of the white ball like she usually did, she almost missed it, only nipping it on its side, damn near ripping up the felt that covered the table.

"If that's all it took to beat you in a game of pool, I would have gotten you drunk a long time ago," Tye said with a wink as he sipped his beer and then sat it back down.

"I figured you already knew that trick about women. I mean, after all, if just getting a girl drunk gets her to spend the night with you, then what made you think it wouldn't work in beating her in a lousy game of pool?"

"Oh, it ain't even like that, Ma," Tye said as he grabbed his pool stick and then got into position to take his shot. "Just like with a game of pool, it's not about how drunk you get the girl." He paused in order to take his shot, where he blasted the balls, sending three solids in. "It's all about how you hit it." He licked his lips and gazed into her eyes.

I know my pussy does not have the nerve to have tears in its eyes, Dinah thought to herself. *I'm wet.* She couldn't believe she was feeling this way about Tye for the first time ever or that Tye was making her feel this way. She stared at him, and it was like she was staring at Wade. Suddenly she didn't see him as Tye; she saw him like she had seen him for the past years, as her best friend's twin brother. *What the hell was I thinking?* she asked herself. *I won't even entertain the thought of Tye and me getting together. I mean, he's Wade's identical twin brother. How could I look at him without thinking of Wade? But then again, would that be so bad?*

"Damn traffic," Cory said as he approached the table. "I don't know why Bush keeps coming to Ohio anyway. They close down all the roads and shit on his route. Fucked up my fares and shit again."

A few minutes later, Wade approached them as well. "What's up, peoples?" he said, giving everybody a hug or some dap. "Who's up next?"

"Cory beat you here, so right after I finish your girl off, I'ma whip his ass and then I'll take care of you," Tye said as he made his next shot.

Tye stared down at the pool table with a puzzled look on his face. He then walked over to Dinah. "Dinah, you feeling okay?" Wade said as he jokingly touched her forehead. "You letting him whip you like that?"

"I'm fine," Dinah said, shooing Wade's hand off her forehead. No way did she want him detecting the little tiny beads of sweat that were dancing on her forehead from the wave of heat Tye had not too long ago flushed over her.

"Oh, she's got the fever all right." Tye smiled as he made his next shot.

Clearing her throat, Dinah said, "Well, it is kind of hot in here." She downed the last of her drink. "I'm gonna go grab me another drink. I'll just grab a pitcher for everybody."

"Hey, where you going?" Tye shouted as Dinah proceeded to walk off. "It's still your game."

Dinah turned around and checked out the table. Tye had only two more balls to pocket to her six balls. "Wade, why don't you finish the game off for me? You've got a better chance of taking the game back than I do. After all, you did teach me everything I know."

Dinah's words came out more sensual than she had wanted them to. And the timing couldn't have been more wrong because just as soon as she made the statement and turned around to head to the bar, she ran smack into Slim.

"Oh, did he?" Slim said in a tone low enough that pretty much only Dinah could hear her. "Now why doesn't that surprise me?" She sucked her teeth, rolled her eyes, and then bumped Dinah's shoulder as she walked over to greet Wade with a hug.

Dinah shook her head and smiled, brushed her shoulder off, then headed over to the bar to get the drinks. She then made her way back over to the pool table where she proceeded to have fun with Wade and the gang this night, like she had all the others. Even with the antenna of Slim's woman's intuition up and standing at attention, she didn't try to put any more space between her and Wade than usual; not even for Slim's sake.

Strangely enough, although Dinah didn't distance herself from Wade at all, for some reason, she did begin gravitating more toward Tye. And in turn, he reciprocated this newfound connection that seemed to be going on between him and Dinah. Wade hadn't really noticed, but of course Slim had, and it wasn't going to take her long at all to bring it to Wade's attention. She just had to wait for the right moment, which was a sharp left around the corner.

It was Wade's turn to host the next game night, but Slim, in order to make herself feel like she was a part of the gang, offered to have it at her place.

"I told y'all sorry-ass Dallas fans that whoever took game five was taking the championship," Tye yelled. "The Heat did the damn thing. I mean, a star was born in Dwayne Wade; and the Diesel, hell, them punks ain't wanna play the game, so they thought they could stop him with fouls. Shit. Who got the ring? Who got the ring?"

Tye stood up from his spot on the floor in the middle of Slim's living room and began pumping his fist. Of the seven people in the room watching game six of the NBA finals, Tye had been the only Miami Heat fan.

"Man, sit your happy ass down," Mike said, shooing his hand at Tye and then slipping his arm around his date. "Had the refs called a foul when Dallas went for that three, we'd be preparing to watch game seven with a different outcome."

"No excuses! Y'all just got whipped is all," Tye said as he made his way into the half-bath of Slim's condo.

"You ready to go, baby?" Mike said to his date, ignoring Tye's final comment. She nodded and they stood up to leave. "Thanks for having us over," Mike said to Slim.

"Oh, anytime, Big Mike," Slim said, rising up from the floor where she had been sitting between Wade's legs. She then extended her hand toward Big Mike's date. "It was nice to meet you."

"Nice to meet you too, Shelby," Big Mike's date replied.

"Excuse me," Slim said, snapping her neck. Everyone else started clearing their throats or swallowing chuckles.

"It's Slim, baby," Big Mike said to his date, grabbing her and pulling her toward the door. "We'll uh, catch y'all later." Big Mike waved and made a quick exit out the door.

"Shelby." Cory snickered under his breath with his fist to his mouth.

"What was that?" Slim said, turning sharply toward him.

"Oh nothing," Cory said as he stood up from the couch. "I better get going too. It's a Tuesday night and I gotta work tomorrow."

"Do you wanna take a plate with you for Big Shirley?" Slim said sarcastically. "Ooops, I mean your girlfriend, Ronnie."

"Uh, Cory, we still on for the gym tomorrow?" Wade said, standing up to run interference. "We need to be working out after eating all those chicken wings and meatballs and stuff that the girls cooked up." Wade was referring to the spread of appetizers that Slim and Dinah had taken the liberty of supplying.

"Yeah, man," Cory replied to Wade, but rolling his eyes at Slim. "I'll catch you tomorrow."

"All right, then, dude. Holla." Wade gave Cory some dap and then showed him out the door. He then sighed as he leaned up against the door. The last thing he wanted to do was judge a segment of *Yo Mama* between Cory and Slim.

"Man, everybody bailed?" Tye said, coming out of the bathroom and almost bumping into one of the

Atlantis wall fountains Slim had hanging on each side of the doorway. She had ordered the intricate décor that had water cascading down burnished copper-finished bowls into a resin sculpture from the same catalogue she had ordered Wade and Tye's couch. "We still got all night to celebrate my team's victory."

"Folks gotta work tomorrow," Slim said as she started tidying up the place.

"I know my brother ain't gon' turn in on me," Tye said to Wade, holding out his hands in question.

"Dude, I'm beat and I have a nine AM appointment all the way out in Pickerington somewhere that I still gotta go home and MapQuest," Wade said.

"Come on, one game of pool? One drink?" Tye pleaded with his twin brother.

"Oh, stop begging, Keith Sweat," Dinah jumped in as she rose out of the chair she had been sitting in. "If you wanna spend the rest of the night celebrating your team's win by getting your ass whooped in a game of pool, *come on den, Cletis.*"

"See, that's my girl right here," Tye said, walking over to Dinah and putting his arm over her shoulder. "She gon' hang with me. She ain't gon' let me down. Are you, bu?"

"Yeah, yeah, yeah," Dinah said, rolling her eyes. "I'm your girl because I'm the only one crazy enough to celebrate my team's loss."

"Oh, you know you my girl," Tye said as he started planting kisses on Dinah's cheek.

"Stop it, boy, before I hurt you." Dinah giggled.

"Oh, didn't my brother tell you? I like it rough." Tye winked.

"Ugh, let's go before I change my mind," Dinah said, grabbing her purse as Tye helped her into the white denim jacket that matched her white denim skirt.

Wade and Slim stood off to the side watching Dinah and Tye interact like two high school kids who liked each other but didn't want to admit it.

"I'll catch you later, Wade," Dinah said as she and Tye headed out the door.

"Yeah, I'll catch you later, bruh," Tye added as he walked down the steps, right before yelling, "You too, Shelb." He then let out a Morris Day–like laugh.

"Bye, Slim," Dinah said, holding in her laughter as she pulled the door closed.

"What's up with that?" Slim said to Wade as she walked toward him.

"I don't know." He shrugged his shoulders as he threw a piece of broccoli from the veggie tray Dinah had brought over into his mouth.

"Have you noticed that they've been kind of clingy these past couple of months?" Slim fed Wade another piece of broccoli and then ate one herself.

"I really haven't paid it much attention. I mean, we're all always together, so I just guess everything seemed normal."

"Well, I'm a woman and I'm here to tell you that it's not normal. I mean, you just saw 'em," Slim said, pointing toward the door as if they were still standing over there. "When have you ever seen your brother help a woman into her jacket? I don't care if she just sucked his dick hanging upside down over the side of a bed, he ain't gon' give her as much as a 'thank you.'" Wade chuckled. "And you know I'm right."

"Yeah, I guess you are," Wade agreed.

Slim popped one last piece of broccoli into her

mouth before she wrapped the tray up and slipped it into the fridge. "Well," Slim said in a pleasing tone, "looks to me like there's a little love connection brewing." She closed the refrigerator door and leaned her back against it with her arms folded.

Wade thought for a moment as Slim studied his face. "Nah," Wade said, shaking the thought. "They just cool like that is all. Dinah's like a sister."

"Maybe to you, but definitely not to our Tye." Slim smiled. It was a smile so huge she couldn't have hid it if she wanted to. Just the thought of Dinah pairing up with Tye gave her happy goose bumps. That would be all the security she'd need to crush the idea of Dinah and Wade someday crossing the boundaries of their friendship. After all, what kind of woman would sleep with two brothers?

"I can't believe what I'm hearing," Wade said to Tye as he lay in his bed while Tye stood in his doorway after hanging out with Dinah until the wee hours in the morning.

"Believe it, dawg. I'm feeling her and shit," Tye said with the most serious look on his face Wade had ever seen. This made Wade sit up in bed and take note. "I know it sounds crazy." Tye walked over and sat down on his brother's bed. "But there's something there that ain't been there before. I can't explain it. It seemed like just one day out of nowhere I started looking at her as not just my brother's best friend," Tye confessed. "And then tonight, after spending time with her one-on-one and not just hanging out with everybody . . ."

Tye paused for a minute while he tried to get his words together. And as Wade watched his brother try to gather his words, a thought popped into his head. "Y'all didn't . . . you and Dinah didn't . . ." Wade tried to ask.

"Hell, naw, man," Tye said, almost offended. "That's your tight peoples. You think I'd go and do something like that without bringing it to you first? We better than that."

"So is that what you're doing right now—bringing it to me?" There was silence as Wade stared down. His silence only affirmed Wade's latest query. "Look, you're my brother," Wade said, putting his hand on Tye's shoulder, "and Dinah's my ace boon coon. What could be wrong with having two of the people I love most in the world—and who love me, too—get together?"

Tye sighed in relief. "You sure, man? 'Cause lately I've been feeling this way about her, and I think I've been ignoring it because of what you and Dinah have."

"We don't have anything," Wade said, almost defensively. "We're just friends."

"That's what I mean. I didn't want things to get weird is all I'm trying to say."

"Now you know you are my brother and I love you to death, and I'd never put anyone before you. You know how it was back in the day; if you didn't like a motherfucker, I didn't like a motherfucker. If a motherfucker didn't like you, then a motherfucker didn't like me. But if something were to go down between you and Dinah and the shit didn't work out . . ." Wade's voice trailed off.

"I know, man," Tye stopped him. "I know how close you two are. And anything that happens between Dinah and me is just that—between Dinah and me. I can accept that. It ain't got shit to do with you. If things don't go the way I want them to with us, then I don't expect you two to stop hanging out. I know blood is thicker than water, but I also know what your relationship with Dinah means to you."

"I just don't want to jeopardize my relationship with Dinah, or with my brother for that matter."

"You won't, dawg. Dinah's a beautiful person. She's different. She's a friend. Mama and Daddy were friends before they got married."

Wade chuckled at how his mother used to remind him and Dinah of that all the time. He even thought about, for just one minute, cock blocking his brother's feelings for Dinah and telling him how their mother had always predicted that it would be him and Dinah who got together and how it had pretty much come to pass with their one night together. But then he thought about the fact that it was just that—one night. Nothing more had ever come of it. He had pretty much suppressed the memories of the night, the feelings, but now, rising to the surface was just a hint of jealousy. But it could be one-sided for all he knew, so why ruin a chance for his brother to be happy? At this point, if he had to see Dinah with any other man, it might as well be his brother.

"Is that what you want with Dinah?" Wade asked his brother. "To maybe even marry her someday? I mean, you really feel like she's the one, Tye?"

Tye sat quietly for a moment and then began nodding his head yes as a smile crept across his face. "Yeah, man, I think I do. I really think I do."

Wade started laughing. "Man, I think that's the liquor talking."

"Yeah, I'm a little full, but the alcohol is only making me speak the truth."

Wade laughed again at how, out of the blue, Tye

was saying that Dinah was "the one." Sitting here before him was his brother who had never had a steady girlfriend in his thirty-three years; he had definitely had his share of women but never claimed any as his girlfriend. Now overnight it seemed as though he was falling for a woman who had been in his life almost forever. *Hmmm,* Wade thought, *sounds familiar.* Suddenly the thought didn't sound so unbelievable anymore as his laugh faded.

"Seriously, bruh," Tye said to Wade, "don't laugh. I ain't making this shit up just to get no drawz or nothing. Pussy is a dime a dozen. I'm coming at you real, or otherwise I would have just hit that, and your ass would have never known about it."

Wade could tell that Tye was dead serious in his expressions for Dinah. "Then what can I say, my brother?" Wade said, sticking his hand out to Tye, "other than that you have my blessings?" The two brothers shook hands and then hugged. "Now turn my light back off and get the hell out of my room. I got work in the morning."

Tye got up, walked over to the door, and turned out Wade's bedroom light. He then exited the room, putting the door back in the closed position. After closing the door, he stood there for a moment and then walked into the living room.

"Well, what did he say?" Dinah, who had been waiting quietly on the couch, stood up and asked in a soft whisper.

Tye walked over to Dinah, put his arms around her, and French-kissed her. It was something he had been compelled to do prior to then, but he didn't want to make a move without discussing the situation with his brother first.

"I've wanted to do that for about a month now," Tye said.

"And I've wanted you to do that for about a month now," Dinah confirmed. "I take it Wade is all right with the idea of you and me."

"He is." Tye nodded with a smile. "But in all honesty, I think I would have come out here and kissed you anyway, even if he hadn't been."

"But I thought blood was thicker than water," Dinah said with a mischievous smile. "At least that's what you told me earlier when we were discussing the two of us getting together."

"It is, but pussy is a muthafuck!" On that thought, Tye lifted up Dinah and carried her into his bedroom.

For a moment it was like déjà vu for Dinah. She flashed back to that night when Wade had lifted her in his arms and carried her into his bedroom; how good it had felt to make love to someone she cared about and who cared about her so deeply. Not many women could truly say that the person they allowed into their bodies was truly their best friend and that they had years of friendship under their belts. It was such an amazing feeling that Dinah hadn't been with another man since; she had been afraid that they wouldn't even be able to come close to what she and Wade experienced.

For a brief second, as Tye carried her in his arms, Dinah fantasized about being in Wade's arms again, about being with him for more than just a night. But he had Slim. If he had wanted it to be her in his arms, then certainly he would have made a move by now; certainly he would have told her—after all, he'd always been able to tell her everything that was on his mind. She didn't dare make a fool out of herself by even giving a hint of how she really felt about him since that night. So at the thought of her feelings for Wade being one-sided, she quickly blinked her eyes back into reality and lived in the moment here and now—with Tye. He just might be the person who could come close to Wade.

For the next few months, Dinah and Tye's relationship was like a tornado that had picked up each of their individual lives and tossed them into one heap. Tye, who had an unspoken rule that he never spent the night with a girl, found himself damn near living with Dinah. He spent more time at her place than he did at his own.

Meanwhile, Slim appeared to be more than thrilled that Dinah was caught up in the rapture of Tye. She noticed that Dinah was hanging out less and less with Wade and his boys and doing more individual things with Tye—like going to romantic restaurants and taking weekend getaways to amusement parks. That definitely opened up the door of opportunity for Slim to woo her man, and she had every intention of doing so no matter what the cost.

"Keep your eyes closed," Slim said to Wade as she covered his eyes with her hands and led him in a wobbly expedition down the basement steps. "Tah-dah!" she said once they had reached the bottom. She removed her hands from Wade's eyes. There, sitting in front of them, was a billiard-style pool table. It was top of the line; Slim had maxed out her newly opened Visa charge card to purchase it.

"Slimee Slim!" Wade said with excitement, rushing over and rubbing his hand down the pool table as he circled it. "This is top of the line, woman."

"And so is my man," Slim said as she walked over

and kissed him. "So I figured if I wanted to keep him, then I'd better learn how to play his favorite pastime."

"You da best, Ma," Wade said, puckering his lips out far and kissing Slim, who was puckering hers out just as far. "So, you wanna initiate it?" he said, removing the two pool sticks that were lying across the table.

"Yeah," Slim said seductively as she slid the pool sticks from Wade's hand and threw them down onto the thick Madrid orange carpet. "But I was thinking that we could more like christen it." Before Wade could say another word, Slim began to undo his pants and lift his shirt over his head. Once she had him fully naked, she stood up in the middle of the pool table and performed an amateur striptease. She then immediately lay across the table and welcomed Wade into her womanhood. Determined to wear out his welcome, Wade joined her on the pool table.

"Oooh, ahhh," Wade moaned as he entered Slim. She wrapped her legs around his waist and began swallowing in Wade's thickness with her pussy. "Oh, Slim," he groaned as he dipped in and out of her, getting high off the sound of his dick plunging into her wetness. "You hear that?" he said to Slim. "That's your pussy talking to me. That's right," Wade said as he began to quickly pound deep inside Slim until he released his warm lava.

"Oooh, baby," she whispered as she stroked her hands up and down his back.

Wade lifted his head, kissed her on the lips, and then said, "Rack 'em," as he hopped off the pool table. Slim followed behind as the two proceeded to shoot pool, Wade showing her a thing or two about the game—both still butt naked.

Chapter V

A Fool in Love

Dinah and Tye sat out on the balcony of Dinah's apartment enjoying a nightcap. This was something they often did, when weather permitted, after making love. But one time, it began to pour as they sat on the balcony, and instead of running inside, they made love in the rain.

Tye had tried to hurry up and go into the house, but Dinah grabbed him by his waist from behind and began puncturing him with burning kisses. As the rain fell, he just sat there, his back to her, while she slid his pajama pants down. She cupped and massaged his ass while licking the back of his neck. Her tongue then made its way down the small of his back. She knew how whenever she did that the hairs on his body would stand at attention. She'd always stop at his oval-shaped birthmark and trace it with her tongue. But on that particular time, she didn't stop there; she allowed her tongue to go all the way down south, blowing the hell out of Tye's mind. No woman had ever made him feel that way before. He knew right then and there that there was something special about Dinah, something different from any other woman he had been with, something that made him one day want to make her wifey.

"So tell me, Dinah," Tye said, taking her hand and looking deeply into her eyes as they sat there on the balcony. "What do you want? What do you really want?"

"I don't know," she said coyly. "What made you ask me that out of the blue?"

"I don't know. I'm just sitting here staring at you, knowing with every ounce of certainty what I want in life. I was just wondering if you knew what you wanted too."

Dinah paused, deep in thought. "I want what Mary J. and the rest of the world want," Dinah said, gazing up at the stars in the night's sky. "I just wanna be happy." Dinah put her head down. "I just wanna be loved, man. Really loved." She closed her eyes and smiled. "Kind of like this." She placed Tye's arm around her and nestled up in his armpit.

"Is that all?" he asked, kissing her on the forehead. "Of all the things God's green earth has to offer, that's all you want?"

"Yeah, man, that's all. I mean, happiness . . . being happy is immeasurable. It's priceless. If you had happiness, I mean consistent happiness, on a regular basis—I'm talking every day—then what more could you possibly want?"

Tye stared down at Dinah's sincere and genuine smile. He then got up out of the double-seater chaise patio lounge and stood over her.

"What?" she asked, staring at him with a confused look on her face. "What's wrong?"

Without saying a word, Tye got down on one knee at Dinah's feet. "If being happy is all you want," Tye replied to Dinah's statement, "then I just wanna make you happy." With all of his heart Tye continued. "I think, no, I know the way I love you can make you happy if you would let me do it with God's blessing."

Dinah's eyes watered as she looked into Tye's eyes. She could feel the honest affection of his words through the depths of her soul. "Marry me, Dinah," Tye begged. "Please marry me." He rubbed her hand and fought back tears. "No, I don't have a two-carat diamond ring to slip on your finger. This wasn't planned. I mean, I didn't plan any of this; from falling in love with you to proposing at this very moment. But I promise that if you say yes, I'll run out to the mall first thing in the morning and buy you one."

Dinah began to whimper as tears fell from her eyes. She shook her head and put her hand over her mouth. Although they hadn't been an official couple for even a year, their past few months with each other had felt like a lifetime. They seemed to have crammed more in their short time together than some couples did in years of marriage. And although they might not have already been in love for several years, they had definitely had love for each other for several years as friends. Once again, Dinah found it special to actually share herself with someone who was truly a friend and not just some man she met when she was ready to settle down. But there was still the fact that she had slept with the brother of the man who was now proposing to her. A cloud of darkness suddenly shaded her face.

"How long have we known each other?" Tye said before Dinah could even respond to his proposal. He had sensed the hesitation in her expression.

"Forever, I guess," Dinah said, shrugging her shoulders. "Forever, it seems."

"Right," Tye agreed. "It does feel like forever." He interlocked his fingers with hers. "It feels like I've been loving you forever and that you've been a part of me forever. So it's not like we are two strangers just up and getting married."

"I know, baby," Dinah said, rubbing her hand down Tye's face. "But—"

"But what?" he interrupted. "But I love you and you love me?" he suggested.

"Tye, even though we've known each other a long time, we've only been officially dating for less than a year. You don't think all of this is happening too fast?"

"It hasn't happened fast enough, if you ask me," Tye responded as he stood up. "We love each other now, and that's all that matters." He leaned down and grabbed her hand. "Do you love me, D?" Tye said, squeezing her hand. "Do you really love me?"

"You know I do," Dinah said, loosening her hand from Tye's and standing up. "I've always loved you. You know that. You're my best friend's brother. We grew up together. I watched you play ball in high school. I've watched you play pool; I've watched you play women." Dinah laughed.

"Well, I don't wanna be a player no more," Tye said seriously.

"I know. I'm not saying that. It's just that . . . I think there's something you need to know."

Dinah walked over to the balcony railing with her back now toward Tye.

"Fuck all that," Tye said, getting up and walking over behind Dinah, who was looking up at the sky. "I know everything I need to know." He pressed up against her and kissed her on the cheek. "Are you in love with me?" he whispered in her ear.

Yes, Wade, I am in love with you, she wanted to say, if only it were Wade who was the one asking her the question. But it wasn't. Dinah closed her eyes and took in the warmth of Tye's body against her back.

"Are you in love with me, Dinah?" he repeated. "Because I'm sure as hell in love with you." Tye wrapped his arms around Dinah and kissed her on the back of her neck.

His touch sent chills down her body. It was a touch that, once she really thought about it, felt damn good. As she stood there wrapped up in him, she could have kicked herself for not recognizing it before now. If she hadn't been so caught up in pretending in her twisted thoughts that he was the man she couldn't have, then she would have seen that he was in all actuality the man she could have.

There was just so much about him that she had never allowed herself to notice, and for years she saw him as nothing more than Wade's brother. Given the opportunity, she could have been experiencing his touch, the way he treated her, the way he spoke to her, the way he made her feel, for years now. There wasn't anything she could do about the past, but there was plenty she could do about the future.

Getting impatient with waiting on Dinah's response, Tye turned her around to face him, and before he could ask her again if she would marry him, she blurted out her response.

"Yes!" Dinah said, quickly spinning around to face Tye as he turned her. "Hell yes," she repeated, tears falling from her eyes.

"Yes . . ." Tye started.

"Yes, I'm in love with you and hell yes I'll marry you," Dinah shouted.

For a minute Tye just stood there cheesing at Dinah as her words sank in.

"Wahooooo!" Tye yelled, lifting Dinah off her feet and spinning her around. He then put her down and ran over to the balcony and started yelling, "Yes! Did you hear that, Columbus, Ohio? My baby said yes!"

Dinah stood there laughing and crying at the same time, watching Tye, her husband-to-be, act like a fool in love.

"Let's honeymoon in Copacabana," Tye said excitedly, running back over to Dinah.

"Well, I always have wanted to go to Rio," Dinah said.

"Then Rio it is," Tye said, kissing her all over her face. "Where's the phone?" He began looking around.

"Huh?" Dinah asked.

"Where's the phone?" he repeated. "I gotta call my brother. He's going to faint when he hears this. His brother is getting married to his best friend. Wahooooo!" Tye opened the patio door to go inside to retrieve the phone, but before entering the apartment, he said, "I wonder if he's going to serve as my best man or your maid of honor." Tye laughed and then ran into the house to make the call.

A lump formed in Dinah's throat. "Yeah, I wonder,"

she said under her breath as she closed her eyes and inhaled.

"So I hear congratulations are in order," Wade said with a nervous smile as soon as Dinah opened her front door. "These are for you, my future sister-in-law." He handed her the bouquet of mixed flowers that he held in his hand.

"These are lovely. Thank you, Wade," Dinah said as Wade stepped inside. "Tye's not here," she said as she walked the flowers into the kitchen and laid them down on the counter while she searched for a vase.

"Damn, it's like that now?" Wade said, following her into the kitchen. "A girl plans to get married and already she forgets about her friends?" Wade joked as he walked over to the sink and turned the water on so that Dinah could fill the vase she had just retrieved from under her sink. "I came to see you."

"Oh shoot, I'm sorry, Wade," Dinah said, placing the vase under the running water. "I don't know where my mind was."

"The same place mine has been," Wade said, turning off the water when the vase was full. Dinah placed the flowers in it.

"And where's that?" She sat the flowers down on the counter and turned around. Wade was standing close behind her, so close that she almost ran into him. Instead, they just stood inches apart from each other.

"Wondering if we should tell him," Wade answered.

"Tell who what?" Dinah asked with a puzzled look on her face.

"Don't, Dinah," Wade said, shaking his head. "Let's not play this game. We've come this far without playing any games; let's not start now."

Dinah just stood there fighting back tears of anxiety and confusion. She knew exactly what Wade was referring to, and he was right; that is exactly where her mind had been from the moment Tye mentioned Wade's name after the proposal. She was so afraid that when Tye walked through those patio doors to tell his brother about their engagement, his conscience would get the best of him and he'd tell Tye about the two of them having slept together. She thought that each day Tye walked through the door, it was going to be the day that Wade had decided to confess. But none of those days had been the one, but with Wade showing up on her doorstep to talk about it, would today be that day?

"So, are you going to tell him?" Dinah said as tears began to pour down her face, so many that she could have used them to fill the vase instead of water. Before Wade could even answer, she began crying harder and stated, "Please don't tell him, Wade. I know I'll lose him. And believe it or not, I love him. I love your brother so much, and he loves me too. I know you know that. You'd be the first person to know if he didn't. I didn't see this coming, Wade. I didn't see falling in love with Tye coming; not in a million years. If I had, I would have never crossed that line with you. What you and me did was a mistake. A mistake that I wish I could take—"

"Shhh, shhh, shhh," Wade said as he pulled Dinah's head to his chest. "Just calm down. Calm down, Dinah." Not only did Wade want to stop Dinah from crying, but he wanted to stop her from taking the memory he had of the two of them making sweet passionate love together and turning it into some god-awful mistake. It was crushing him to know that she didn't remember their night together as something just as special as he would always remember it to be. Just like he had expected, his feelings about the whole night were one-sided. "Don't worry, Dinah. I won't tell him," he said in a low-pitched tone.

"Huh? What did you say?" Dinah said, lifting her head from Wade's chest.

He pushed her away, almost with a hint of anger. "I said I'm not going to tell him, Dinah, damn it." He beat down on the counter. "That's my brother, man." Although Wade hated that he would be lying to his brother by omission of the truth, he was even angrier that Dinah was showing absolutely no concern or feeling for what the two of them had shared.

"I know," Dinah said, racing over to Wade to comfort him by stroking his muscular arm. "And I know you love him. But I love him, too, Wade. And he loves me. You and me fucked up and crossed the line just one time, and then we went on with our lives as if nothing had happened. That's what we need to keep doing. I think telling him now would do more harm than good."

Dinah was right as far as Wade was concerned. The perfect time to have told his brother would have been that night in his bedroom when Tye had first told him about his feelings for Dinah. But Wade never honestly thought that if Tye pushed up on Dinah she would give in to his advances. She had already slept with Wade, and even though they were still the best of friends, the truth still remained that they had been intimate. Wade just never pegged Dinah as the type of woman who could sleep with one brother after having slept with the other. Anyone on the outside looking in might have taken her for some desperate whore, but because Wade knew her heart and the type of person she was, he knew that only love would be the force strong enough to put her in such a compromising and seemingly immoral position.

"I hear you, Dinah, and you're right," Wade agreed. "What would telling Tye about us really do besides lift the hundred-pound weight off our shoulders? I'm not going to be that selfish as to cause my brother despair in order to get rid of my own."

"Oh God, thank you, Wade," Dinah said as she threw her arms around him.

"Don't mention it," Wade said as he stood there allowing Dinah to hold him, wishing that the same feeling that went through his body when they touched each other went through hers as well.

Sure, Wade had appeared to have been unaffected by his and Dinah's intimacy by pretending that nothing had changed between them. When she had showed no signs that anything had changed between them, he reciprocated her actions right back, not wanting to make a fool out of himself by expressing his true feelings. But now he was strongly reconsidering his actions, wishing that he hadn't hidden his true feelings—feelings that made him want to kick Slim to the curb and spend the rest of his life with Dinah. But with his brother engaged to Dinah, that was no longer an option. Now, for the sake of the love he had for both his brother and Dinah and for their happiness, he'd have to sacrifice his own happiness and sit back and watch his brother live out the life that he was certain was meant for him.

Chapter VI

Broy oh Broy

"And just who are you to sit here and tell me what is and what isn't going to make my man happy?" Slim said to Broy, digging her index finger into the tub of rainbow sherbet and inhaling it off her finger as they sat at the half-moon seating bench and table set that rested in front of the window in her condo's eating space.

"Honey child, I might be gay, but I'm still a man, and don't you eva fo'gct it," Broy said, jokingly snapping his finger with each syllable, pretending to be flamin'. He was, indeed, a homosexual, but not one that walked around twitching, snapping his wrists and exaggerating the *s* sound. But once he was in his element and around his friends, he always played around with the traits society had stereotyped gay men with.

At work, and when in business mode, Broy didn't appear gay. He could be placed against any heterosexual male in a three-piece suit and he'd look like straight Mr. Corporate America with a nice house on a hill where a lovely wife, two children, and a dog were waiting for him. Even though the accounting firm that he and Slim worked for had adopted the business-casual dress code, he still dressed as if he were an attorney due in court in a half hour with a judge who had a strict dress code. But his gayizm was something that he was proud of and did not keep in the closet. He just didn't feel it was necessary for him to wear his gay pride on his sleeve. There was a time and a place for everything, and whenever he was at Slim's place, he could always let his true colors show.

"I mean, do I want to go on a trip to Rio?" Slim said. "Hell yeah! But do I want to be that bitch's maid of honor? Hell no! And besides, she didn't ask me, Wade did. 'We're her only friends, and you know that, Slim,' he said to me." Slim continued imitating Wade's conversation from the night he asked her to be Dinah's maid of honor at a wedding they had booked in Rio, which was just a month away. It would be small and intimate, with just the bride and groom, the best man, and the maid of honor.

"Look, fish," Broy said to her, taking his spoon and scooping up some sherbet, "if you won't take advantage of a free trip to Rio with one lousy stipulation being your boyfriend's best friend's maid of honor, then hell, I'll do it. It ain't like I ain't worn a dress before." Broy licked his sherbet off the spoon and then stared at Slim bug-eyed, waiting on her response.

"I know." Slim sighed. "Sounds silly, but you know

she's more than just Wade's so-called homegirl; she's like my archenemy."

"You mean archrival?" Broy said, taking another lick of the mound of sherbet that sat on his spoon.

"What are you talking about?" Slim said with a dumbfounded look on her face.

"Bitch, please, you know you been fighting that girl for Wade's attention since day one."

"That is so not true."

"Don't bring that white girl talk over here, missy, because you know *that is so true*," Broy said, moving his head from side, teasing her. "And now, to top it all off, the bitch is getting married to your man's brother after only sleeping with him a few times— give or take—and here you been fucking Wade and sucking his dick, sometimes swallowing, for years now and ain't been down the aisle."

"Fuck you, Broy," Slim said angrily, pushing the tub of sherbet toward him.

"You're not my type; besides, best friends don't sleep together." Broy raised one eyebrow and stated, "Or do they?"

"You know what? I think lunch break is over," Slim said, snatching the tub of sherbet from Broy, barely allowing him to get his final scoop out of it. "Time to head back to the office."

"Oh, bitch, don't get mad at me," Broy said, standing up and walking over to Slim, who had just slammed the freezer door. "You know I'm your friend, and I tell you like it is, whether the truth is going to hurt or not. I ain't gon' let you walk out into the world with your slip showing, girlfriend. You know that." Slim looked over at her Broy, who put his arm around her shoulder. "Love you."

Slim knew Broy meant no harm, but he was right

about everything he had just said to her. He could always read her like a book, forcing her to face the truth on the pages even when she wanted to live a lie.

"I love you too," Slim said almost inaudibly.

"What was that?"

"I love you too, Broy. You know that."

"Did you love me even that one time when you showed up at the gay club wearing that black, tight-ass pleather miniskirt, red tube top, and tall, red pleather boots thinking you were going to fit in? Child, I laughed at you all night; told you that you looked like a hoe on crack . . . in drag." Broy burst out into laughter, remembering that night three years ago when he was having his thirtieth birthday celebration at Club Wet, a downtown premier gay spot. As beautiful a woman as Slim was, all the gay men were hitting on her because they thought she was a dude in drag.

"Okay, enough already," Slim said, chuckling as she recalled the night. "Yeah, I loved you then, too, and I love you now." As Broy continued to laugh, Slim began pouting somewhat.

"All right, I'm sorry," Broy said, calming down. "Here." He pushed his spoon that held the last bit of sherbet he had been licking into Slim's face. She graciously accepted his apology by wrapping her mouth around the spoon and taking in the last bit.

"Thanks," she said.

"You're welcome," Broy said, kissing her on her cold lips. "Now when are we going to get that dress so that you can look like the stunning diva of a maid of honor that you are?"

"Thanks, but no thanks, Broy," Slim said as she grabbed her purse and keys. "That's another condition of my trip to Rio; I have to go shopping for the dress with her. I guess we're supposed to bond and become the best of pals or something? Yeah right. File that shit under never."

"Umph, you shopping with Dinah. Now that should be fun," Broy said as they headed for the front door.

"Fun? I don't know," Slim said with a mischievous look in her eyes. "But interesting; yeah, I'm sure with a few pointers from you, the queen of interesting, I can make my little shopping spree with the bride-to-be one to remember."

"Oooh, bitch, you are so bad," Broy said as he spanked Slim on the ass and they headed back to work.

"Are you serious? You're really going to wear white?" Slim asked Dinah as they stood in David's Bridal. Dinah had just come out from the dressing room modeling a beautiful ballroom-style white gown.

"What's wrong with your face?" Dinah asked Slim, noticing the disfigured look on her face as she frowned all up. "You smell something rotten or something? Why are you making that distorted-looking face?" Dinah said, putting her hands on her hips.

"Nothing . . . I guess . . . I mean," Slim stammered on purpose.

"What?" Dinah said. "You don't like the style or something? Does it look funny on me?"

"It's not that. It's just that . . . Well, are you sure it's okay to wear white when you're not a virgin?" Slim repeated the line Broy had told her to say. "I mean, it's no secret that Wade and I have been intimate; that's why I'm going to save myself the embarrassment and just wear cream when the two of us get married."

Dinah stood there furious at Slim's rude comment. She wanted to walk right up to her and slap the shit out of her, but instead she refrained from doing so. After all, she had promised Wade that she would try to start a fresh relationship with Slim—for his sake. That's the only reason why she let him talk her into having Slim be her maid of honor. If it was up to her, she wouldn't have one at all. She didn't give a damn about a bridal party. All she wanted to do was become Mrs. Tyler Preston.

"Since me and the guys are your only friends," Wade had said to Dinah, *"and none of us are going to show up wearing a dress on your behalf, you might as well have Slim do it. Besides, Slim's always felt left out. I think that's why she's so envious of our relationship at times. This is the perfect opportunity to show her that she is a part of us,"* Wade had said in convincing her.

As Dinah stood in the bridal shop with Slim, she thought, *Why did I let him talk me into this bullshit?* Just then, Dinah's eye caught a glimpse of a dress that was hanging behind Slim. It was the most hideous deep-olive-green, throw-up-colored dress she had ever seen. Slowly she started making her way straight toward Slim.

Slim had the look of death in her eyes as Dinah made her way toward her. With a look of displeasure and anger on Dinah's face, Slim wished she could take her words back, but it was too late. Dinah was right up on her. Dinah raised her hand and Slim flinched, closing her eyes and preparing to take the blow she just knew Dinah was sending her way. After a couple of seconds, when she didn't feel a sharp, sudden pain, she opened her eyes only to see Dinah holding the dress she had retrieved from the rack of dresses that were behind her.

"You know what, Slim?" Dinah said, holding up the god-awful dress. "I don't even think cream is your color. I think green is. And I think this is the perfect shade of green to complement my beautiful white gown. I mean, you're going to look just delightful in the pictures that we'll have to remember this day forever. And the place where we are getting married even puts the wedding photos on the Internet."

Slim looked at the gown with the same twisted look on her face she had used to look at Dinah in her white wedding dress. "You're kidding me, right?" Slim asked.

"No, I'm not. Now run along and let's get a sneak peek at how you're going to look on my wonderful wedding day," Dinah said, pointing toward the dressing room.

Slim snatched the gown from Dinah's hands and stomped off into the dressing room. As Slim pulled the curtain closed behind her, Dinah looked over to the bridal consultant who had been helping her and who had decided to wait over on the sideline until the end of round one. The consultant shook her head and giggled at the apparent joke Dinah was playing on Slim. Dinah had made it clear on the phone when she scheduled a fitting appointment that her wedding colors were white, black, and peach or tangerine, so the clerk knew that Dinah was just yanking at Slim's strings to get a rise out of her.

A few moments later, Slim came charging out of the dressing room, rolling her eyes. Obviously, Dinah's little trick was working.

"Slim, you look just stunning," Dinah said, putting her hands over her mouth as if she was spellbound. "This is the best I've ever seen you look." Dinah walked up behind her and whispered in her ear, "And I've looked at you quite a bit." She paused, still set on taunting Slim. "Yep, and this is, hands down, the best you've ever looked, my dear."

"You're full of shit," Slim quickly turned around and spat.

"And you look like shit in this dress, but guess what? I don't give a damn. It's me, the bride, who has to look good. I don't give a fuck about you, Miss Always a Bridesmaid, Never a Bride." Dinah let out a taunting chuckle that just did it for Slim.

The next thing Slim knew, and before she could hold back her fist, she had slugged Dinah upside the head. Not believing she had just done that, Slim turned and started to run because she knew, this time, Dinah wouldn't be reaching for a dress from behind her; she'd be going for her throat.

Unfortunately, as Slim turned around, Dinah grabbed at her and pulled her down to the ground, her acrylic nails clawing down the back of the dress like a tiger, completely ripping the zipper off. Once Dinah had Slim on the ground, she began throwing jabs to Slim's eye until the consultant was able to pull her off.

"I hope you like green, ladies," the consultant said, breathing heavily, almost out of breath from all the strength it took to pry the women apart. "Because you've just bought that dress!"

"Well, how did it go?" Broy said, opening his front door for Slim, dying to hear the details about her shopping outing with Dinah and wanting to see the maid-of-honor dress they chose. But of course he was more interested in hearing about what he knew was an interesting Saturday afternoon.

"You don't want to know," Slim said, storming through the front door wearing her favorite pair of dark Gucci shades, carrying a dress bag over her shoulder.

"The hell I don't!" Broy corrected her. "Looky there," he said, pointing to his living room where a bowl of popcorn and two cans of sodas sat on the coffee table. He then started walking toward the setup. "Now get your high-yellow tail over here, sit down, and spill it." He sat down on the couch and patted the spot next to him.

Slim sighed and dragged herself over. "You wanna know how shit turned out?" she asked. "Good, take a look at this." She threw the dress bag over the couch and unzipped it. "There! There's the damn dress."

Broy's mouth dropped open. "Child, you gon' look like a frog shit all over you," he said about her dookie-colored maid-of-honor gown.

"Yeah, thanks to you and all that advice you gave me on what to say to make our little outing more *interesting*," Slim said in an accusing tone, "it all backfired and now I gotta show up at the wedding looking like I fucked Kermit the frog the night before at the bachelorette party and he came all over my dress. But in that case, you could just say that I'm going to look like a green White House intern."

Broy put his hand over his mouth, but then he couldn't hold it in anymore. He burst out laughing. "Whew, child, you right. I can't believe I didn't come up with that one, but that's exactly what you are going to look like."

"Hell, you think that's the worst part?" Slim said as she proceeded to pull the dress completely out of the bag. "I gotta find a fuckin' seamstress to clean this thing up."

Immediately, Broy's laughter came to a halt. "What the hell?" he said as Slim turned the dress around so that he could see the back of it. It looked as though a cat had taken its claws and ran them down the back. "Sweetie." Broy's tone was now more empathetic. "What happened?"

"We got into a fight," Slim confessed. Feeling stupid and embarrassed, her eyes began to water. "Can you believe a grown-ass woman like myself was out in public fighting another grown-ass woman? And in gotdamn wedding party dresses no less?"

"Well, did you win, honey?" was the question Broy felt was most important. "Did you windmill her? Did you beat her ass?" Broy said just as Slim removed her shades to wipe her tears away.

She stood there with a look on her face that said, "Do I look like I won?" as her swollen eye stared back at Broy.

"Oh, Slim." Broy hugged her. "I'm sorry. I'm so sorry. I didn't know it would lead to this." He softly touched her eye.

"Ouch!" She flinched.

"Wait right here. I'm going to get you some ice." Broy dashed off into the kitchen and put some ice cubes in a plastic baggie. He then returned to Slim, who was sitting on the couch crying. "Did you at least tear up the gown she had on too?"

"No," Slim said with failure lacing her tone. "I don't know why I let her get to me, Broy," Slim said.

"You were right the other day. I've always felt like I've been in competition with Dinah for some reason. I love Wade and I know he loves me. Dinah is just his friend and nothing more. I mean, in a month, she'll be married to his twin brother, and I won't have to worry about her at all. I should be grateful. I should be ecstatic, but instead I'm getting in all the last bits and pieces of anger and jealousy toward her that I can. And just maybe had I let it go a long time ago, it would be Wade and me jumping the broom and not . . ." Slim couldn't finish as she got choked up.

"It's okay." Broy hugged her. "Let it go. I know you've been wanting to do this for some time now. Instead you've just played the hard 'I've got my shit together and ain't nobody gonna take my man' girlfriend. But let it go, Slim. Let it go forever." Broy took the bag of ice and placed it softly on Slim's swollen eye. She began to regain her composure. "You feel better now?"

"As a matter fact, I do," Slim said, taking deep breaths, getting herself together.

"Don't worry about nothing," Broy comforted her. "Everything's going to be all right. You are going to call Dinah and apologize, and you're going to mean it because I can see it in your eyes that you really want to just let this thing go."

Slim jumped in to concur. "And you're right, Broy. I do. I don't want to use all my energy trying to make her miserable. I want to use all my energy in making Wade happy. Had I done that before, maybe I would be the one getting married now. So the jealousy and the silly games stop here."

"That's my girl," Broy said, hugging her again.

"Thanks, Broy," Slim said, squeezing him tight.

"Everything is going to be all right." Just then, she looked down at the puddle of green lying on the couch. "But what in the world are we going to do about that dress?"

"Ugh," Broy said as he picked up the dress with his thumb and index finger like it had the cooties. "Now, I can help you get in trouble, and I can help you get out, but this hot mess right here is a job that Boo-Boo can't help you get out of. But I know who can."

Broy dropped the dress, and it hit the couch like a bowl of pea soup splattering. He then raced to the phone and started dialing.

"Who are you calling?" Slim asked curiously.

"Child, I'm calling nine-one-one," Broy answered. "This is a job for the fashion police!"

Chapter VII

The Green-Eyed Monster

"Thank you for hearing me out, Dinah," Slim said after she had spent the last twenty minutes apologizing to Dinah for her behavior over the past years, and especially in the bridal shop.

"No problem, Slim. I really do understand. Thanks for calling, though. I really do appreciate it," Dinah said into the phone. "And I'm sorry, too, for everything. I know I haven't made it easy for you either."

"We've both made it hard for each other, and as black women, we should be ashamed. But that's all water under the bridge. All I know is that you are going to be the most beautiful bride in your lovely white gown, and you're going to love what I've done with that maid-of-honor dress." Slim looked over at her closet door where the gown was hanging.

That day after the fight in the bridal shop, Broy had called for help with Slim's dress dilemma, and he put her in touch with a guy he used to date who did a little sewing on the side. Actually, he designed most of his own clothes and was honored to work on the dress that had been described to him as "hideous," even before it had been shredded down the back. He accepted the challenge of taking an ugly duckling and turning it into a swan, and that is exactly what he did. He couldn't do anything about the color of the dress, but with the tough makeover he gave it, it could have been orange with purple polka dots and Slim would have still looked beautiful in it.

"Speaking of the dress, Slim," Dinah said, "I really wasn't going to make you wear a green dress in the wedding. I just wanted to see your face when you thought that there was even a remote possibility that I would choose that dress for you. But when we got to fighting and the dress ripped and the store made us buy it, well, we didn't really have any other choice, now, did we?"

"I know, and again, Dinah, I'm so sorry," Slim apologized. "The last thing I want is to ruin the best day of a girl's life, even if the girl is you." There was silence. "Wait, that didn't come out right." Both the women laughed.

"I know what you meant, girl. Don't worry about it. You're sorry, I'm sorry, we're sorry. Now let's get to packing. We leave in two days."

"All right, Dinah. And it really is an honor to be a part of your wedding. I'll see you in a couple of days," Slim said, and hung up the phone.

She sat for a moment and then looked over at Wade, who was lying next to her in bed, sipping a nightcap of gin and juice. He had a huge grin on his face. She then leaned over and kissed him, at first with just a little peck, and then with a deep, passionate tongue kiss.

"You don't know how good it makes me feel to see that after all of these years, you and Dinah are able to put your differences aside," Wade said to her.

"I know," Slim said, throwing her hands up. "It's just been silly."

"But just like a woman who cheated on her husband with the pool boy and is waiting on her period to come . . . it's better late than never." He laughed.

"Who told you when you're drunk that you were funny?"

"Uh . . . nobody."

"Good, because you're not," Slim said as she touched the side of Wade's face and stared into his eyes. "Cute," she said, looking into his eyes, which were only two more drinks from being drunken eyes, "but not funny."

"Cute, huh?" Wade asked as he sat there staring back into Slim's eyes. Suddenly it felt like déjà vu to him. Those were the exact words Dinah had said to him the night they made love. Then the next minute he felt as though it were Dinah's eyes he was staring into and not Slim's.

"Wade, you okay?" Slim asked, noticing that he seemed to be staring off. "Wade, you all right, honey?" she asked again after not getting an answer the first time.

"Oh yeah, baby, I'm okay," Wade finally responded.

Slim took his face into her hands and began kissing him again, thrashing her tongue in and out of his mouth. She then reached over and pulled Wade's dick out of the slit in his boxer shorts, slid off her panties from underneath her T-shirt-style nightgown, and then climbed on top of him.

Although Wade's hardness was automatic once Slim gripped it in her hands and stuck it inside of her wetness, he was not automatic in putting his head into the sexual act. Dinah was still on his mind.

"Oh, Wade, I love you," Slim moaned as she popped her pussy faster and faster onto Wade's hardness. He didn't hump back. He just laid there allowing Slim to get hers off. With her eyes closed and head thrown back, she was none the wiser that she was the only one who was into the sexual act.

Her clit tingled as it pressed down upon Wade's dick as she slid back and forth, side to side. "Oh, Wade. Wade! I'm about to cum!" she yelled as she grabbed her knees, legs spread wide open, and began fucking Wade wildly. Within a few seconds, Slim's juices were dripping down into Wade's pubic hairs, and her tiny frame collapsed onto his chest.

Breathing heavily, she asked, "Did it feel good to you?"

Wade said nothing. He just kissed her on the forehead, closed his eyes, wrapped his arms around her, and pretended he was holding Dinah.

"I now pronounce you Mr. and Mrs. Tyler Preston," the minister said as Tye proceeded to kiss his bride.

The sun that set behind them looked as though it had been drawn on a canvas, a prop in the wonderful future they planned on having together. The white sand and beautiful water of the beach on which they had just been joined in holy matrimony made Tye and Dinah feel as though they were truly in paradise.

After their lips parted from their first kiss together as husband and wife, Dinah lifted her long, flaring, off-white gown, allowing her French-manicured toes to show as they sank into the sand. There she stood barefoot in the sand with her new husband, who also stood barefoot. Tye bent over and cuffed his pants.

"Congratulations, brother," Wade said, grabbing Tye by the shoulders as he stood back up. Wade then gave his brother a kiss on the cheek and hugged him.

As Slim watched them, she figured she should at least congratulate Dinah as well, so she walked over to her.

"Congratulations, Dinah," Slim said as she hugged her.

Dinah was still gripping her dress, so she wasn't able to hug Slim back, but she did whisper in her ear. "Thanks for the tip about the white dress," Dinah said. "You were right. This color is more appropriate, and you of all people know that I ain't no virgin." Dinah then winked.

If anyone knew that the real reason Slim despised Dinah so much was because of the dark, hidden secret Dinah held over her head, they would not only be surprised, but they'd also be shocked. Slim had only shared with Broy what happened between her and Dinah back in Cancun, Mexico, during the All-Star Fiesta weekend when she was just a freshman in college. She and Broy never talked about it, though; he just called her "fish" every now and then—a term he used to tease her about the fact that she walked around as a girly heterosexual but probably still liked pussy on the down low. She had pretty much managed to bury it deep in her own mind until the day the man she wanted to spend the rest of her life with introduced her to his best friend.

The idea of the new guy she was digging having a female as a best friend was enough to deal with, but meeting her face-to-face and seeing that it was the girl her friends had talked her into making out with, after drinking more than her share of margaritas while on spring break in Cancun, was more than she could stomach. The two were so drunk at the time that Slim thought for certain that Dinah hadn't remembered who she was, but then when Dinah started making those slick little sly-ass comments on the side, like the one she had just whispered in her ear, she knew for certain that she remembered her all too well.

Once Slim had sobered up after her rendezvous with Dinah, it made her sick to think that her first sexual experience had been with a woman. Slim had taken pride in being a good girl, unlike the two girls she had been with who had been sexually active since they were fourteen. The rest of the trip was miserable for Slim. She cried and moped in her hotel room the entire time. Finally her friends told her that tit licking, clit rubbing, and fingering couldn't be considered intercourse, so she was still a virgin and hadn't technically had sex. They also assured her that what went on in Cancun stayed in Cancun and that her secret would be forever safe. Slim felt some comfort in that, but every time a new *Girls Gone Wild* video came out, she cringed at the thought that it would be the one that displayed her and Dinah, two good girls doing very bad things, thanks to the influence of alcohol.

"You ready, Mrs. Preston?" Tye said to Dinah before Slim could comment on Dinah's last statement.

"More ready than you'll ever know, Mr. Preston." Dinah smiled.

"We'll see you two in the morning," Tye said to Wade and Slim as he linked his arm through Dinah's. After one more peck, the two dashed off toward the water; they ran along the beach, close enough to the water so that the waves could roll up on them and wet their feet.

"They look like a postcard," Slim complimented as she and Wade stood there watching them.

"Yeah," Wade said in a dry tone. "Come on. Let's go get something to eat. I'm hungry."

That evening, Wade and Slim spent their time enjoying each other's company as they explored Copacabana. Tye and Dinah spent their time enjoying each other's company as they explored each other's bodies in ways unimaginable, well into the next morning. For the first time in her life, Dinah allowed a man to enter her from the *back* back, but not just any man—her husband. It was explosive and stimulating for them both, to say the least. Tye told her he felt as if he had taken her virginity because it was so tight.

"I feel like a virgin with you, Tye Preston," Dinah told him the next morning as he lay on top of her, their bodies sweating from making love all night and into the morning. "Every time with you is like the first time." She kissed him on his soft, thick lips. "I might have had sex before, but that was the first time I've ever made real, true love."

"Well, seeing how you've had sex before, and now you've made love, can we just do one other thing?" Tye asked.

"And what's that?" Dinah said, almost afraid to ask.

"Fuck," Tye said as he flipped her over onto her stomach, pulled her up on all fours, and plunged deep inside her pussy lips, which were slightly swollen from all the lovemaking they had done the night of their wedding.

"Oh, Tye, oh, baby!" Dinah yelled at the top of her lungs as she looked over her shoulder and watched Tye pound in and out of her pussy. Seeing him go to work on that ass made her insides throb.

"Throw that ass back on this dick," Tye ordered her while he remained still, allowing her to back it up on him.

Dinah submitted to her husband and began pulling forward, just enough where the tip of Tye stayed inside of her; then she'd push backward into him. First she started off slowly, and then she quickly slid on his pole. He began smacking her ass with one hand while he fingered her clit with the other. He then began grinding himself into her.

"Ewww shit, Tye. I love it when you fuck me like that. Don't stop fucking me," Dinah begged.

Tye plunged into her so hard that the headboard began beating against the wall. Between the headboard slamming into the wall and the two of them crying out in ecstasy, they hadn't heard Wade knocking at the suite door.

"You guys in there?" Wade called from the other side of the door. He then stopped knocking and pressed his ear to the door. After a couple of moans and groans and the thumps of the headboard, he realized that they were in there; he also realized why they hadn't heard him knocking.

He heard the muffled moans of Dinah begging Tye not to stop fucking her, and he heard the muffled groans of Tye promising her that he would never stop. Wade knew that he should have walked away, but for some reason he couldn't. He stood there at the door listening, wishing that he was the man on the other side of that door and not his brother.

"I'm about to shoot these babies up in you," he heard Tye yell, along with the smacking sound of perhaps him spanking Dinah's ass as he fucked her.

Wade slammed his eyes tight and balled his fist. He wanted to beat on that door and cock block; the selfish part of him wanted to do just that. But before he got the best of himself, and just as he heard a final outcry from both Tye and Dinah, signaling they had each reached their climax, he headed back to his and Slim's hotel room.

"Were they in their room?" Slim came out of the bathroom with a towel wrapped around her body when she heard the hotel room door close, indicating Wade had returned to their room. She was still a little wet from the shower she had just taken.

"No, I mean yeah," Wade stammered.

"So did they want to join us for breakfast or are they getting room service?"

"I don't know, fuck! What's with all the gotdamn questions?" Wade snapped.

Slim just stood there silently with hurt feelings. Here they had been having a wonderful time, and now all of a sudden Wade had an attitude.

"Sorry," Slim said sadly as she turned and went back into the bathroom.

"Wait, Slim," Wade said, going in after her. "I'm sorry," he said as she dried herself off.

"It's okay," she said.

"No, it's not." He walked over to her and kissed her on the forehead. He ran his hands down her wet body and then kissed her lips. He closed his eyes and in his head heard the sound of Tye and Dinah having sex. He could only imagine how they had spent the night as one, inside each other's bodies. He could only imagine it had been him deep inside Dinah's warmth.

Without warning, Wade threw Slim onto the tiled floor, forced her legs open, and held them open by planting each hand on her thighs. He then lay down on her with all of his body weight.

"Wade!" she called out as he entered her dryness. "Wade?" she called out again, but he had her on mute as he stroked in and out, pumping her into the floor. "Damn it, Wade," she cried out as she tore her nails down his back, creating wounds that mirrored the rips down the back of the maid-of-honor gown before it had been repaired.

"Ugh!" Wade yelled as he arched his back while digging deep into Slim's pussy.

Slim didn't know if he was yelling from the pain of the scratches down his back or from the pleasure of cumming inside of her as his dick began to jerk and spit.

"Oh God, Slim," Wade said as he trembled inside of her. "You make me feel so good. So fucking good." After lying on top of her frozen body while breathing heavily for a few seconds, Wade jumped up and got into the shower.

Slim peeled herself from the hard, cold floor and sat up. She watched Wade's silhouette through the frosted shower door as he hummed the tune of the latest rap song. A puzzled look came across Slim's face. She knew that Wade didn't even like rap music. Tye did. Wade preferred smooth classical and R & B. Rap music was too rough to listen to for him, but hell, as far as she knew, he didn't even like rough sex, but what she had just experienced with him was beyond rough. Slim felt as though Wade had walked out of that hotel room and returned as a different man. Now it was up to Slim to find out just who this *different* man was.

Chapter VIII

"Somebody's Sleeping in My Bed"

Slim sat at the bar alone, talking on her cell phone while Wade, Tye, Dinah, Cory and Mike all played one another in pool. Dinah may have gotten married to Tye, but as far as Slim was concerned, shit still hadn't changed, not for the better anyway. Wade still continued to spend time with Dinah and the gang. In Slim's opinion, that was the only time he seemed happy; the only time the two of them could manage to get along was if there was someone else around as a distraction. And if Slim wasn't mistaken, Wade made it a point to spend more time with Dinah and Tye than ever before, almost as if he purposely didn't want them to have any alone time. And any alone time he had with Slim was usually consumed with arguments as a result of his new arrogant attitude. Wade was starting to act like a complete asshole. He had even gone as far as constantly accusing her of cheating on him. Slim couldn't imagine wanting to have any alone time with the man she now shared her condo with ever since Tye and Dinah got married and Dinah moved in with Tye, pretty much forcing Wade out.

Wade stood back, sipping on a gin and juice while supposedly watching Dinah whup Cory in a game of pool. Tye, noticing that his brother wasn't really watching the game but was glaring over at Slim who was giggling and carrying on with her private phone conversation, approached his brother.

"You all right, man?" Tye said, putting his hand on Wade's shoulder and then following the direction of his brother's eyes over to Slim.

"Yeah, man, I'm good," Wade said, still glaring at Slim.

"You sure, partner?"

"Yeah, I'm sure." Wade finished off his drink.

Tye looked over at Slim and then back at his brother. "Let me go grab you another one," Tye said, taking the glass from his brother's hand.

"Cool, I gotta go piss," Wade said as he headed for the bathroom.

Tye made his way over to the bar.

"Another gin and juice for my brother and another beer for me," Tye said to the bartender. Just then, Slim quickly ended her call.

"Okay, talk to you later, Broy," she said, closing her flip phone, tucking it safely into her purse and then taking a sip of her wine spritzer.

"Oh, no need to end your call on the count of me," Tye said.

"Don't flatter yourself," Slim replied. "I just happened to be getting off the phone when you walked over."

"Really?"

"Yes, really," Slim said, rolling her eyes and taking another sip of her drink.

"I know you might think that this ain't none of my business, but when I see that my brother isn't happy, then I make it my business," Tye said to Slim, looking at her through the oblong bar mirror.

"Oh, don't you fucking start too," Slim said, a little tipsy but a lot tired of the accusations Wade had been making against her and was now feeding to his brother.

"I'm serious, girl," Tye said, grabbing hold of Slim's arm just as she was about to take another sip of her drink.

Slim looked down at her arm, where some of her wine spritzer had splashed on it. She then looked up at Tye, cutting him with her eyes. He released his hand and she yanked her arm away.

"What goes on between your brother and me is our business. You don't see me in your and Dinah's business, so stay out of mine. You got that?" Slim said, poking Tye in the chest. "But to put your mind at ease, no, I am not cheating on your brother if that's what he's telling you." Slim downed her spritzer. "I gotta get out of here. Tell Wade I stepped outside to get some fresh air." She looked Tye up and down before saying, "It stinks up in here." She then whisked away and walked out the door, but little did she know, Tye was right behind her. When they made it outside, Tye grabbed her arm once again.

"If you think I'm going to let you play my brother, then you've got another thing coming," Tye told her.

"Get off of me," Slim said, snatching her arm from him once again. "I'm not cheating on your brother. He's paranoid. I mean, he's even insinuated that I'm sleeping with Broy."

"Well, are you?"

Slim shook her head and sighed. "Trust me when I say that I'm the last person on earth that Broy would want to crawl into bed with. He's gay. He was born gay, for Christ's sake. He's never been with a woman in his life. We are friends, just like your wife and your brother are *just* best friends. Now, you wouldn't ever catch those two sleeping together, would you?" There was a hint of sarcasm behind Slim's tone.

Tye looked away, not responding to Slim's question. "Look, I'm not trying to fight with you, Slim. It's just that he's my brother is all. I don't like to see him hurting."

"And I don't like to see him hurting either, Tye." Slim pointed at her chest for emphasis. "You know that." Her eyes began to water. "And I would never want to hurt him." She quickly wiped away any tears before they could fall.

"I'm sorry, Slim," Tye said in a consoling tone. "I know that you would never *want* to hurt him. It's just that I know how it is sometimes, how shit can just happen when you least expect it to, or no matter how much you don't want it to happen, it does. And sometimes when that thing happens, somebody gets hurt. It's easy to get caught up. You and I both know that all too well. We don't *want* to hurt the people we love. Sometimes we just do."

Slim looked at Tye with fire in her eyes. "Maybe you know how it is sometimes, but I don't." Slim turned her back to Tye as if she couldn't look him in the face.

"Now don't go getting amnesia on me, girl," Tye said. A mischievous grin covered his face as he circled around Slim until he was facing her again. "I may be hard to remember, but I ain't that easy to forget," Tye said, rubbing Slim's chin with his index finger.

"Don't fuckin' touch me," she said, shooing Tye's hand away. "That was a long time ago, Tye, and if I remember correctly, it was something that I soon wanted to forget."

Although she had spit her words at him like swords, they didn't cut him. As a matter of fact, they humored him.

"But you didn't forget, did you?" Tye chuckled. "You crack me up, Slim. I mean, you always try to put on this persona as if you can do no wrong. Well, we all make mistakes, and a few years ago you made one. I made one. We made one together."

"So what's your point, Tye? Once a cheat always a cheat? What happened between you and I was stupid. I was hurting. Your brother and I had just had one of our split ups, and I was vulnerable. You took advantage of that."

Slim had wanted so badly to forget all about that night she had called herself as getting back at Wade by sleeping with Tye. It was one of those instances where she had accused Wade of sleeping with Dinah. At that point, Slim and Wade had never had intercourse with each other. He had sucked her titties, eaten her out, and finger-fucked her, and she had sucked his dick and jacked him off during their heavy petting and grinding encounters, but actual intercourse was something she wanted to give to her husband. But it was her fear of Wade not being able to wait on her that kept getting the best of her. It only made her think more that Dinah was giving Wade what she wasn't.

Wade had gone out of town with Dinah to visit

her parents in Oregon. Slim had been calling Wade all day and night, and he had finally answered his phone around midnight, claiming that he and Dinah had been out sightseeing and that he had left his phone at her parents' place. Slim didn't buy it. And then there was just something about the way Dinah's voice chimed in in the background during their phone conversation that just really made her feel jealous, insecure, and like something was definitely going on between the two.

For two hours Slim shouted out her suspicions into the phone until, finally, Wade hung up on her and turned his cell phone off. That was the straw that broke the camel's back for Slim. She figured if Wade wasn't alone at two o'clock in the morning, then why should she be? That's when she called Tye, crying. Her speech was so muffled from crying so hard, that all he heard was that something was going on with his brother. He jumped out of bed and made his way over to Slim's to find out just what in the hell was going on.

When he arrived, the door was unlocked and Slim was sitting on the couch with her chin on her knees, rocking back and forth, crying.

"What's wrong?" Tye had asked her as he walked over and sat down next to her. "Is everything okay with Wade?" He put his hand on her knee.

"No," Slim cried. "Everything's wrong." She put her feet on the floor and embraced Tye. At first he didn't know what to do. Usually women were throwing themselves at him in tears, begging him not to leave them, so in this case, with this crying woman, he didn't know what words to say to calm her.

"It's going to be okay, Slim," he said, telling himself, *What the heck* as he wrapped his arms around her. He never really cared a great deal for his brother's girlfriend. She didn't cut loose enough for his taste and was always stressing his brother out with her far-fetched insecurities.

"It's not; it's not going to be okay because I can't give him what he wants and now he's getting it from somewhere else." Slim pulled herself away from Tye and looked him in the eyes. "He's fucking her, Tye. I know he's fucking her."

"Who?" Tye asked, confused.

"Dinah. He's fucking Dinah."

Tye burst out laughing. He knew that was the furthest thing from the truth. Wade shared everything with Tye, so Tye knew better than to believe Slim's far-fetched idea that Dinah and Wade were more than friends. Matter of fact, he had joked with Wade by telling him that he needed to either learn how to play the harmonica like Stevie Wonder or the piano like Ray Charles because he was going to go blind from jacking off so much.

"Woman, you're crazy," Tye said as he continued laughing.

Slim couldn't believe her heart was hurting and here Tye sat laughing at her. His laughter was starting to anger her so much that out of nowhere, but surely out of anger, she slapped him, immediately ceasing his laughter. Tye balled his fist and flexed on her, taking everything in him not to punch her. She flinched and had the look of fear in her eyes.

Tye grabbed her and started shaking her. "Don't you ever do no shit like that again. Do you hear me? Huh?" He began to shake her harder.

"Get off of me!" she yelled as she began to swat at him. The next thing she knew, the two of them were tussling on the couch. Tye grabbed her by the wrists, and in her effort to pull away from him, they fell to the floor, him landing on top of her.

Breathing heavily, they'd stared into each other's eyes, and then Slim lifted her head off the floor just high enough for her lips to reach Tye's. She'd kissed him. She'd pulled away from him, stared at him for a reaction, and then kissed him again. He found himself kissing her back, and within seconds, Slim felt him growing rock hard against her. She reached down and massaged his hardness.

Still breathing heavily, she spoke. "Teach me how to do it. Teach me how so it can be right for your brother. I need to know how to please him, how to make him happy. Teach me, Tye," she begged.

Still holding on to her wrists, Tye pushed his tongue back into Slim's mouth and parted her legs with his leg. He then released one of her wrists and stuck his hand down her pajama pants. It felt like he was soaking his hand in a bowl full of water. Her wetness was immeasurable.

"Oh fuck, your pussy is wet," Tye moaned as he began fingering her. She was so wet that his fingers slipped in and easily got lost. "I can't believe this pussy ain't never been fucked," he mumbled. Tye could feel himself creaming his boxers. No broad had ever made him precum, and here he felt like he was going to explode at just the thought of being all up in her wet stuff.

"Teach me," Slim moaned as she squirmed on his hand, rocking herself against his fingers.

Tye removed his hand from Slim's crotch, released her other wrist, and pulled her pajama pants off. He then pulled his T-shirt over his head, unbuckled his belt, unbuttoned his jeans, unzipped them, and pushed them down to his knees. Forgetting—not considering or just plain old caught up in the moment—that Slim was a virgin, he then immediately threw his fishing pole into her deep waters.

"Ahhh," she screamed at the top of her lungs. "Tye!" she cried out as he pounded her profusely. Within seconds, Tye was cumming inside of her with his eyeballs rolled in the back of his head. That had been the best sex he had ever had in his entire life. They both had wanted it. And Slim wanted him to do it too; the fact that she had just stood there and accused him of taking advantage of her vulnerability had only pissed him off.

"I took advantage?" Tye said angrily. "You called me over to your house at two o'clock in the morning to supposedly talk about my brother. Bitch, I know a booty call when I get one." Tye caught himself, realizing that he had slipped up and called a woman the B word, something he had never done before, at least not to her face.

Slim's face froze. The truth hurt, but not nearly as much as the slap she laid across Tye's face. Tye only smiled and brushed off the blow, even though it stung the shit out of him.

"Don't hate the player," Tye said, hoping his next words would hurt Slim as equally as a slap would have. Oh how he wanted to lay one on her, but he would never consider hitting a woman. "Do you know how many nights I had to listen to my brother talk about his sweet little Virgin Mary? It took everything in me not to let him know that I had hit that. Then when you finally gave him a taste, that fool thought your pussy was molded to the shape of his dick. But the way you strung him on, for a full year almost, before you gave him any was almost comical to me. He wanted nothing more than to be your first. Little did he know that I was. Less did he know that he didn't have much to look forward to."

Once again, Slim raised her hand to haul off and slap Tye across his face. He tried to dodge the blow, but she caught him on the mouth. He bit down on his lip upon impact, causing it to bleed. He touched his lip, then saw that there was blood on his hand. He then licked the blood off his lip and, once again, smiled at Slim.

"You might want to stop hitting me. Remember what happened last time," he teased, "when you couldn't keep your hands to yourself?" He winked at Slim and then headed back into the bar.

"So who the fuck is he? Who you fucking around with, Slim?" Wade said as he held on to Slim's wrist. "Cory told me that he saw you downtown the other day when he was on a taxi run. You were coming out of a hotel."

Slim had barely had enough time to set her briefcase down when she came in after work. Wade was home waiting to accuse her of yet another act of infidelity.

"And he probably did see me, Wade," Slim explained. "I had a conference over at the Convention Center. Remember? I told you about that? The Convention Center is attached to a hotel, you know. You should have thought about that before you listened to your little friend who doesn't really like me anyway. Cory's probably just mad because he and his woman split up for good, and he wants you to be just as lonely and miserable as him. You know what they say: misery loves company."

Wade stood in their living room feeling real

stupid. He didn't think about that fact that Cory could have been blowing everything out of proportion just so that Wade could be in the same boat as he was.

For the third time in the past two months, he had suspected and accused Slim of being on the creep, but once again she had a clear and believable alibi and reason for being where she was or where she wasn't supposed to be. Wade's accusations were starting to get the best of Slim, though. She almost wished that the two of them had never moved in together.

After Tye and Dinah got married, Wade moved out of his and Tye's apartment and moved in with Slim. At first, Slim was more than excited to have him there. It was their first big step toward marriage, she thought. Slim figured that after living together and spending all of their time together, Wade would see that they might as well just get married. But after only six months, things weren't going quite as well on the home front as she thought they would be.

"You always got an excuse," Wade said, after his ego made the choice, even though Slim had explained herself, to still push the issue a little further. "When I found that receipt for that flower delivery, you claimed it was for a client of one of your big new accounts. When I found the dinner receipt for the M restaurant, you claimed that was business too. Since when has business become the front and center of your life?"

"Ever since I haven't become the front and center of yours," Slim retaliated, wiggling her wrists. "Let go of me, Wade," Slim said, snatching her wrist away from him. "What's gotten into you? You've been acting like some jealous, deranged boyfriend. You never even acted like this when we didn't live together, and hell, then is when I could have had any dude I wanted up in here fucking him."

After the blow to Slim's face, there was shocked silence.

"Oh, God, I'm sorry, baby!" Wade said, more shocked than Slim over the fact that he had just slapped her across the face. He tried to reach out to her.

"Get away from me!" she yelled, pushing him away. She began crying hysterically. She couldn't believe Wade had put his hands on her. He was the sweetest man she had ever known, but in the past few months, he had turned into a complete stranger.

"I'm sorry," Wade said as he still tried to reach out to comfort her.

"No! Don't you fuckin' touch me," she warned him, putting her hands up as a shield. She frantically looked for her keys and her purse until she found them sitting on the table by the door.

"Don't leave," Wade begged her. "I'm sorry. I've had a lot on my mind, and I'm just trippin'. I'm not myself. You know I would never hit you. I've never done anything to hurt you, woman." Wade grabbed his head as if it were about to explode. "You don't understand. There's just so much on my mind." He fell to his knees.

"What? What's on your mind, Wade? Make me understand. Just talk to me," Slim pleaded as she cried. "I've been trying to talk to you, to get you to talk to me, but you've put this brick wall up between us. I thought with you moving in things would be different, that we would get closer, but instead we've grown miles apart. You haven't even really touched me—made love to me—since that day in Rio when you threw me on the floor and practically raped me." Wade put his hands on his ears as if hearing those words coming out of Slim's mouth was the bloodcurdling truth that he had suspected about his unexplainable actions in Rio. "Maybe one or two times you've touched me, but even then it was rough and quick like I was just some hole in the ground you were sticking your dick into, and now you want to accuse me of cheating? If anything, I should question you."

"I know, I know, baby," Wade said with his hands up in surrender. "And I'm so sorry. Just hear me out. I want to talk to you. I want to talk to you now, baby; just put your keys and your purse down. Please don't leave me." Wade got down into a ball-like position, putting his head between his knees, and began to cry. He covered his face with his hands and just cried out. Slim's heart began to hurt for him more than the sting on her face hurt from his abuse. She slowly made her way toward him. She reached her hands out to let him know that she was there for him, but before she made it over to him, he spoke. "Please don't leave me," he cried into his hands. "Please don't leave me, Dinah. I love you so much. Please don't go."

Slim stopped in her tracks as her mouth dropped open and her eyes flooded with new tears. She began choking on her tears as she walked backward, away from Wade, until she disappeared behind the other side of the slamming door.

Chapter IX

"If I Was Your Girlfriend"

"I'm coming!" Broy shouted as someone stood outside his front door with their finger on the doorbell. "If this ain't gotdamn Ed McMahon with my ten million dollars, then someone is going to get their ass kicked straight-dude style," he yelled in warning to the person on the other side of the door. He opened the door, and before he could even say a word, Slim fell into his arms in tears.

Not knowing what was wrong with her, and therefore not knowing what to say, he just held her. "It's okay, baby," he said as he kissed her and rubbed her head. "It's okay." They just stood there for a few minutes, Slim crying in his arms and Broy rubbing her back, kissing her head every now and then.

Finally, Broy managed to get Slim inside the house and close the door behind them. She clung to him like she was born attached, not releasing him while he maneuvered. After soaking his shirt, she finally stopped crying and pulled away from him, which was when he saw her swollen eye. Without asking any questions, he immediately sat Slim down on the couch and made his way into the kitchen. He returned with a bag of ice and placed it on Slim's swollen eye.

After several minutes, Broy finally broke the silence. "Bitch, you gon' have to learn how to fight, take up karate or something because this shit is just ridiculous," he said, still holding the bag on her eye. "I thought you and that fish had kissed and made up anyhow."

"Dinah didn't do this, Broy," Slim said, pushing the bag of ice away.

"Who did, then?" Slim stared at Broy, letting her eyes do all the talking. He heard them loud and clear. "No, that fool didn't!" Broy said as he jumped off the couch. "Oh, his ass is going to jail. Any man that hits a woman is a punk and needs to be in jail taking it in the ass anyhow."

"What are you doing?" Slim asked Broy when she saw him pick up the phone.

"Calling nine-one-one," he stated matter-of-factly, "the real nine-one-one, the Columbus Police."

"No, don't do that," Slim said, racing over to him, taking the phone out of his hand and setting it back down in its cradle. "I don't want the police involved."

"Why the hell not?" Broy was curious to know.

Slim put her head down. "I just don't want to have to tell them that I let a man hit me. Besides, this was the first time anything like this has ever happened." Broy raised his eyebrow. "Broy, you know it is. I would have told you of all people if Wade had ever raised his hand to me before. I just don't want to go putting my business out there like that."

Broy closed his eyes and took a deep breath. He then opened them and shook his head at Slim. "Sweetie, you don't have to be ashamed to tell. There is nothing to be ashamed about. This is not your fault, and you didn't deserve it. Telling the police that you were assaulted is not putting your business in the street. This is reporting his ass so that the next woman doesn't have to go through this or maybe worse. You cannot let that man put his hands on you. You're his girlfriend, not his punching bag." He put his hand to her eye. "If you were my girlfriend—"

Slim looked up at Broy and cut him off. "I know, Broy. If I were your girlfriend, you would never hurt me, but I don't think Wade meant to hurt me either," Slim reasoned as she made her way back to the couch. The words *the next woman* had sent chills down Slim's spine. Although she was pissed the fuck off at Wade right now, the thought of him with another woman made her stomach turn. Not after all she had been through with his ass. She'd be damned if she let another broad just take over. Oh, hell no. "And I don't want him to have to go to jail. I mean, I know he didn't mean to do it. Something's going on with him. He's not himself. I mean, even before I left the house, he called me by another woman's name, Broy." Slim was too humiliated to even look at Broy.

"What? And you don't want me to call the police on his ass? That bastard needs to go to jail on GP alone for calling out another bitch's name. Who is she? Who'd he call you?"

First looking down in embarrassment, Slim then

turned to look at Broy and allowed her eyes to give him the answer to the question he had asked while adding, "Who do you think?"

Broy's eyes widened. "Oh, honey," Broy said as she walked over to Slim and sat down next to her just in time for her to go limp in his arms again in tears.

"I can't do it, Broy. I can't do it anymore. I love him to death, but I can't compete with her. I can't compete with Dinah." Slim pulled away from Broy and wiped her tears away. "I have to admit it; he's jealous. He's jealous that his brother married the closest friend in his life."

"Well, I can understand that to some degree. You do know that it's kind of an unspoken rule—you just don't fuck with your best friend's sister or brother. I mean, hell, if you had a fine-ass brother, I wouldn't get with him no matter how much I was diggin' on him. It's just something you don't do. It taints the friendship for some reason."

"No, Broy, you don't get it. He's not jealous that Dinah broke the unspoken rule. He's jealous because he wishes she had married him."

"Wade, what are you doing here?" Dinah said as she opened the front door, holding a bottle of red nail polish in one hand that had a fresh, dry coat of polish while blowing the fingernails of her other hand that were still wet.

"Where's my brother?" Wade asked, walking through the door like it was still his place.

"He's out at some weeklong manager-tenant training the complex sent him on. He won't be home for a couple of hours. He's been getting in late all this week." Dinah sensed something was wrong with him. "Wade, what's going on? You don't look too hot." She followed him over to the couch where he had sat down.

"Me and Slim just got into it," Wade informed her.

Dinah closed the door. "Do you want something to drink?"

"No, I'm good."

Dinah sat down next to him. Wade watched her pull her knees up to her chest where all he could see was her beautiful, thick legs hanging out of her tight-fitting little cotton shorts.

"Well, don't just sit there watching me paint my toes—tell me what's going on," Dinah said as she unscrewed the cap to the nail polish. "I might be your sister-in-law now, but I was your confidante first. Nothing's changed, Wade. Get to talking."

He stared at Dinah, who hadn't started polishing her toes yet but was picking at them. *You're wrong,* he thought as he stared at Dinah. *Everything has changed.*

"No, I don't want to talk about her. I just want to forget about the whole thing," he said, taking the bottle of polish from Dinah.

"What are you doing?" she inquired.

"Helping you out."

"Well, thank you." She smiled.

"Stretch your feet out over here on my lap."

Following Wade's instructions, Dinah placed her feet on his lap. This wasn't anything new. He had polished her toes before. She had even talked him into allowing her to polish his two big toes. She convinced him by telling her that if she had to play pool, watch basketball, and work out at the gym, then the least he could do was polish a couple of toenails. But she had repaid him plenty of times by giving him nice, friendly back massages on the occasions he had overexerted himself at the gym. Besides, she told him that if he was one of her girlfriends, part of girlfriend-hood was polishing each other's toes.

"You've got some really nice feet," Wade complimented as he sat the bottle of polish on the arm of the couch and started rubbing them. Before, when he had polished them, he never really paid that much attention to her evenly filed toenails and her soft heels. Nor had he noticed the sexy curve of her foot.

"Mmm," Dinah moaned, allowing her head to fall back. "A girl's best friend always knows what she likes." Dinah closed her eyes as Wade continued to rub her feet.

"I know we're friends and all, but what would Tye think if he came through the door right now?" Wade asked as she allowed his hands to grip her ankles. She squirmed and opened her eyes.

"I . . . I don't know. I guess this does look a little weird," Dinah said as she attempted to pull her feet off Wade's lap.

"No!" he said, pulling them closer to him. "You said nothing's changed."

Dinah paused for a moment and took in the seriousness of Wade's tone and the expression on his face. She then watched as he continued rubbing her feet, but he then raised one of her feet to his mouth and began kissing each toe with tiny pecks until he found himself French-kissing them. Dinah squirmed.

"Does he know?" Wade said, looking at her sensually while he flickered his tongue across her toes. "Does Tye know you got a thing about these feet of yours?" He shot her a sexy glance before inhaling her big toe.

"Ahhh," Dinah moaned as she sank down into the couch. Dinah couldn't even reply to Wade's question. She was too busy moaning and crooning from the wonderful sensation Wade gave her. Wade knew about her little foot fetish. She had told him about the time this guy she had gone out with sucked her toes until she came in her panties. She told him how embarrassed she was that a man had actually made her cream on herself without even touching her womanhood.

As she felt her clit begin to tingle, Dinah quickly opened her eyes. "Wade, stop it," she said, removing her feet from his mouth. "This isn't right." She went to get up.

"No, wait! I'm sorry." Wade rested her feet back on his lap. He picked up the nail polish and proceeded to polish her toes. "You're right. That ain't even cool." He slowly stroked each of her toenails with a coat of the red hot polish by Mary Kay until all ten were polished. "They're all done," he said as he twisted the cap back onto the bottle.

"Thank you," Dinah said.

"Let me blow 'em dry," Wade suggested.

"You don't have to do that." Dinah chuckled.

"I know I don't have to. I want to. Friends do things like this."

As Wade began blowing on Dinah's toes, he might as well have been blowing on her clit. The soft, gentle breeze was an aphrodisiac. Then out of nowhere, and to Dinah's surprise, the words "I love you, Dinah" dripped out of Wade's mouth.

Dinah just sat there for a moment. She knew that

the way Wade had just told her he loved her wasn't the way a person told their best friend that they loved them. It was the way one would tell their lover. Dinah exhaled. She exhaled the breath she had inhaled that day in her kitchen when she swore Wade to secrecy, not to tell Tye about their sleeping together. She hadn't really been able to breathe since.

Deep down in her soul, she knew she loved Wade on a much stronger level than just a friendship, but it was something she didn't want to deal with, so she buried it within her being.

She turned her head as if she had a pimple on her face and if she had allowed Wade to look at her long and hard enough, he would have discovered it.

"You know what I mean, Dinah, and no matter how much you've tried to hide it, I know you love me, too, the way that I love you."

At first Dinah wanted to deny it, but she couldn't. She did love Wade, more than he'd ever know, but she loved Tye, too, in a different way. If she were to just be honest with herself for once, she'd admit that being with Tye was the next best thing to being with Wade. It was easy for her to pretend that while Tye was making love to her that it was really Wade inside of her. She had even caught herself once from screaming out Wade's name during her love-making with Tye. But she had managed to bury her true feelings and cover it with cement, but now here Wade was with his jackhammer, drilling right through it. The feeling was too strong for her to hide anymore.

"Wade," was all Dinah could say as she crawled over into his lap. Straddling him, she began kissing him. "You don't know how bad I've wanted you inside of me again," Dinah said as tears fell from her eyes. "Wade, it's been so hard. I never wanted to feel this way. I swear I didn't. I love Tye, I really do, but I'm so in love with you, Wade. You are such a big part of me, a part of me that no man will ever be."

"Me, too, baby," Wade confessed as he palmed her ass in his hands. "Me too. I love you, too, and it's been harder for me than you'll ever know." He hugged her tightly in his arms.

After a couple of minutes, Dinah got off Wade and stood over him. Slowly she removed the gray T-shirt that matched the shorts she was wearing. She then stepped out of the shorts, where she wasn't wearing any panties, before grabbing Wade by the hands and leading him into her and Tye's bedroom. At the moment, though, she didn't see it as her and Tye's bedroom; right now the world and everything in it belonged to her and Wade. It was theirs.

After undressing, Wade found himself inside of Dinah, slowly pleasing her as her legs wrapped tightly around his waist.

"You feel so good inside of me," Dinah told him as she stared into his eyes as he moved in and out of her. "No man could ever make me feel the way you make me feel, Wade, ever. Make love to me, Wade. Do it like only you can." Dinah's words caused Wade to begin taking faster and longer strokes as he dipped in and out of her. "That's right, Wade. Right there, baby. Right there."

Soon there was nothing but the sound of wet, sweaty bodies smacking against each other as Wade and Dinah pleased each other. With an hour left before Tye was expected home, Wade decided to take a quick shower. After he turned on the water and lathered himself up, Dinah soon joined him in the shower where they made love again, standing up in the shower. It was like making love in the rain.

After they finished, Wade exited the shower first and got dressed. Dinah remained in the shower and washed up and got her hair together, which had gotten ruined in the shower during their love-making. Just as Dinah came out of the bedroom, Tye walked through the front door.

Chapter X

The End of the Road

"Bruh, what's up?" Tye said, walking over and hugging his brother while shaking his hand.

"Hey, nothing too much. I just stopped by to see if maybe you wanted to go out and shoot a game of pool or something. Slim and I got into it, and I guess I just wanted to talk. I know you just getting off work and stuff, so I'll drive and bring you back here."

"Man, you ain't said nothing but a thang. You know I'm here for you," Tye said. "Let me go get out of this suit and throw on a change of clothes and we can head out." Tye headed toward the bedroom where Dinah was still standing by the doorway. She nervously ran her hands down her hair, which was now slicked back in a ponytail. "Hey, baby," Tye said as he stopped to kiss her.

"Hey, sweetie," Dinah said. "I missed you."

"I missed you too," he replied. "Me and Wade are going to head out for a second."

"Yeah, I heard. That's cool."

"Did you cook?"

"I made a seafood pasta salad."

"Cool. I'll eat when I get back home," he said, kissing her one more time and then heading into the bedroom.

Dinah quickly walked over to the couch and gathered her T-shirt and shorts that she had thrown onto the floor. Thank God Tye didn't notice them.

After Tye changed his clothes, he and Wade headed out. Two hours later, Tye was on his second beer, they were on their third game of pool, and Wade was on his fourth gin and juice.

"Do you have any idea who she might be bonin'?" Tye said nonchalantly as he chalked the tip of his pool stick.

"Don't be so insensitive," Wade said, studying the pool table for his next shot.

"Oh, my bad, bruh. Do you have any idea who Slim might be running around with?"

Wade sighed, as if he hated to say the name that was about to come out of his mouth. "I think it's ol' dude. Her partner from work and shit."

"You mean the faggot?" Tye said, turning his nose up.

"Yes, Broy. The gay guy."

"Gay, faggot, drag, homo, whatever," Tye said. "Either way it goes, dudes fucking dudes is some sick shit. I'm not talking about being homosexual is sick; I'm talking about sleeping with one is sick. You know, a woman sleeping with a man who sleeps with men. You know what I'm trying to say?"

"Yeah, yeah, yeah. I get it already." Wade took a shot and scratched. "Fuck!"

"Look, man, enough pool. Let's go sit down at the bar and talk," Tye said, walking over to his brother and putting his arm over his shoulder. "I mean, your mind could just be playing tricks on you, homie."

"No, I seen the shit with my own two eyes," Wade confessed as they went and sat down at the bar.

Tye froze in shock. "You caught Slim bangin' ol' dude?"

"No, but I saw her with him," Wade said. The bartender then came over and took Wade's order of another gin and juice. "You want another beer?" he asked Tye.

"Naw, man, I'm straight. Two beers was enough for me tonight," Tye responded. "And I think you've had enough, too, my man."

"Aw, man, you know my tolerance level is high," Wade informed him.

"So anyway, what did you see going on with Slim and this Broy cat?"

The bartender handed Wade his drink, and Wade took a sip before beginning. "After we got into it and she left the house, I got in my car and followed her. I really wanted to apologize to her. Man, you know I've never hit a woman in my life. But anyway, when I was following her, she went straight to dude's house and knocked on his door. He opened it and they didn't even say 'hi' and shit. He just hugged all up on her and was kissing her and shit. I mean, it wasn't some quick little friendly hug either. They were embracing, and then he kept putting his lips on her, man. I knew if I got out of that car, I might do something that I'd regret even more, so I kept it moving."

"Damn, Wade man," Tye sighed. "You know you can stay with Dinah and me if you want to. Your old room is the guest room. Be our guest."

"Naw, man. I'm straight. I just need to go home and get my head right. From the looks of it, she'll probably be spending the night with Broy anyway. But even if she doesn't, I have to face her. I can't run from the situation."

"You sure? 'Cause you know I'm here for you." Just then Tye's cell phone rang. He looked at the caller ID, then answered it. "Yo, D, what's up?" Tye said as a huge smile took over his mouth.

Wade glared at his brother, wishing he was the one wearing the smile.

"Still hanging out with my brother," Tye said into his phone. "We're getting ready to call it a night. Why? Is dinner getting cold?" he said, laughing at his own joke.

"Where y'all at?" Dinah asked.

"Same old spot. Just at the bar shooting some pool."

"And without me?" Dinah asked, faking jealousy.

"Girl, stop playing," Tye said, rubbing his chin, grinning ear to ear. "Although a jealous woman does turn me on."

"Well, if you really want to get turned on," Dinah said in a sensual tone, "then you'd be wrapping up that game of pool and bringing your ass home right about now."

"Nuff said," Tye said anxiously. "Give me a few minutes and I'll be right there." He then cupped his hand around his mouth and the receiver and whispered, "And ya better be waiting butt naked in some high-heeled shoes." Dinah began to laugh. "The clear ones."

"The clear ones, huh?"

"Yeah, the Cind-hoe-rella shoes," Tye said.

"All right, baby. Just hurry home."

Tye hung up the phone and said to himself under his breath, "This honeymoon shit just never ends." He tucked his phone into his jacket pocket, then turned to finish up his conversation with Wade, but Wade was nowhere in sight. He had left the bar.

"Oh God, Dinah! Where is he? Is he all right? Where's Wade?" Slim yelled, running down the hospital corridor as she spotted Dinah, Cory, and Mike standing outside a hospital room. "Where is he?" Slim tried with all her might to get into the hospital room, but Cory and Mike blocked her.

"Slim, you don't want to go in there," Dinah said, shaking her head as tears began to fall.

"Damn it! Move the hell out of my way," Slim ordered.

"He's not in there, Slim," Dinah told her.

"Then where is he? Where did he go?" Slim screamed. "Somebody better fuckin' answer me right now!" She looked to Mike and Cory, who were silent and teary eyed.

Finally, Dinah shouted, "Wade is gone. He's gone." Dinah ended up breaking down while Slim stood in complete shock at the words she had just heard spoken.

The nurses began to stare at the commotion that was going on outside of room 599.

"Slim, I'm so sorry. I'm so sorry," Dinah cried.

The next thing anyone knew, Slim had hit the floor. When she finally came to, she was lying in an examination room of the hospital. As soon as she saw Dinah, Cory, and Mike staring over her, she remembered the final moments prior to her hitting the floor. Tears seeped from her eyes as she spoke. "Dinah, please tell me that it was all just a nightmare. Please tell me that Wade and Tye didn't get into a car accident and that they're both doing just fine," Slim begged as tears fell from her eyes.

"I wish I could, Slim," Dinah said, grabbing hold of Slim's hand. "Tye is going to be all right, but Wade . . ." Dinah's voice faded off.

As Slim lay there, she couldn't imagine how she was going to live without Wade. She wished their last few months together, their last minute together, had been better, but there was no turning back time now. As hard as it was to learn how to live with him, Slim knew that it wasn't going to be easy living without him. She knew that the same would be for Dinah too; she knew deep down in her heart that Dinah and Wade were closer than she could have ever been to him, and now none of that seemed to matter.

It would be Tye, who was lying in the hospital bed in the room next to Slim, who, once he woke from his drug-induced coma, would be absolutely devastated to learn that his brother was dead.

"Dinah?" the nurse said as she stuck her head into the examination room. "He's coming to and he's asking for someone named Dinah."

"That's me!" Dinah said. "I'm his wife. That's me."

"Come right away," the nurse said as she led Dinah over to Tye's room.

"Dinah!" she could hear him call. "Dinah! Where's my Dinah?"

"I'm here, baby. I'm right here," Dinah said, entering the room. She ran over to Tye's side, leaned

down over him, and began to weep on his chest.
At first she was weeping with joy that he was okay,
but then her weeping was for the loss of Wade and
the fact that she didn't know how she was going to
tell her husband that his brother was gone.

Tye began to rub Dinah's head. "It's okay," he
said to her, his eyes opening and closing, still a little
drowsy. "He's in a better place now."

All of a sudden, Dinah lifted her head and stared
at Tye in shock. She then looked over at the nurse.
Her eyes said to the nurse, "Did you tell him?" The
nurse shrugged her shoulders and shook her head
in the negative as if to suggest that she didn't know
how he knew his brother had passed.

"Who are you talking about?" Dinah asked, just to
make sure she was clear on what Tye was saying.
"What are you saying?"

"Wade . . . he is dead, isn't he?" Tye said, staring
at Dinah.

"Yes, he is," Dinah said softly as she nodded her
head.

Tye's eyes blinked a couple of times and then
they stayed closed, a single tear falling from his eye
as he fell back into a drowsy sleep.

Dinah just stood there watching him. She knew a
big part of him was missing now, so much that he
had felt in his spirit that his brother was no longer
with them. She knew as his wife, she would have to
do everything she possibly could to try to fill the
void that was now in Tye's life. But who would be
able to fill the void in her own?

Chapter XI

Double Life

As Tye lay across the bed on his stomach in all of his nakedness, Dinah began to slowly kiss the back of his neck. She had a gut feeling that this time their lovemaking would be what it once used to be—good. For a minute there, their lovemaking had been stagnant for the both of them. With all of their mourning over Wade's death, their bodies hadn't had the strength to want to interact with each other.

Mike and Cory had been very supportive, bringing them dinner, coming over to clean the house, and forcing them to go out to dinner just to get them out from between the four walls they had imprisoned themselves in. Even in Slim's own mourning, she was able to show support. For a couple of months she and Dinah talked on the phone constantly, reminiscing about their times with Wade. But then their phone calls became fewer and farther between as the healing process took place and they felt back to themselves again.

Soon Dinah and Tye found themselves smiling again, laughing at the good times they had had with Wade. So instead of being set on mourning his death, they celebrated his life.

Although it was hard for Tye and Dinah to get over the loss of Wade, with the love and support they had for each other, they managed to get through it. Six months later, they were just starting to fully get back to living a normal life.

As a result of the car accident, Tye had suffered some minor head injuries, which had caused him to forget some things, particularly certain things that had taken place in his and Dinah's relationship, but there was one thing he would never forget, and that was the way he felt when they made love.

"Oh, baby," Tye said as he reached back and rubbed Dinah's hair.

Slowly she continued down his back, planting her teeth softly into his flesh every now and then. She licked up, she licked down, stroking his back with her tongue like it was a paintbrush and his back was the wall she longed to cover in her warm, sweet saliva.

Dinah allowed her tongue to run over the arch of Tye's back, right down to the crack of his ass. And then she stopped all of a sudden.

"What's wrong? Why did you stop?" Tye asked when Dinah abruptly ceased her act of foreplay. When Dinah didn't respond to his query, Tye looked over his shoulder at her. She was frozen stiff and beads of sweat had formed on her head. "Baby, you all right?" he asked, concerned. Tye got up and ran his hands down her hair as she began to tremble. "Sweetheart, talk to me," he said, slightly shaking her. "Come on, honey, talk to me. You don't look good. You look as though you've seen a ghost."

Dinah stared into his eyes as tears formed in her own. She slowly lifted her hand and ran it down her husband's face. She opened her mouth, but only air came from her throat.

"Dinah, please talk to me," Tye said worriedly. "Please."

As the tears escaped Dinah's eyes and as she continued to rub her husband's face, softly spoken words flowed from between her lips. "Wade?" she said. "Wade?" Noises of crying began to softly wail from her throat.

He swallowed. He swallowed hard. Dinah repeated herself as she took small, deep breaths and the tears continued to flow.

"Wade?" She began nodding her head up and down. "It's you, isn't it?" He looked down without answering. "It is you." Dinah broke down in tears. "Wade. Oh my God, Wade?"

"Shhh," he told her as he pulled her against his chest, holding her head tight to him while rocking her. "Shhh. It's okay."

Dinah continued to cry freely. "Oh God, Wade, I don't . . . I don't understand. I knew something was different about you; your personality and the way you were acting, but I just thought the death of your brother had changed you. I thought maybe I had changed or that you weren't acting yourself as a result of the accident and I didn't want to say anything because—"

"Shhh, listen," he whispered softly as he comforted her. "Shhh."

Dinah just shook her head. "What have you done? Wade, what have you done?"

He took her face into his hands and stared into her eyes as she cried a puddle of tears that raced from the palm of his hands down his arms. "I've made it so that we can be together for the rest of our lives, Dinah. That's what I've done," he answered.

"But . . . but I—"

He cut her off. "I love you, Dinah." He leaned in toward her, going in for a kiss. But he moved slowly in order to get a feel of where her head was. His lips touched hers. He pulled back to look at her reaction. She trembled as tears continued to flow. "Yes, it's me, Dinah. It's me, Wade." He kissed her again. He pulled back to look at her again, and this time her eyes were closed as tears forced their way out from under her lids and flowed down her face. He then kissed her again, and when he parted her lips with his tongue, she accepted it. For a moment the two just sat there kissing like long-lost lovers. Then Dinah slowly pulled away. But Wade wanted more of her.

"Oh God, Wade," Dinah said as she allowed him to pull her head back by her hair and kiss and roll his tongue across the front of her neck. "Oh God, Wade," was all she could say as he laid her down on the bed and parted her legs.

As he kissed her mouth, his hand found its way down to her pussy where he proceeded to finger-fuck her while he tongued her down. Her hips slowly rose up and down to the rhythm of his finger strokes. Her pussy was the violin strings to the romantic tune he was playing.

"Oh, ahhh, Wade," she moaned through kisses as he fondled her hot and bothered womanhood with his fingers. "I missed you." Tears streamed out of her eyes as she lay there, feeling a puddle of wetness underneath her from her own juices.

"I've been here, Dinah," Wade told her as he stopped kissing her and looked into her eyes. "I've been here for you all along. It's been me."

Dinah touched his face as if she still couldn't believe that it was Wade. The moment she saw his birthmark, she knew it was Wade and not Tye. She had given him enough back massages to identify it. She had to admit, however, that she felt as though Wade had been with her all this time, that it hadn't been Tye at all. But she just passed it off for being one of her old twisted feelings of the past when she would imagine that Tye was actually Wade. But once she noticed that the birthmark on his lower back folded into the shape of a heart instead of the oval shape that she knew Tye's was, there was no doubt in her mind that the man she had been with for the past six months wasn't Tye at all but was Wade.

After staring into Wade's eyes for a few more seconds, realizing that it wasn't a dream, that it really was Wade, Dinah put her hand behind his head and pulled it down to her and began kissing him hard. Even though for the past few months she thought she had been kissing Tye and it was really Wade all along, something about now knowing who the man, in fact, really was that had been lying next to her at night only made her more excited. It excited Wade as well.

He placed himself deep inside of Dinah and exhaled. It felt good to have Wade inside of Dinah with her finally knowing that it was his dick, and not his brother's, that was embedded in her walls. It was the love vessel of the man who had loved her since forever and a day.

In and out Wade pumped, and Dinah humped back with him. As they climaxed together, they were both overcome with such emotion that as their bodies erupted, so did the tears from their eyes. And then they lay there, still wrapped up in each other, weeping.

After making love, weeping for joy and then making love again, Dinah and Wade finally decided to take a rest from loving each other's temples. But just as Wade expected, Dinah had one hundred and one questions for him that she wanted answers to. Dinah sat up on the bed with the sheet pulled over her naked body, sticky with her and Wade's sweat and juices, as she listened intently as Wade described the night of the car accident.

"It was all his idea," Wade started. "It was all Tye's idea. I had had way too much to drink that night. Slim and I had gotten into it and you and I had just . . ." He paused and took a deep breath. "I remember my brother and I were at the bar and his cell phone rang. You called him. From the minute he said 'hello' into that phone receiver, his entire world changed. I could see it in his eyes. Your voice trickled into his ear, and I just watched his face light up as he talked to you. Knowing what you and I had just done . . ." Wade shook his head and took a deep breath as he forced himself to continue. "I couldn't bear that cross of both jealousy and guilt that was branded in my heart. I couldn't take it. So I just got up and left the bar. Well, Tye came right out after me just as I was getting in the car."

"'Hey, bruh,' he called to me, 'wait up!' He got into the passenger side and I just sped off. He detected that something was wrong other than my fight with Slim. He said that he knew that I was hurting bad because he, himself, could feel my pain through his own heart. He said that he couldn't stand to see me hurting, so he begged me to tell him what was going on with me." Wade paused for a minute. "And so that's when I told him."

The hairs on Dinah's head stood up. The hairs on her arm flared and tingled. She swallowed and then spoke. "That's when you told him what?" she asked nervously.

"That's when I told him about us, Dinah," he said, looking up at her.

Dinah put her hand over her mouth as tears formed in the corners of her eyes. She closed her eyes and was able to send the tears back to where they had come from without falling down her face. "He knew about us? He knew about me and you? He died knowing that . . ." Dinah broke down in tears just trying to fathom what her husband's last thoughts of her probably were. "Oh God, Wade, no! Why did you tell him? You promised." She put her head down and cried in shame. "You promised."

"It's okay, Dinah. He forgave you. He forgave us." Wade put his hand on her knee. "He forgave us," he repeated.

Dinah looked up at Wade. "Did he say that?" She was anxious to know. "I mean, were those his exact words, because I swear, Wade, if he didn't, I don't know what—"

"Shhh," Wade said, cutting her off by placing his index finger on her lips. "Those were his exact words."

"Oh God, thank you," Dinah said, looking up to the ceiling. She felt some solace in knowing that Tye had forgiven her for her act of adultery she had committed on the very evening of his death. "What did he say?" Dinah hesitantly asked. She didn't know whether she should leave well enough alone and just live with the fact of knowing that Tye had forgiven her, or if she should ask for details. But she felt that not knowing was one of the worst things in life, so curiosity got the best of her. "What exactly did he say?"

Wade paused for a minute. "Well, he didn't say anything at first. He just had this blank look on his face. I knew he felt as though a knife had just gone into his back and out of his heart, because I felt the pain in my own heart. Being twins is crazy like that." Wade took a deep breath as he fought back tears before he continued. "After I told him that you and I had slept together, not only prior to his marriage to you, but that very night, I wanted to take my words back, but I couldn't. I looked over to him for a reaction, but he just sat there in shock and disbelief. I was so busy staring over at him that I didn't realize I had gone left of center until the horn from the car I was about to smack head-on started blowing. That's when I swerved over from hitting the oncoming vehicle, lost control of my car, and we went over the embankment."

Wade had an intense look on his face as he described the accident. "The world was spinning and turning. Glass was shattering and flying everywhere. There was darkness. There were trees. The car went flipping out of control into this field. It felt like it was never going to stop, and it probably wouldn't have if we hadn't slammed head-on into that tree.

All of a sudden the car just stopped. BAM!" Wade smacked his hands together in demonstration. "I felt the life seeping out of me, like a part of me was evaporating. I automatically started moving parts of my body to make sure my limbs were still in place and working. But still, I just felt like death, like I was on my last breath. I looked down at myself, but yet I didn't even seem to have a scratch on me. That's when I looked over at Tye and saw that his neck was broken."

"How could you tell?" Dinah inquired, trying not to cringe at the painful details.

"I don't know," Wade said as he shrugged his shoulders. "I could just tell. I guess it was the way he was just sitting there—limp and lifeless and not moving. I asked him if he could feel anything." Wade's eyes began to flood. "I asked him to try to move a little, to try to move anything—something— just wiggle a toe, but he couldn't." Wade couldn't fight back his tears as they streamed down his face. "He couldn't lift a finger, Dinah. He told me he couldn't feel anything. He couldn't feel any parts of his body. He couldn't even feel his lips moving."

"Oh God, baby, I know it must have been hard for you to see him like that; to watch your brother . . ." Dinah paused. "Wade, I'm so sorry you and your brother had to go through that. I'm so sorry," she said as she wrapped her arms around Wade and they wept together. After a few seconds she said, "But I still don't understand . . . how was this Tye's idea?"

"He knew that he was going to die, Dinah," Wade answered. "He could feel it. I could feel it in my soul. His last breaths felt like my own. He also knew that I had had way too much to drink that night and that I would have gone to jail, not only for DUI, but for vehicular homicide. So . . ." Wade started crying as he continued, repeating to Dinah his brother's last words to him. "'Try to move me over into the driver's seat, man,' he instructed me. 'Tell 'em I was the one driving. Tell 'em it was me.'"

"And what did you say?"

"I refused at first, of course. I mean, I didn't think I would be able to, but we weren't pinned in the car or anything."

"So what did you tell him?"

"'I can't move you, Tye,'" I tried to tell him. 'You can still make it, man. Even with a broken neck you can still live, but if I move you, Tye . . .' I tried to explain, but then he just got angry with me and shouted to me that his fuckin' neck was broken. But I kept telling him that didn't mean that he had to die, that he could still live with a broken neck. But then he just kept telling me of the quality of life that living with a broken neck would entail. Life in a wheelchair. Never being able to feel again; never being able to touch again." Wade looked up at Dinah. "He asked me to imagine him having to spend the rest of his life with you as his wife and never being able to touch you again."

Dinah swallowed her tears and shook her head in the negative. She couldn't imagine how awful life would have been for him. After calming herself down, she asked, "So you moved him?" Dinah asked, wiping her tears.

Wade broke down in sobs. "Yes! Yes!" he cried out. "I moved him anyway, damn it!" Dinah got up and wrapped her arms around Wade. "I reached over to lift him, and before I moved him, he said to me, 'I want you two to be happy. Tell Dinah that I forgive her. I forgive you both. Take care of her, bruh.'"

Wade and Dinah sat there in a ball weeping and holding each other.

"He said for me to tell you thank you for making his last days the happiest days of his life. Can you believe that?" Wade turned to Dinah. "He told me that he forgives me because he knows how it felt, how easy it was to be in love with you and how hard it was not to be."

"I loved him, too, Wade, I really did. In spite of everything, you've gotta know that."

"Dinah, I know that you loved my brother. I loved my brother. But whether I know how much you loved him doesn't matter. He knew, Dinah. He knew."

"Thank you, Jesus," Dinah said to herself as she closed her eyes. "Thank you." She wiped her face, hoping it would be for the last time, and then a sudden thought entered her mind. "How come the hospital didn't know that you weren't who you said you were?" Dinah asked.

"What reason did they have not to believe me?" Wade reasoned. "Besides, I learned by watching an episode of *Forensic Files* a long time ago that no two people in the world have the same DNA except for identical twins. There was no way that the hospital could have ever known that it was actually Tye who died in the car accident and not me; that was, unless they had known about our birthmarks, which they didn't."

"But I guess what I still don't understand is the part about you pretending to be Tye. I mean, you could have easily walked away from that car accident as yourself. After all, you had moved Tye to the driver's seat, so the matter of you being charged with driving the car was no longer an issue."

Wade took a deep breath, ran his hands down his face, and gathered himself. "I didn't want to hurt Slim," Wade confessed, staring off. "I guess you could say I 'pussied out.' Sure I could have just walked away from that accident as myself, but then I would have had to face my own life, a life that I never wanted to look back on. I would have had to put some closure to it, which would have meant hurting Slim. I didn't want to hurt her. I had already hurt her enough."

"I understand not wanting to deal with everything, but, Wade," Dinah said sincerely, "Slim loved you. I mean, hell, you were at the funeral. You saw how tore up she was. You could see the loss in her eyes whenever we were around her. That wasn't an act."

"I must admit, at first I did feel bad. It was hard seeing the effect my death had on her. But then, just like I figured, Broy came to the rescue. I mean, I honestly thought about what I was doing to her sometimes and would just want to pick up the phone and call her from the grave, so to speak, to tell her that I was sorry. But that day she waltzed over here announcing that she had moved on with her life and was seeing someone because she knew '*that's what Wade would have wanted*,'" Wade said, mimicking Slim, "and that she wanted to tell us first before we heard about it; something told me that the minute you asked her who this new someone was, she was going to say 'Broy.' I just knew it. Low and behold, that was the name that came out of her mouth." Wade let out a sarcastic chuckle. "Can you believe it? Slim and Broy, a couple? Boyfriend and girlfriend?" He chuckled again. "Gay my ass. More like bisexual. I knew that dude liked pussy. He may have liked dick, but he liked pussy too."

Wade was right. Slim had mourned hard for him for a couple of months. But of course Broy was there to help her get through it. It would be Wade's death that would end up bringing the two of them together as a couple.

"Now I know why you were so angry that day Slim came to the house to tell us that she was seeing someone and that it was Broy," Dinah said. "You weren't upset that she had moved on so quickly after your brother's death; you were upset because you had suspected all along that the two of them had been sleeping together and you wanted to call her on it, but you couldn't or else you would have blown your cover."

"Tye always tried to tell me that Slim wasn't the woman I thought she was," Wade said. "I should have listened to him. He said that girls who pretended to be as pure as her were usually the biggest hoes out there, running around screwing everybody. He was right. Tye always did have a sixth sense about those kinds of things." Wade chuckled and stared down at the ground. "But, hell, knowing my brother, he probably fucked her himself behind my back. But I guess that would serve me right. You know what they say about that bitch named Karma."

"So now what?" Dinah said, shrugging her shoulders. "Where do we go from here? What's everybody going to think when we tell them the truth?"

"Truth?" Wade said, grabbing Dinah by the hands. "We can't tell anyone else the truth. I could go to jail for this, Dinah. If that was the case, I might as well have kept my black ass behind the steering wheel of the car that night. If we tell anybody, then that means everything my brother went through would be in vain."

"But, Wade," Dinah started, trying not to become emotional.

"But nothing, Dinah." He caressed her hands and smiled into her eyes. "Let's make this our truth. Dinah, I'm serious," Wade said, looking into her eyes. "Has there ever been a time in your life when you wished you could just end it? I mean, not die or kill yourself or anything like that, but to just walk away from the life you are living and just start a brand-new one? Be an entirely different person?" Dinah just sat there, knowing that everyone during the darkest times of their days has wished they could just start life over as a different person, erase their past. "Have you?" Wade repeated.

"Yeah." Dinah nodded.

"Well, I had that opportunity that night six months ago in that car. And you have that very same opportunity now."

"What are you saying?" Dinah asked Wade, somewhat confused.

"I'm saying that let's just pick up and go." Wade stood up and spun around with his arms raised. "Let's leave all of this behind and start new lives somewhere else."

"Wade, we can't just pick up and go. That takes money and believe me when I tell you that my paycheck alone isn't enough," Dinah stated matter-of-factly because she knew that Wade hadn't gone back to work in Tye's position as property manager, or any other job for that matter. Dinah had been flipping the bills alone.

"We don't have to worry about money. I was the beneficiary on Wade's, I mean Tye's, I mean . . . you know what I mean. I was the beneficiary on the life insurance and the accidental death policy. I have almost a half million dollars sitting in the bank. But I wasn't going to touch it, Dinah. My conscience wouldn't allow me until I came clean with you."

"Until you came clean with me?" Dinah questioned with a puzzled look on her face. "So you had actually planned on telling me all of this someday?"

Wade proceeded to tell Dinah how he knew that if he lived as Tye, that eventually they would grow a bond so strong and unbreakable that he could someday share the truth with her and explain why he had lied about his identity. He hoped that she would understand that he didn't want to live without his brother, so he would live as his brother. He told her that on a sudden impulse, in addition to allowing him to walk away from his own life, that it was, although twisted, a way of keeping Tye alive. He also told Dinah that he hoped that by giving up his own identity and taking on that of his brother's in order to share a life with her, that she would see just how much he truly loved her.

"Wade, I do love you," Dinah assured him. "And there is nothing more that I want than to live life with you—my husband—forever."

"Oh, Dinah," Wade said as he hugged her and held her tight in his arms.

Suddenly, Dinah pulled away from him.

"Dinah, honey, what's wrong?" Wade asked her. "What is it?"

"But there's just one thing," Dinah started. "If we are going to start over and leave our past behind, then there's something I need to tell you now so that I can get it off my chest, leave it behind and not take it with us into our new lives."

"What is it?" Wade asked.

Dinah took a deep breath and proceeded to tell Wade about her tryst with Slim. She didn't know what type of reaction to expect, but what she didn't expect was him to burst out into laughter.

"What's so funny?" Dinah asked Wade.

"That explains everything," Wade said, trying to tone down his laughter. "She wasn't jealous of you because of our friendship. She was angry at the fact that ultimately you ended up with me instead of her. Deep down inside, I think she wanted to be with you." Wade ran his finger down the brim of Dinah's nose and winked. "You're just addictive, girl."

Dinah thought about Wade's analogy for a moment and agreed. "I never really thought about it that way, but I think you're right. At first I thought she just hated the fact that I was carrying around her dirty little secret to dispose of anytime I wanted to. But I kept asking myself why she would think that because I had just as much to lose as she did. I mean, what would you have thought of me had you known I—?"

Wade cut her off by placing his index finger over her lips. "Nothing less than what I think of you now," Wade assured her, placing a kiss on her forehead.

Dinah looked up into his eyes. "I love you so much, Wade, and our new life together is going to be better than anything you could ever dream of." Dinah threw her arms around Wade and just held him.

Wade was relieved that Dinah had decided to believe in him and his love for her and agree to start life over with him. They decided that they would move to California, where they were sure they could get lost in the shuffle and just live life carefree. But what had Wade even more relieved was that Dinah believed all of the lies he had told her about the night of the car accident when his brother lost his life, or rather, when he took his brother's life.

Everything about that night that Wade had told Dinah had been true up to the part after the car hit the tree. That's when he embellished the story in order to get Dinah to start a relationship with him with a clear conscience. He knew that unless she thought that their affair had been put out in the open and that Tye had forgiven her, she wouldn't be able to move on and share a life with Wade. The guilt would get to her. But in all reality, forgiving her was the last thing on Tye's mind before he took his last breath.

"Are you okay?" Wade asked Tye as they sat in the wrecked vehicle. "Are you hurt?"

"Am I hurt?" Tye was able to manage through the pain of talking with his broken ribs. "Hell, yeah, I'm hurt, man." He grabbed his ribs. "But I'm more hurt that my brother is a Judas and my wife is a whore."

"Please, man, I'm sorry."

"I know," Tye huffed. "Sorry that you aren't me."

"What?" Wade said with a confused look on his face.

"You heard me. You've always wanted to be me. I've seen it in your eyes ever since we were kids."

"Tye, you're talking crazy. Let's just get you out of the car," Wade said as he reached over to give his brother a hand.

"I hope you don't think that by telling me about you and Dinah, that that means I'm just going to divorce her and turn her over to you. You can forget it, so you're going to be the same miserable bastard after all of this that you were before."

Something in Wade just snapped and instead of leaning over to help Tye out of his seat belt, he found one hand *around Tye's head and one hand around his neck and then SNAP!*

That night Wade proved that blood might be thicker than water, but not even blood could dilute the power of love.

And Cain talked with Abel his brother: and it came to pass, when they were in the field, that Cain rose up against Abel his brother, and slew him.—Genesis 4:8

THE END

The Ghostwriter

*How far is one willing to go to
turn fantasy into reality?*

Chapter I

Beautiful One

"Mr. Irving, you have a call on line one," Rhain said through the intercom on her desk that she used to communicate with Mr. Irving from 8:00 A.M. through 5:00 P.M. Monday through Friday.

"Thank you, sweetheart. Put it through," Mr. Irving replied.

Rhain put the call through, rolling her eyes up in her head. She hated when her boss called her "sweetheart" but never verbally expressed her dislike for it. For seven years he had been calling her "sweetheart," and for seven years she had detested it, but in order to keep the peace, and her job, she said nothing.

Even as a little girl, Rhain was always a peace-keeper. She never liked to make waves. Making waves brought attention, and the last thing she wanted was attention. She felt that the more attention people would pay her, the more they would notice her. The more people noticed her, the more people would be able to detect her flaws—her flaws that she was so very insecure about.

Rhain was twenty-five years old and had never experienced intimacy with a man, or even the mere companionship of a boyfriend, because she was too busy keeping the world at bay. If anyone got close to her, they'd notice the slight acne problem she had been battling ever since her teenage years. She gave up soda pop and chocolate bars, thanks to the myth that those were the things that caused pimples. But in all actuality, the bumps came from the stress of her worrying about her so-called imperfections. One of which was her lazy left eye. It was hardly noticeable, and she could probably correct it herself by wearing a patch over her right eye to train the left one. But even if she were to correct it, there was always that gap between her two front teeth that prevented her from engaging in open-mouthed smiles. Thank goodness for the acting community and the lovely actress Lauren Hutton, who never let something like a gap between her teeth stop her from getting in front of the camera. Instead of just looking at these things as unique individual trademarks, Rhain chose to round them all up into a huge pile of shortcomings.

"Rhain, sweetheart, before you go, can you bring me the Coleman file?" Mr. Irving said through the intercom after he had ended his call.

"Certainly," Rhain said as she shut her computer down and then headed over to the file cabinet. She then grabbed her sweater from the back of her chair, put it on, and then headed into her boss's office.

She always made it a point to wear a sweater whenever she went into his office. It was guaranteed to be freezing cold in there, something Rhain concluded that her boss was doing deliberately. She felt that he kept the temperature down so that every time she entered his office he could watch her soft brown nipples grow into chocolate fudge pops as they hardened from the coldness.

Now I got something for that ass, she thought as she closed her sweater and folded her arms in front of her.

"Here you are, Mr. Irving," Rhain said as she walked into his office and handed him the file. "Is there anything else you need before I go?"

Mr. Irving paused and then gave Rhain *the look*. A look that replaced the words, that if he had dared spoken, would have landed him a sexual harassment charge.

"Yes, there's something else," she imagined him saying. *"How about a cup of coffee and a blow job?"*

Dirty old pervert, Rhain thought to herself. *Men and what they'll stick their dicks into. I'm the least attractive girl working for this company, yet that makes no never mind to his horny ass at all. Sad.*

"Can you think of anything else?" was Mr. Irving's reply to Rhain's query as he licked his lips and stared at her with those googley brown eyes of his.

He wasn't bad-looking for a man in his late forties; well, not to a woman in her late forties anyway. His chiseled brown skin, full beard, and mustache were very becoming. The fact that he used the company gym every morning before clocking in did wonders for his well-cut physique, that and the fact that he got a great workout after business hours doing push-ups with Evelyn, the new receptionist.

It was just last week when Rhain realized, while in the grocery store line, that she had left her wallet in her desk and had to go back to the office after hours to get it. Once she arrived at her desk, she could hear the moaning, groaning, humping, and bumping through the closed office door. She learned that Mr. Irving loved being called "Daddy" during sex because every time Evelyn shouted out the word, the clapping of their skin got faster and harder. It was when Evelyn first called out the word "Daddy" that Rhain was able to recognize her voice.

After grabbing her wallet, she wanted to just head back out the door and go claim her merchandise that the clerk had bagged and set aside for her at the counter, but curiosity got the best of her. Tiptoeing over to Mr. Irving's door, Rhain placed her ear against it and listened.

"Oh, Mr. Irving," Evelyn called out. "Fuck me just like that, Daddy."

"Mmm, you like it from the back, huh?" Mr. Irving said as he dipped his forty-something-year-old hard dick into Evelyn's twenty-one-year-old pussy.

"You know I do," she answered. "Now make it cum. Make it cum for me, Daddy."

"Oh shit," Mr. Irving yelled out as he began thrusting faster and harder into Evelyn. "Oh, look what this young, tight pussy is about to make me do. Oh shit, I'm about to fuckin' bust!"

"Oh, uhh, ahh, yes, yes, yesssssssss!" Evelyn roared.

Rhain stood at the door trembling, with her clit tingling, squirming in her panties.

"Oh God," she whispered under her breath as the intensity of their sex had her hot and bothered. She swallowed hard, placed her wallet under her armpit, and hurried off to her car. Once inside, she threw her wallet into the passenger seat, looked around to make sure no one else was in sight, and then quickly placed her hand down her pants.

"Oh, uh, uh, uh, uh," she moaned as she allowed her index finger to quickly rub back and forth over her thick throbbing clitoris. It didn't even take one minute for Rhain to make herself cum in her panties. Who knew that just listening to Mr. Irving and Evelyn have sex would have that type of effect on her?

Initially, Rhain had assumed that it was Kenya, the input clerk, he was screwing, considering she was the one he was getting free feels from under the table at their last departmental lunch. All Rhain knew was that no way was she going to become another notch on the belt of the president of the claims department of Heigan National Insurance.

"As a matter of fact, I can think of something else I could do for you, Mr. Irving," Rhain said, looking over the rims of her brown-framed *Essence* eyeglasses. "Valentine's Day is right around the corner, a little less than a month away. It will sneak right up on you before you know it. Would you like me to pick up something for *Mrs.* Irving?" Rhain said with a subtle smirk. Whenever she made mention of his wife in the premature stages of his sexual innuendos, that always seemed to make his horniness go down.

Why he chose to cheat on Mrs. Irving was beyond Rhain. His wife wasn't a bad-looking woman at all. Word was that he had met her in a strip club twenty years ago, where she used to dance to make money to survive. So Rhain knew this woman had to recall some of her old moves that she could utilize in the bed to keep her man happy. But men like Mr. Irving were one of the reasons why Rhain was still a virgin. *Dogs,* she would think. *They're all dogs, and if*

they think they're going to be wagging their tails all up in
my cat, only to run off with the next kitty, they are sadly
mistaken.

"Uh, yeah, well, uh, that would be nice," Mr.
Irving stammered. "Valentine's gift, yeah. Perhaps
you should pick one up."

"Very well. You have a good evening, sir," Rhain
said as she headed out of his office.

"You do the same." He sounded defeated.

Rhain couldn't help but grin as she grabbed her
coat and purse and headed to her car. After looking in the rearview mirror and patting down her
reddish-brown hair that was neatly concealed in a
tight bun, Rhain started up her five-year-old Toyota
Camry and headed for home.

On the way, Rhain made her customary stop at
Carlos' Place for her usual, a Cobb salad with extra-
grilled chicken. Rhain typically ate out more than
she ate at home. For single people, it was sometimes
cheaper eating out than cooking up a meal and
wasting the majority of it because there was no one
else in the house to partake in it. And it never took
long for her to get burnt out on the boxed or frozen
dinners that filled her cupboards and freezer. So,
since Carlos' was right around the corner from her
apartment, it quickly became her favorite place to
get takeout. It was a restaurant/bar and one of the
most popular joints in Bexley, a suburb of Columbus, Ohio. They had the best happy-hour prices in
town. If Rhain had been a drinker, she might have
ordered one of their famous half-priced margaritas
to down while she waited on her order, but instead
she sipped on her usual cherry Coke.

It was Friday night, so the place was filled with the
regular Friday happy-hour customers. After getting

her salad, Rhain went home and placed it in the refrigerator while she took her shower. She always liked to shower and get comfy before settling down to her dinner. Afterward, she flipped the switch to turn on her living room gas fireplace. She then sat down on the floor in front of the television to catch the last of the evening news while enjoying her salad.

After the news went off, Rhain headed to her bedroom that was decorated in an Old English style with high oak bedposts that were only a few inches away from touching her ceiling. She turned on her computer that sat in the corner of her bedroom on a Queen Anne–style whitewash desk. She then nestled into bed while it booted up. She leaned over and pulled out a pen and her journal from the night table drawer that contained her original poetry. She flipped through the journal and read a couple poems that brought a smile to her face.

Her writing was something, the only thing, that she wasn't modest or embarrassed about displaying. Whenever someone in the office had a birthday, she always created a special poem for them or created a card in Photoshop with one of her original quotes or sayings inside it. Pretty soon, whenever a birthday or special occasion came up at the office and someone had forgotten to at least go out and buy a card for her coworkers, they would pay Rhain to create a poem or make a card. One of "Rhain's Originals" is how they referred to her work when making a request. It got to the point where people would pay for a Rhain's Original for their friends and family members as well.

Rhain started to invest in card stock and scrapbook crafts to enhance the appearance surrounding her written words. Each card or poem was made specifically for that individual. This added a personal and unique touch to the already moving words she created, a touch that couldn't be bought in any Hallmark card shop, making it, indeed, an original. Rhain even had a special stamp created at Staples that read "Rhain's Original" and had her e-mail address on it. Little did Rhain know at the time, but that would be the beginning of a very profitable side gig.

She started receiving e-mails left and right from people who had used her services before or who had been the recipients of one of her originals. In a matter of months, the request went from just poems and cards to speeches and letters. Rhain had to create a PayPal account to start receiving payments for her services online. Depending on the caliber of the client, Rhain got paid anywhere from $5 to $10 for a poem or card, and $100 to $1,000 to write speeches and letters. Because her business was computer-based, she knew most of her clients only by their screen name, but every now and then she'd be watching the news and hear a tidbit of some politician's or community leader's speech and knew that it was her work.

Rhain turned her journal to a blank page and began to write, allowing words to just flow through her spirit.

"Beautiful One"

Today look at yourself in the mirror,
and this is a guarantee,
you'll see the most beautiful woman in the
world that there ever was to see:
A naturally darkened tone with no makeup

or help from even the sun's brightest ray;
Full-figured lips; dark brown eyes;
and versatile strands of hair to display;
strong bones, and wide hips to support
such a lovely foundation.
The black woman, the most beautiful woman,
that ever existed across the nations.

"Hmm," Rhain said with a chuckle after reading the poem. "What irony, for me of all people to write this poem. I have no idea where this one came from. This poem is definitely not about me. I'm the black woman God decided to leave out on this one."

She closed the journal upon reading the poem. Rhain then placed the journal and pen back in the night table drawer and headed over to the computer to check her e-mail. Tonight there were three new requests from potential clients. One was for a poem someone wanted to put in the program for their uncle's funeral. They gave Rhain a few lines on what type of person he was. *Easy enough*, Rhain thought. The second was from a man who had gotten into an argument with his wife and wanted to break the ice with a letter of apology. "Great. Another 'Baby, I'm sorry, please forgive me' letter," she sighed. "Which always confirms my theory on men—they're always screwing up!" The last was someone wanting Rhain to take the written testimony they wanted to give in front of their church congregation and put some order to it. They said that they weren't good at talking in front of others and knew that if they didn't have a blueprint to follow, they would freeze up and just get to rambling on. "Hmm, this is a first," Rhain said to herself, always ready to take on a request outside of the ordinary ones.

In a matter of three hours and fifteen minutes, Rhain had completed each of the three jobs. "An easy hundred dollars," she said as she logged off her computer. *Thirty-three dollars an hour . . . can't beat that,* she thought as she turned on her thirty-two-inch television that sat on a mahogany entertainment stand and climbed back into bed.

After flicking through what seemed like a million channels on her DirecTV satellite, Rhain stopped at HBO where *She Hates Me* was showing. Rhain had never heard of it before, much less seen it. She hit the Info button to see what time it had come on. She never watched a movie that was already over fifteen minutes into it. She figured after that point, it was too hard to get into, and if it was a mystery, she would have already missed some major clues to help her solve it. It had just come on, so she decided to watch it. Based on the first few minutes, she thought it was going to be a movie about white-collar whistle-blowing, so when all of sudden the lead male actor was screwing a different woman every other minute and women were screwing each other like they had dicks, Rhain began to feel the throbbing of her clit, a throbbing so strong that for a minute there, she felt like she had a dick, a dick she wanted to grip her hands around and jack off until it erupted all over her. But instead, she closed her eyes and allowed the tip of her index finger and thumb to fondle her clit.

Twisting and rubbing it like it was clay she was shaping into a one-of-a-kind mold, she slowly began squirming at the wonderful feeling she was subjecting herself to. Twice a week, at a minimum, this was Rhain's foreplay for full-blown masturbation. After a few minutes Rhain proceeded to take her middle finger and glide it up and down her clit.

"Oooh, that's right," she moaned to herself, pretending that she was talking to her lover, the lover she had never had. "Right there. Ohhh yes, damn it, right there!"

Elvis had nothing on the way Rhain was gyrating her pelvis. One would have thought she had a real live dick between her legs the way she was fucking her finger. Once she was good and wet, she allowed the tip of her finger to enter her pussy on the down stroke.

"Mmm, yeah. Oh God, yeah," Rhain screamed as she was now taking in half of her finger. Aside from that silver thing her gynecologist stuck inside of her to perform her annual Pap smear, her finger and a tampon were the only things that had ever been admitted inside her walls. If she ever did meet the right man, preferably her husband, she would at least be somewhat open to receive him, she thought.

"Oh, baby, you are so wet," she complimented herself. Turned on by the compliment and the sound of her finger dipping in and out of her pussy, Rhain began thrusting harder and harder. She lifted her ass off the bed and grabbed the edge of her mattress with her free hand while she continued to please herself with the other. She then turned over on her stomach, her hand still between her legs, and she started humping the bed as if she was on top of her lover, fucking his brains out. "Oh yes, yeah, yeah." Her ass went up and down, her finger in and out of her wetness.

The sound of the headboard hitting the wall finally brought Rhain to her climax as she trembled in ecstasy while her sticky cum poured into her hand. *With a nut like that, who needs a man?* she thought as she wiped her hand down the sheets, turned the television off with the remote, and fell fast asleep.

The next morning, Rhain got out of the bed to answer a knock at the door. The knocking didn't wake her. She had been lying awake in her bed for a few minutes, gathering the energy to actually get up. It just so happened that as she was finally rising up, the knocking began.

"Just a minute, Sylvia," Rhain said, already knowing exactly who was on the other side of the door. Unless receiving a package she had to sign for, the chances of anyone else knocking on her door at nine o'clock on a Saturday morning were slim to none.

"Come on in," Rhain said after unlocking and opening the door without even looking through the peephole.

"Here," Sylvia said, handing Rhain a foil-covered plate while she carried another in her other hand. "Sunny side up on an egg and honey bagel with two strips of bacon."

"Sylvia, as Mr. Irving would say, you're a sweetheart." Rhain grinned, taking the plate from Sylvia's hand.

"Don't mention it. My mother-in-law's birthday is next week. You can repay me by making her one of those Rhain's Originals for me," Sylvia said as she sat down on Rhain's black rolled-arm settee couch and removed the foil from her plate. "I checked every drugstore in the city, and there wasn't a card on the shelf that said what I wanted it to say— Happy birthday you meddling bitch!"

"Sylvia." Rhain laughed as she sat down on the

floor in front of the round leather ottoman that also served as a table. "I'll be a little more diplomatic than that."

"Fair enough. I trust you'll know what to say. Because Lord knows what I, myself, have the right mind to say in that card, especially after she volunteered me to host this year's St. Patty's day family dinner. I mean, my apartment is the size of a shoebox, not nearly enough room to house a drunken Irish family. You and I both know there'll be no designated driver, so half of them will end up camping out and puking in every corner of my place."

Rhain took the foil off of her plate and took in the wonderful scent of her breakfast sandwich, compliments of her neighbor. She sat the plate down on the table in front of her and then sank her teeth into a bite as Sylvia rambled on.

"You know I could go on and on," Sylvia said, taking a bite of her sandwich, "but enough about me." She chewed a couple of times and then spoke with her mouth full. "Did you finally give up that cherry that's been rotting up inside of you by meeting some dark and handsome stranger at a bar and then bringing him home for a night of wild sex with no strings attached? Or did you finally give in to your boss's advances and bring him back to your place and allow him to fuck your brains out last night?"

"Neither," Rhain said, sucking her teeth and rolling her eyes. "That's your fantasy, Sylvia, remember? Not mine."

"Look, sistah," Sylvia said, pointing her finger. Rhain always found it entertaining when Sylvia started to talk "black." She was a black woman indeed, but underneath a white woman's skin, and she was married to a white Irishman. Not that she was being phony when she talked "black," but she just rarely used the same type of language around her husband and his family as she did with Rhain. Abandoned by her natural mother at the age of two, Sylvia was raised by an older black woman who had lived next door to them and who took legal custody of her. "You can lie through your teeth all you want, but the sound of your headboard banging into my wall doesn't lie. Hell, you had my husband pouncing on me all night; he got so turned on by the sound."

"Geez, Sylvia," Rhain said, setting her sandwich down on the plate and then standing up to go into the kitchen. "You want orange, apple, cranberry, or grape juice?"

"Can you mix the cranberry with orange?" Sylvia shouted.

"You got it." Rhain proceeded to prepare their drinks and then returned to the living room to join Sylvia. "Here you are." She handed Sylvia her drink.

"Thank you, but speaking of juice . . ."

"You are so nosey," Rhain said, taking a sip of her apple juice and then sitting down on the couch next to Sylvia. "You'd think you and your mother-in-law would be the best of friends. After all, you each enjoy getting into other folks' business."

"I can see I'm not going to get an answer out of you," Sylvia said, taking a sip of her drink.

"Then it's safe to say that you're not blind."

"Rhain, you're so boring. I'm a thirty-five-year-old woman married ten years and you're a twenty-five-year-old single beautiful young woman. Do you think I really come over here just because I like you? Hell no! I want to live vicariously through you.

I want sex stories. I want to hear about promiscuity and all the other shit you can get away with up until you're thirty."

"Beautiful? Yeah, right," Rhain said, begging to differ as she reached over to pick up her plate and take a bite of her sandwich.

"Rhain, seriously. I can't believe you don't see just how gorgeous you are, girl. Come here," Sylvia said as she sat her plate down on the table, got up, and took Rhain's plate from her hand and sat it down next to hers. She then grabbed Rhain by the hand and led her into the bathroom. "See, look," Sylvia said as she stood behind Rhain in the mirror. "Look at those beautiful hazel eyes. Do you know how much money some people spend on contacts to have eyes like yours?"

"Sylvia." Rhain blushed, putting her head down.

Touching Rhain gently by the chin and lifting her head back up so that she was staring at herself in the mirror again, Sylvia continued. "And this hair." She removed Rhain's hair from the bun she always wore it in. It fell to her shoulders like puffs of clouds falling from the sky. "Do you know how much money some women spend on weave and extensions to get hair as long and as full as this? And this natural reddish-brown color . . . Child, white girls buy this stuff by the bottle." Sylvia began to run her fingers through Rhain's hair. "You're beautiful," she sincerely said as her eyes met with Rhain's through the mirror.

You're beautiful yourself, Rhain thought about Sylvia as she admired her brunette hair that fell down each side of her face in huge, roller-set curls. Not wanting to dye her eyebrows the same way she had dyed her hair, the thick blond brows were a dead giveaway as to Sylvia's natural hair color. But no one paid attention to her eyebrows anyway, not with those gray cat's eyes of hers. If it wasn't for the fact that Sylvia wasn't even five feet tall, she could have very well had a career as a runway model. Instead, she opted to be a stay-at-home wife who sold Mary Kay cosmetics on the side, but only to herself and the few instances Rhain might need a product or two. With Mary Kay products covering Sylvia's dresser and her bathroom, Sylvia was definitely her own biggest customer.

The feeling of Sylvia running her fingers through Rhain's hair caught Rhain off guard. Perhaps it had something to do with the movie she had just watched the night before, but she could have sworn there was something sensual about Sylvia's touch.

A few seconds more than necessary elapsed as the two women stared into each other's eyes through the mirror before they both realized it. Suddenly Rhain dropped her head again and Sylvia quickly removed her hand from Rhain's hair and cleared her throat.

"Come on, let's go finish breakfast," Sylvia said as she walked away.

Rhain stood in front of the bathroom mirror a few seconds more, staring at herself, trying to see the same thing in herself that Sylvia had seen and wondering if someday a man would see it too.

Chapter II
That Bitch Katrina

Because of the hurricane that ripped through the home of the Mardi Gras, Jazz Festival, and Essence Music Festival, insurance claims were pouring into the office. Before that bitch Katrina made her presence known, profits at Heigan National Insurance had been great, but from the looks of things now, the midsize, midwest corporation could be in trouble with all of the payouts it predicted having to make. Rhain knew that things weren't going all too well when on Monday the employees were informed that the owner of the company would be flying in for a mandatory meeting to be held that Friday.

The week seemed to drag on and on for all of the employees. Rhain could have even sworn that Wednesday rolled around twice, back-to-back. By the time Friday finally arrived, the employees were on edge as they stood in the company's conference room, standing room only, to learn the fate of their company.

"I just want to let all of you know that I consider the employees of Heigan National Insurance as family," the owner of the company said during the meeting. "But I'll clear out every bank account, sell every company stock, and file bankruptcy on behalf of this company before I put those good people of New Orleans through any more suffering. Wind damage, water damage, I don't care. Every claim is to be treated with sensitivity and paid out according to the coverage."

The owner shook almost each and every employee's hand as he exited the conference room in which the meeting was held. It was as if it were the last time he would ever see his employees again. The company's parent company was in Louisiana, so Heigan insured a decent amount of homes that had been destroyed by Hurricane Katrina. It was only a matter of time before the company would be underwater too.

Rhain had been an employee of the company since high school. It had been the only place she had ever worked. She started out as a high school senior intern through her Cooperative Office Education class at Linden High School. After graduation, she remained on intern status as a college intern because of her age but was eventually promoted to an entry-level clerk. She held the position of receptionist for a while before she was eventually promoted to the position she currently held. Intelligent, graduating at the top of her high school class at the age of fifteen and graduating summa cum laude from Capital University in Bexley, Rhain knew when she took the job that she had the skills and education to damn near run the company herself, but that would have required too much of her time and would have kept her from ultimately living out her passion—to become a famous published author of sexy and romantic mystery novels.

Sylvia had always asked Rhain how in the world she planned on going from writing poems to full-length novels when she never went out and experienced anything in life. "In order to write a good juicy novel," Sylvia would tell her, "you gotta go out and get you some inspiration, girlfriend, and you're not going to find it sitting behind a desk at Heigan National Insurance."

Ignoring her neighbor's advice, Rhain decided that she would hold the mediocre position so that she could easily walk away from her job and, at the same time, hold a position that wasn't so demanding, thus allowing her time to write and maybe someday even look into internships related to writing. She sometimes would even envision herself as writing for a popular daytime soap opera someday, wearing holey, ripped jeans, T-shirts, and tennis shoes, sitting around a table hashing out story climaxes with other members of the writing team. But most of Rhain's drive was lost after the death of her mother four years prior, as a result of breast cancer.

Every day after that, she seemed to become less and less motivated to pursue her big dream, but she didn't throw out the idea altogether. But there were those times when she did threaten to give up the dream altogether and just take the easy way out and retire from Heigan National Insurance. But now, after the meeting, a fear brewed inside of her that her time there wouldn't be much longer, that she'd be forced to seek employment elsewhere. And the only thing Rhain hated more than her personal flaws and imperfections was change.

She had lived at the same apartment, driven the same car, wore her hair in the same style and worked for the same company since she could remember. She was comfortable and content. The last thing she needed now was a change.

Rhain wasn't really hungry for dinner when she left work that Friday. Something about that meeting had ruined her appetite, but it was a norm for her to stop by Carlos', and she didn't want to jinx herself by changing her norm. After all, one thing changes, and before you know it, everything starts to change.

When Rhain entered Carlos', the hustle, bustle, and excitement of the patrons thanking God that it was Friday was mute to her ears. She just couldn't seem to shake the dreary not-so-hopeful words cast out by the owner of the company that was sticking to her like lint on wool pants. Her plain future that she could have been content with for the rest of her life now seemed to be so unpredictable.

"Your usual, Miss Garrett?" Woodrow, the bartender who always took her order, asked as Rhain approached the bar.

"Yes, Woodrow, with extra grilled chicken," Rhain replied.

"Cherry Coke while you wait?"

"That would be nice," Rhain answered as Woodrow went to put in her order and fix her soda. She just sat there gazing down at the shiny black bar that Woodrow had just wiped down and was now so clean and clear that it allowed her to see herself in it. All Rhain saw staring back at her was a miserable reflection.

"Your Cherry Coke, Miss Garrett," Woodrow said, setting the glass down in front of Rhain and then walking away.

"Looks like you could use something much stronger than a Cherry Coke," a deep voice said up from behind her. "Please, let me buy you a drink?"

"Oh, no, thank you," Rhain said without even turning around to see who the voice belonged to.

"Please, it would be my pleasure. Besides, I hate drinking alone," the gentleman, to whom the voice belonged, said as he took a seat next to Rhain at the bar.

"Really, thank you, but no—" Rhain started as she turned around to face the gentleman. Her words froze in midsentence. When her eyes met his, she almost froze stiff and fell over. He had to be the most sensual man she had ever encountered. It had nothing to do with his baritone voice, his beautiful eyes, his clear, smooth skin, or the way he licked his lips and then slightly bit down on his bottom lip. It was just a pure aura that settled over him like an angel's halo. His presence simply demanded the attention that Rhain was so freely giving him. She could have sat there in that same position and stared into his eyes all night, but obviously the feeling wasn't mutual as he quickly turned his attention away from Rhain and to the bartender who was heading over to take his order.

This sexy muthafucka, Rhain thought as she clenched her teeth. For years she had had to create an image in her mind to fantasize to while pleasing herself. And she'd be damned if that very image hadn't just appeared before her in the flesh. It was surreal. She had literally dreamed of this man before. He was her mental creation; only now he was real.

Rhain wanted nothing more than to grab him by his face and turn him around so that he was looking dead into her eyes again, just to make sure he was really real and that she hadn't dozed off while waiting on her order and was in dream state. But of course, she wasn't that bold. She'd never be that bold. And on top of that, he didn't seem like he'd go for that type of wild animal instinct thing. A man had never looked at her before the way he had—so innocently and with such purity. It was as if all he truly wanted was to buy her drink and wanted nothing in return from her.

Rhain quickly let that thought escape her mind as she went back to staring at her reflection in the bar. Perhaps there really wasn't anything different about his look than any other man's. Perhaps he was just the first man she had ever really looked at. Rhain usually saw to it that she didn't make eye contact with a man, not wanting to give him the wrong idea, forcing herself to bruise his ego by rejecting the advances that would soon follow.

"I'll have two rum and Cokes on the rocks, please," the gentleman said. He then turned his attention toward Rhain. "That is fine, isn't it?" Rhain didn't realize that the gentleman was talking to her, so she didn't reply to him. "Excuse me, miss, rum and Coke is fine, isn't it?" he repeated.

"Oh, who me?" Rhain said, sitting straight up. "Oh yeah, that's fine," she stated, not quite certain of what she had just agreed to. She was still swimming in thoughts of him, so she never even witnessed him throwing the life jacket to her.

"You heard the lady," the gentleman said to Woodrow. "Rum and Coke is fine."

Rum, Rhain said to herself. *Alcohol.* She wanted to tell Woodrow not to make her drink, but then she looked over at the gentleman, who was all too quickly engrossed in the basketball game that was showing on the television, and decided not to. She didn't want to seem like a baby. Besides, there was something about this man that was making her feel all grown up.

"Yes, that will be just fine," Rhain affirmed with Woodrow.

"Miss Garrett!" Woodrow said, surprised. In the two years he had been bartending at Carlos', he had never seen her drink anything stronger than a soda. Rhain nodded, letting him know that it was okay to bring her alcohol.

"Two rum and Cokes coming up," Woodrow said as he walked away and proceeded to make their drinks. "I'll make yours nice and special, Miss Garrett." He winked.

Rhain watched as he poured the liquor into the glass. It seemed as though he kept pouring and pouring and the damn glass wouldn't fill up. *Oh God, what am I thinking?* Rhain thought, now feeling like a scared little kid who was fighting against peer pressure. *Why didn't I just tell the man that I don't drink?*

"Miss Garrett?" the gentleman asked in a tone that suggested he wanted to know her first name.

"Oh yes," Rhain replied. "Rhain Garrett." She watched him not taking his eyes off the game, still waiting for him to look into her eyes again.

"I like that name. Rhain," he said. Finally, he turned and looked at her. "Fred, Fred Simmons," he said, extending his hand. Rhain was too busy looking into his eyes to notice that his hand was extended. "You just gonna leave me hangin'?"

Rain looked down at his hand. "Oh, my apologies," Rhain said, extending her hand and shaking his.

"So you want to talk about it?" he asked. Now that a commercial was on, he seemed to find the time to direct more attention to Rhain.

"Excuse me?"

"Do you want to talk about it?"

"Talk about what?" Rhain said, shooting him a puzzled look.

"It only took me a few seconds of looking at you to know that today your world came tumbling down—your world as you knew it anyway."

"Here's your drinks," the bartender interrupted as he sat each of their drinks in front of them.

"Thank you," Fred said as he handed Woodrow a twenty-dollar bill.

"Thank you," Rhain said to Fred as the bartender made change for the twenty.

"Don't mention it," Fred replied. He took his change from Woodrow, tipping him three dollars.

"To your new world," Fred said, raising his glass. "To your new world as you don't know it, which makes life a lot more interesting." Fred slightly raised his glass and winked.

Rhain raised her glass and allowed a slight smile to cross her closed lips. She watched Fred swallow most of his drink in one gulp. She then attempted to follow suit by taking a huge gulp from her glass, in which the Coke went down one pipe and the rum the other.

"You all right?" Fred asked as Rhain began choking.

"Yes," Rhain managed to say, "I'm fine, thank

you." She then took a small sip, one that she could handle.

"Your salad, Miss Garrett," Woodrow said, placing a plastic bag in front of her.

"Thank you," she replied, digging in her purse and pulling out ten dollars. "Keep the change." Although initially she wasn't hungry, she knew she needed to put some food in her stomach with that alcohol she was drinking. She then took her food out of the bag and began pouring Italian dressing on it. She lifted up a forkful and took a bite.

"Ummm, that looks good," Fred said, watching Rhain's lips go in circles as she chewed.

"Carlos' makes the best salads in the world," she stated as Fred continued to watch her chew. After a few seconds of feeling his eyes staring at her, she turned to him with a forkful and asked, "You want a taste?" She knew he would decline, but it was just that his stares were making her feel a little awkward, so she felt the need to say something, anything.

Rhain waited to see if he was going to give her that googley-eyed look, the one Mr. Irving would have given her if she had addressed him with that question, but instead, Fred looked down at the delicious salad and replied, "Sure."

"Oh, okay, sure," Rhain said, surprised that he had said yes. She took the lid from the plastic container that held her food and forked half her salad into it. She then slid it over to Fred.

"Thanks," he said.

"It's the least I can do. After all, you did buy me a drink."

Fred had Woodrow bring him a fork so that he could enjoy his portion. For the next few minutes, neither Fred nor Rhain said two words as they inhaled their food and drank their rum and Cokes, Fred ordering a second drink for himself.

"You don't talk much, do you?" Fred finally struck up conversation.

"I guess I never really have that much to say," Rhain said, taking a bite of her food.

"I like that."

"What?"

"Someone who talks only when they have something to say. I'm used to people who talk all the time and don't have anything to say, anything worth listening to anyway."

"My mother always told me that there is power in remaining silent."

"Your mother is a very smart woman."

"Yes, she *was*," Rhain said, fiddling in her salad with her fork before dropping it into the container and pushing it away.

"I'm sorry," Fred said, realizing that the mention of Rhain's mother had made her uneasy. "Did I say something wrong?"

"No, it's okay. It's just that my mother, she's deceased."

"My sincere sympathy," Fred said, placing his hand on top of Rhain's.

Rhain closed her eyes. *What I wouldn't do to have that manly hand be the hand that finds its way between my legs three nights a week instead of my own,* she thought. Taking a deep breath and then opening her eyes, Rhain replied, "Really, it's okay." She slid her hand from underneath Fred's and finished off her rum and Coke.

Fred looked down at his watch. "Well, I think I'm going to call it a night."

His words almost disappointed Rhain. He had

been good company. He hadn't tried to hit on her. He hadn't talked her head off with a one-sided conversation about himself. As a matter of fact, he hadn't done much at all, giving new meaning to the term *less is more.*

"Thank you for the drink," Rhain said with a tight-lipped smile, careful not to reveal her gap.

"Thank you for the salad . . . I guess we're even." He stood up and put on his coat.

"Yeah, I guess so," Rhain said. *Why did I have to go and offer him some of my salad?* Rhain asked herself, wanting to kick herself. *Had I not, I'd definitely owe him. I could have made it up to him by inviting him to dinner or something. Now I'm sure to never see him again.*

"We'll have to do this again sometime."

BINGO! "I'd really like that," Rhain said, not realizing that she had a huge smile on her face, showing almost every last one of her teeth.

Fred paused and gave her a look.

"What? What's wrong?" Rhain said right before realizing that she had the widest smile on her face that she had ever allowed to show and that he was staring right at her mouth. *Oh no! My gap.* She quickly closed her mouth and looked down.

"Oh, nothing's wrong. I was just admiring your smile. You should smile more often. You have lovely teeth."

"Thank you." Rhain blushed. *Maybe I closed my mouth in time before he noticed my gap,* she hoped. *I don't care what that chick on* America's Next Top Model *says; if I could afford to, I'd close my gap up in a heartbeat.*

"How about next week or the week after, depending on my calendar?"

"Excuse me?" Rhain asked, afraid she had missed something while concentrating on that gap of hers.

"Doing this again sometime. Did you forget that quickly?"

Before Rhain could catch the words, they fell out of her mouth like drool. "Yes, that would be fine."

"Is there a number I can reach you at?"

"Uhh, yeah," Rhain said, digging in her purse for a pen. *Smooth operator. I like. Far cry from all the other men I've encountered. If this one right here is a dog, then he's top-of-the-line pedigree.* There had to be a dozen pens in her purse, compliments of Heigan National Insurance, but the nervousness that she was suddenly succumbing to prevented her from putting her hands on one of them. The longer she searched for a pen, the more doubtful she got about giving him her phone number. *What was I thinking, making a date with this man?* she thought to herself. *Maybe he doesn't want anything from me now, but certainly the day will come when good conversation won't fill the void of good sex. Then what am I going to do?*

"A business card . . . do you have a business card?" he suggested after watching Rhain rummage through her purse.

Why didn't I think of that? Rhain thought as she managed to get her hand on a pen. She retrieved a business card from her business card holder. "As a matter of fact, I do." *Too late to bail out now.* Rhain went to hand Fred one of her Rhain's Originals business cards, but then quickly pulled it back. "This card only has my cell phone number for business, and since this isn't business, let me write my home number down on the back of it." Rhain wrote her home phone number down and then handed him the card.

"I'll give you a call in a couple of days," he said, taking the card and placing it in his coat pocket.

"I look forward to your call."

"You have a good evening, all right?"

"Thank you. You do the same."

Fred nodded his head and was on his way, Rhain watching him until he was out of the door and no longer in view. She soon followed behind him and headed home.

By the time she made it through her apartment door, Rhain couldn't wait to jump in the shower, a cold one. She didn't know if it was the alcohol or the feeling of being in the company of a man like Fred that had her insides boiling. Her tolerance for both was pretty low.

Leaving a trail of clothing from her front door through her living room to her bedroom, Rhain darted to the shower and turned on the water. She couldn't jump in quickly enough.

Breathing heavily, with her back up against the shower wall, Rhain squeezed and fondled her breasts with one hand while she masturbated with the other. With her index finger racing up and down her clit one hundred miles per hour, it took no time at all for Rhain to allow her cum to flow down her thigh with the shower water.

"God, I'm sick of this," she said, tired, ashamed, and embarrassed of always having to please herself from getting all worked up over the littlest things. "Maybe Sylvia's right. Maybe I need to start living."

After Rhain got out of the shower, she slipped on her mix-and-matched pajamas, some blue satin pants with a cotton shirt she took from another set. She couldn't find the top to the satin ones to save her life. She didn't care, though; it wasn't like she had someone lying next to her at night to model her pajamas for. But hopefully, if she played her cards right, that would soon change. But for now, she climbed into her bed, alone. She tossed and turned to visions of the tall, dark, and mysterious, not to mention sexy as hell, Fred Simmons. Soon Rhain finally fell into a deep, dream-filled sleep.

Chapter III

"Words Escape Me"

"If a man calls you the same night you meet him, steer clear, 'cause all that means is that he is going to be a bugaboo," Sylvia had told Rhain. "Either that, or he's desperate. And if he's that desperate, then something's wrong with him. And if something is wrong with him, you don't want to be the one to find out what that something is."

Although Sylvia's words from the night before were meant to comfort Rhain, she still couldn't help but wonder why it was now Monday, three nights since she had met Fred, and he still hadn't called. *Must have been the rum asking me for my phone number, and the minute he sobered up, he realized the mistake he had made with the homely girl sitting next to him at the bar,* Rhain thought as she sat on the floor at her living room table eating her Cobb salad from Carlos'. She hadn't done anything more than poke at the green leaves with her fork. She didn't even have a taste for Carlos' tonight; what she really had a taste for was Fred and she had hoped that by going to Carlos', there was a chance she would run into him again. Not wanting to confirm the truth of spending one more night waiting for a call she'd never get, she forced down a couple forkfuls of salad and then headed to her bedroom.

Rhain turned on her computer and went to brush her teeth while it booted up. After flossing, she scanned her e-mails, where ten new orders awaited her. With Valentine's Day coming up, Rhain knew that last-minute requests for cards and poems would start to pour in. Amongst the expected requests was a very interesting one, one that wasn't similar to any of the types of request she had received before.

FROM: Carrington69@hotmail.com
TO: RhainsOriginals@aol.com
SUBJECT:The Words Escape Me
Dear Rhain's Originals:
I heard of your services through a friend of mine who was exceptionally pleased with the work you did for her. I know my request may be a little out of the ordinary from anything you've ever done before, but I have to ask anyway; my marriage depends on it. If I sound desperate, that's because I am.
You see, my wife and I have been married for fifteen wonderful years; at least up until last week I thought they were wonderful, but that's when I found out that she was seeing someone else. Of course, we got into this huge fight and I threatened to leave her, but in all actuality, I love her so much that I'm willing to forget about her indiscretion and start over and work things out. I mean, when I look into my children's faces, I

couldn't bear living apart from them or subjecting them to the ugliness of a bitter divorce.

When I asked my wife the million-dollar question— Why? Why she had cheated on me?—she told me because our relationship had stagnated, that is, was boring to her and entailed little romance and excitement. In so many words, I guess she was saying that this other person was everything I'm not: romantic and made her feel exciting and like a new woman. I'll be the first to admit that I am the least romantic person on earth. That's why I am contacting you. What I need from you goes beyond a simple card or poem. I need you to be me.

I know that sounds crazy, but I don't need you to be me in the physical, only in the mental. I need you to communicate with my wife via mail, e-mails, sending flowers with romantic messages, etc. . . . You're a woman. You'd know best what another woman would want, what would make her feel romanced and excited.

Money is no object. I'm willing to pay you $1,000 a month plus any expense you might incur in addition to the regular fee. I would need your services to be indefinite, until I accomplish everything I need to.

Take some time in considering my request, but please, don't take too long. I don't want to lose her. I can't lose her. I won't.

Respectfully,
Carrington69

"Desperate ain't the word," Rhain sighed after reading the e-mail. "Poor guy."

Rhain didn't know what to think. A part of her wanted to delete the e-mail and hope the weirdo who sent it didn't repeat the request. But another part of her felt for the sender and wanted to help, almost to the point where she'd do it for free. Not only was $1,000 per month a great second income, but the job actually did sound kind of exciting. But Rhain didn't want to make a quick decision. At times like this, she wished her mother were still alive. At times like this, even a sistah-girlfriend would do. But since she had neither, she'd have to go to the next best thing.

"Honey child, a grand a month just for sending sweet nothings to some stranger . . . I say go for it!" Sylvia exclaimed as she finished reading the e-mail that was up on Rhain's computer screen. "Besides, don't take this the wrong way, but girl, you are a great big oversized bag of boring. It will do you some good to be somebody else for a change. Somebody exciting and romantic." Sylvia got up from the computer desk and threw herself on Rhain's bed. "Hell, I wish my man would pay some-one a thousand dollars to send me sweet nothings." Sylvia sat up and stared off with a serious look on her face. "Then again, I'd rather have the thousand dollars per month to go shopping with."

"How is pretending to be a man romantic and ex-citing?" Rhain asked.

"Don't look at it as pretending to be a man. Look at it as being someone other than yourself. It will be fun. Like I said, go for it. You have nothing to lose and a thousand dollars a month to gain. I fail to see your dilemma."

Rhain thought for a moment in silence as she bit down on her thumbnail. With a serious face, she looked up at Sylvia, who was waiting intensely on her response. She then broke into a smile and said, "You're right. What the hell? I'm going for it!"

FROM: RhainsOriginals@aol.com
TO: Carrington69@hotmail.com
SUBJECT: Re: The Words Escape Me

Thank you for considering me for your somewhat unique project. I must be honest in saying that at first I was a little taken back by your request, but at the same time I found it intriguing.

You're right; this is a little out of the ordinary from any other project I've ever worked on before. But you know what they say, "There's a first time for everything." So I'm making you my first.

$1,000 a month plus expenses works fine for me. I'm going to need you to supply me with your wife's name, address, e-mail address, and any other pertinent information you think I'll need in order to make this work (what she looks like, her favorite flower, wine, song, anniversary date, birthday, etc. . . .). All payments may be made to me via PayPal using my e-mail address as the payee. Just as soon as you get me the requested information and make your payment, we can get started.

Again, thank you for considering me and I'm excited to . . . well . . . to be you. ☺

FROM: Carrington69@hotmail.com
TO: RhainsOriginals@aol.com
SUBJECT: Re The Words Escape Me

Dear Rhain's Originals:

You don't know how grateful I am to you for accepting this project. I'm glad that we both could agree on the terms. But there's just one thing: is it possible that I could pay you cash through the U.S. postal service? I know you don't feel safe giving out your home address, but perhaps you can get a P.O. box or something and I can mail the payment there. I know this request seems to keep getting stranger by the moment, but if I use PayPal or write you a check or anything else, my wife will certainly become suspicious. I just don't want to leave any trail that might uncover the fact that I had to seek assistance in winning her heart. That would simply defeat the purpose. Imagine how everything would backfire if she found out that it wasn't me at all, my heartfelt, crafted words, that were wooing her back to me. I would hate for all of this to be in vain.

This really is important to me. I just need you to rope her in for me and I can take care of the rest. I don't want my family, as I know it, to end. For your trouble I'm willing to add $500 to the already agreed upon fee of $1000 for your P.O. box and inconvenience.

Please let me know if this arrangement is acceptable. I look forward to hearing back from you soon.

Respectfully,
Carrington69

After reading the e-mail, Rhain thought for a moment. This prospective client's desperation was a little too extreme now, but Rhain knew about love and the things one would go through for it; after all, in her side business she had dealt with enough desperate fools in love. This just happened to be the most desperate, is all. Going out and getting a P.O. box and all that mess sounded like too much trouble. On the same note, it was fine time she got a P.O. box anyway. Perhaps a lot of Rhain's skepticism was the fact that she knew this was a huge project. It could be the one to catapult her writing career beyond anything imaginable. It could bring about an entirely different creative side to her, giving her that inspiration that Sylvia had always said she so desperately needed. Besides, with the uncertainty of her position at her company, she'd be a fool to pass up such an opportunity. This could even be a godsend. Perhaps He was positioning her to be able to be an independent entrepreneur and to live out her heart's desire of being a full-time writer.

With that final thought, Rhain hit the Reply button on her keyboard and accepted the proposal. Eagerly, her new client forwarded her all the information she needed about his wife. The next day Rhain went to her local post office and rented a P.O. box. Within two days, after giving her client her mailing address, she went to her P.O. box and pulled out an Express Mail overnight envelope with $1,500 cash inside it. "Let the game of charades begin," Rhain said as she removed the cash from the envelope.

Rhain set up a dummy e-mail name, MyLove69, on her already existing AOL account, a name suggested by her client, and started sending sweet little poems to his wife at her e-mail address, McKinnyS@rightcorp.net. The S stood for her first name, which was Susan. Susan would sometimes reply with a poem of her own or just a "thank you" or "that's so sweet."

Her client had given Rhain his wife's work address because that's where he wanted any flowers and gifts to be delivered to. He wanted his wife to be the envy of her coworkers, with every other woman telling her how lucky she was to have someone who sent her flowers for no special reason. Eventually, Rhain planned on sending flowers to her job, but she wanted to take things slow. Considering her client claimed not to have a romantic bone in his body, she didn't want him to seem like Casanova all of a sudden with major overkill. But Rhain couldn't wait to keep pouring on the charm. She was excited as if she was the one being romanced. Sylvia was right. It was fun and exciting getting to be someone else, even if it was a man.

Chapter IV

"Are You Wet?"

As she unlocked her front door, Rhain heard the phone start to ring. She knew that after only three rings it would go to her voice mail. Her phone rarely rang unless it was Sylvia, needing to borrow a cup of sugar or something, or a bill collector if she had accidentally overlooked one of her bills and was getting a reminder call to keep her from reaching the thirty-day-late status.

"Hello," Rhain said into the receiver as she raced and answered the phone.

"Are you wet?" the voice on the other end said.

"Excuse me?" Rhain questioned with a weird look on her face.

"I said are you wet?" the voice repeated. "Your name is Rhain, isn't it? Rhain, wet, Rhain, wet . . . get it?" Rhain didn't reply. "I suppose that isn't such a good opening line for my first phone call to you, huh?"

By then, the voice registered in Rhain's head, and she knew just who the caller was. She had been expecting his call. It had been almost two weeks since she had given him her phone number, but nonetheless, she had still been expecting his call.

"Fred," Rhain said, making sure she said his name in a statement form and not as a question. She wanted him to know that she knew exactly who he was, that she didn't just go around giving her number out to men in bars.

"Miss Garrett." He laughed. "I guess I better keep my day job. Comedy's not my thing, huh?"

"Uh, no, it's not," Rhain agreed with a slight chuckle.

"So, how's your day?"

"It's a day. I can't complain. How's yours?"

"Aaah, so-so." There was a moment of silence. "So . . ."

"So, how about that drink? You agreed that we could get together again sometime like we did in Carlos'."

"And I'm a woman of my word."

"Good, because I'm a man of mine."

By now, the bass in Fred's voice was all that Rhain was thirsty for, but she knew that she had to start out with small sips. Perhaps she should have at least made it a point to have had at least one boyfriend before, maybe in high school. Then she'd at least have some experience with how to converse with a man. Thank goodness, her new, big client had her communicating with a woman, because that's about the only sex she knew how to communicate with.

"So, did you want to meet at Carlos' again? This Friday, happy hour after work?"

"Carlos'? Nah, not really."

"Me neither," Rhain agreed. She tried so hard to catch those four words as they leaped off of the tip of her tongue and jumped straight through the phone receiver and into Fred's ear, but she failed. "My place is fine." Rhain stood there holding the phone in her hand with her eyes clenched tight, just waiting and hoping for an affirmative response. If he said yes, it would be the first time she had ever invited a man to her house for a date. If he said no, it would be the first time she had ever been rejected by a man. Either way, her stomach would turn somersaults.

"Your place sounds great. This Friday night . . . happy hour at your place?"

"Yes, this Friday is fine," Rhain said, now able to breathe again. "A drink over dinner. Is seven o'clock fine?"

"Perfect," Fred agreed. "Do you need me to bring anything?"

"No, I'll take care of everything," Rhain assured him.

"Then I won't argue with the lady," Fred said in the most charming voice ever.

"Wise decision, because you can't win an argument with the lady," Rhain said, getting a little chuckle out of Fred. "Is there anything you dislike or are allergic to?"

"No, I'm pretty much game for anything, anything but Mexican. It goes right through me for some reason."

"Way too much information for me," Rhain said jokingly, turning her nose up.

"Look, I have a late meeting I have to run to. I had five minutes for a breather, which is rare, and I wanted to utilize it calling you."

"I feel so special."

"And you should." Fred piled it on. "But like I was saying, I have to run. Do you do e-mail?"

"Huh?" Rhain questioned.

"Do you do e-mail? Do you get online? I'm always on my laptop, so I can manage to squeeze in a hello or two to you sometimes via e-mail."

"Oh yeah. My e-mail address is on that card I gave you."

"That's right. Great. Well, write my e-mail address down, and if you don't mind, e-mail me your house address and I'll MapQuest my way there."

"I don't mind at all."

"Good," Fred said as he rattled off his e-mail address to Rhain while she wrote it down. "I guess I'll see you Friday."

"I guess you will."

"Enjoy the rest of your evening, Fred."

"Stay dry, Rhain."

With a huge smile on her face, Rhain hung up the phone. She just stood there for a moment staring at the phone and then let out a screeching yelp of excitement. It was only Wednesday and Rhain felt like a high school girl counting down the days to the prom. How on earth would she make it for an entire forty-eight more hours? She knew it wouldn't be easy.

Rhain kicked off her shoes and headed to the kitchen to mark her and Fred's upcoming date on the erasable calendar that was attached to her refrigerator door by magnets. Although she would never forget it in a million years, just looking at it marked on her calendar for the next two days would be sure to put a smile on her face.

"Oh my God," Rhain said to herself as she went

to scribble in her date with Fred. To her surprise, something was already written in on that date: a picture of a heart. "It's Valentine's Day." *I wonder if he realized that,* Rhain thought as she rested the bottom of the marker on her chin. *Maybe I should call him back. Valentine's Day is for lovers. I don't want to give him the wrong impression.*

After a few moments of contemplating, Rhain wrote their date on the calendar anyway and prayed to God that Fred hadn't partaken in another shot of rum before he had called to make the date. Otherwise, she would get the razor blades and the tub of water ready, because if she got stood up on her first date ever in her life, she would be well prepared to slit her wrist.

The very next day, after work, Rhain went to the market to pick up the items she would need for her and Fred's dinner date. Now that she was actually trying to plan the meal, she couldn't understand for the life of her why she agreed to cook dinner for him. After all, she was the frozen dinner, boxed dinner, carryout queen. So she knew whatever she decided to prepare as the main course would be basic, something like spaghetti. Boiling noodles couldn't be that difficult.

Rhain picked up a couple pounds of ground turkey. She hoped Fred didn't mind turkey instead of ground beef; Rhain wasn't big on red meat. She grabbed a jar of Prego Traditional, some angel-hair pasta, an onion, a bell pepper, and fresh mushrooms. About the only ingredient she had in her cupboards for the chosen meal was oregano. She picked up a bag of Dole's salad and a couple different salad dressings, Italian and ranch dressing. Everybody loved either Italian or ranch. Hopefully Fred wasn't the exception, preferring something like French instead. With that thought, Rhain picked up a bottle of French dressing as well.

After leaving the grocery store, Rhain made a pit stop at the Asian market in order to pick up a couple of rambutans. She loved the sweet and spiky fruit delicacy, which tasted like a peeled white grape with a hint of lemon, but she rarely engaged in the exotic fruit. She hoped, by Friday though, to be feeling a little exotic herself. Her trip was in vain as she was informed that the fruit was only available during certain months out of the year—May through August and November through January. She had just missed the fruit's availability by a couple of weeks. That explained why she had rarely indulged in it, only thinking to buy it whenever she saw it. She had used it a couple times when she had prepared fruit salad, or as an ice cream topping. But this time she had planned on using it as dessert alone. *Hmmm,* Rhain thought as she exited the market, *looks like I'm going to have to be dessert.*

By the time Friday evening arrived, Rhain was running around the house like a mouse on a hunt for cheese. Sylvia was close on her heels, bathing Rhain in her words of advice.

"Whatever you do tonight, don't fuck him!" Sylvia advised Rhain as she stood over the stove stirring the spaghetti sauce. "I'm telling you, girl, from the way you describe Mr. Fred, he doesn't sound like the type who will think twice about taking a girl who gives it up on the first date to the company Christmas party. Now your first mistake," Sylvia continued, "was inviting him to your home for your first date anyway. I mean, for all you know, he could be Ted Bundy's brother."

"Bundy was an only child, so he wouldn't have a brother," Rhain rebutted as she mixed the salad. "I think. And anyway, it's Theodore. Since when are you on a nickname basis with a serial killer?"

"Whatever. Don't try to change the subject, missy," Sylvia scolded, pointing her finger. "You know what I'm saying. You should always meet out in a public place for the first time."

"We did meet out in a public place for the first time. We met at Carlos', remember?"

"That doesn't count. That was by chance; this is by appointment. But anyway, I can't school you all the way back from puberty years up until now in one sitting, so until I can at least bring you up to when the bird spreads his wings and the bee sticks his stinger in, hold off on fucking him, okay?"

"Gosh, Sylvia, you're so disgusting," Rhain said as she placed the bowl of salad into the refrigerator. "Please, just finish making the sauce for me and go," Rhain said, pointing to the door with a friendly smile on her face.

"Is that any way to talk to the girl who saved your butt with the last loaf of garlic bread she had in her freezer? I'm not even Italian, I'm Irish. Well, I'm not really Irish, but my husband is and the Bible says we're one so that means I'm Irish too. . . ."

"Sylvia!" Rhain exclaimed.

"Sorry, but like I was saying, I'm not Italian and even I know you don't make a pasta meal without garlic bread."

"Thanks, my dear friend, Sylvia. You're a lifesaver. Now be off with you."

"Oooh, aren't we feisty," Sylvia said, putting her hands on her hips.

Rhain took a deep breath and relaxed her shoulders. "Sorry, Sylv," she said regretfully, "but I'm just so nervous. You know. This is my first date ever. I mean, what if this man wants to kiss me good night?"

"Then, hell, you just kiss him. I don't think one lousy kiss will ruin your chances of going to his Christmas party."

"Sylvia, don't you get it?" Rhain said, slightly frustrated. "I don't know how." She threw up her arms. "I've never even kissed a guy before."

"Oh, honey," Sylvia said in a sympathetic tone and with a sympathetic look on her face as she walked over to her and put her hands on her shoulders. "It's okay, sweetie. I mean, if he goes in for a kiss, just follow his lead. It will come natural."

"The only thing that comes natural to me is writing," Rhain assured her.

"Oh God," Sylvia said, shaking her head. "I don't believe I'm about to do this, but here goes. She walked in closer to Rhain and began demonstrating. "If he leans his head this way," Sylvia said, tilting her head to the left, "then you lean your head that way." She placed a hand on each side of Rhain's face and tilted Rhain's head to the right. The two women stood there, staring into each other's eyes.

"And then what?" Rhain's lips softly spoke as she stood gazing into Sylvia's eyes.

"And then meet him halfway; that way there's no question about who initiated the kiss and who didn't. You both just move in together."

"Meet him halfway?"

"Yeah, by bringing your head in toward him." They both slowly brought their heads in until their lips were almost touching. "And then you close your eyes," Sylvia said. Rhain could feel her breath on her lips.

Both women closed their eyes and then somehow their lips touched. Instead of pulling apart, they just stayed there.

"Then you open your mouth," Sylvia whispered.

Still caressing Rhain's face, Sylvia allowed the tip of her tongue to touch Rhain's. Before she knew it, she was sucking on Rhain's tongue. Both women were breathing heavily.

"Now you try it," Sylvia said to Rhain.

Rhain began sucking on Sylvia's tongue. Then the two started taking turns back and forth, sucking on each other's tongues. Sylvia's hands slipped down Rhain's face to her breasts. When Rhain heard herself moan, she pulled away and the two women just stood there, slightly embarrassed.

"See, just like that," Sylvia said, breaking the silence as she wiped her hand across her mouth. "Just lose yourself, Rhain."

"Yeah," she said, still somewhat in a daze. "Lose myself." After another few moments of silence, Rhain snapped out of her daze and realized that she needed to get dressed because Fred would be there soon. "Okay, I need to go get ready," she said in an upbeat tone as she began shooing Sylvia off as she headed into her bedroom to start laying her clothes out for the evening.

"All right," Sylvia called to her. "I'm out." She turned the sauce off. "But you call me just as soon as Mr. Fred leaves so that I can come over and get the four-one-one. And make sure you put me a plate up," Sylvia called before Rhain heard the front door slam.

Rhain slipped into her long but simple black dress. Her first choice was the red dress, trimmed with ruffles, she had bought on sale at Macy's, but Sylvia managed to talk her out of wearing it, saying that the color red would give off the wrong signal to Fred. With a fresh pair of sheer black hose and her Calvin Klein Boyce evening slides, Rhain was all set, and just in time as the doorbell rang right after she slipped on her last shoe.

"Coming," Rhain called after stopping by the mirror to make sure every single hair was slicked back in its neat little bun.

When she opened the door, she gasped. It looked as though standing before her was a rosebush with legs.

"Fred, are you somewhere in there?" Rhain asked, all smiles.

"For you," Rhain heard Fred say from behind the roses as he extended them to her.

"Oh my God," she said, opening her arms wide to accept them. "Fred . . . oh my God." Rhain inhaled the sweet scent and fondled the roses. She knew they had to be expensive because these were the kind with long, healthy green stems, minus any thorns.

"I hope that means you like them," Fred said as he entered the apartment, closing the door behind him.

"I love them!" she exclaimed.

"Good, because I think I fell and hurt my knee trying to get away from the old lady whose yard I dug the bush up from," Fred joked as he pretended to wipe dirt off of his pant legs.

"Silly, come on in and take a seat while I get these into some water." Rhain thought for a minute.

"Into the bathtub is more like it. I don't think I have a vase I can fit all of these into."

"May I suggest using several vases or tall drinking glasses even?" Fred said as he sat down on the couch. "Oh, and I brought something to drink too," he said, referring to the bottle of gin he was carrying.

"Oh good," Rhain said, forgetting all about the fact that the whole purpose of their initial date was to have a drink. She looked down at the roses again. "I think you're right," she agreed with his earlier suggestion, "I think putting these in several vases and glasses is the only thing that's going to work."

"Let me know if you need any help."

"I'll be fine," Rhain said as she went to the kitchen and began to get the roses situated.

Fred began gazing around the room. After a few minutes, he called out, "Do you mind if I turn on some music?"

"Excuse me? What did you say?" Rhain asked, exiting the kitchen.

"I was just asking if it was okay if I turned on some music with your CD player over there," Fred said, pointing to Rhain's entertainment center.

"Sure, I'll get it," Rhain said, walking over to her entertainment center and opening the glass door that held her CD collection. "What type of music do you like to listen to?"

"The same pretty much goes for my music as it does for my food," Fred answered. "I'm game for anything."

"I hope you don't have that same philosophy when it comes to women," was Rhain's comeback. But where it came from she had no idea. *I've defi-*

nitely been hanging around Sylvia's ass too long, she thought.

Fred chuckled. "Why don't I just come over and see what you have in your collection?" Fred said as he got up from the couch and headed over to the entertainment center. He stood close behind Rhain and stared over her shoulder at her CDs. She closed her eyes and inhaled his sexy, manly cologne. Fred reached his arm around her and ran his index finger down the CDs, slightly brushing against Rhain's arm as chill bumps covered it. "Jon B," he said, grabbing the CD from the cabinet. "Is this fine with you?"

"Certainly," Rhain said, slowly taking the CD from Fred's hand. She looked up at him and smiled. With him still standing over her, she removed the CD from the case and placed it in the CD player and hit the button to start it.

As the music began to groove from the speakers, Fred whispered in Rhain's ear, "And just so you know, no, I don't have the same philosophy about women."

"Oh yeah?" Rhain said, turning to face him. "Then what is your philosophy when it comes to women?"

"Actually, I don't have one." He paused. "I don't have a woman, or a philosophy about them."

All six feet and two inches of Fred stared down at Rhain's five feet seven inches. "And any man who says that he has a philosophy when it comes to women or that he understands them is full of himself. There isn't any science to such an intricate creature. Every woman is different and requires different things. You have to really get to know that particular woman in order to be able to deal with her on her own individual level. Even then, you'll never really know what makes her one hundred percent whole. You just have to hope, pray, and try your damnedest to be that missing piece of the puzzle that will complete her life."

A guru for such well-put-together words, Rhain could have melted right there at Fred's feet. She had not ever even written anything that slick in her cards or poems.

Fred leaned down, staring into Rhain's eyes the entire time, and placed a kiss on her lips. Still staring into her eyes, he ran his tongue gently across her lips until she got tired of being teased and began to try to catch his tongue with her mouth so that she could suck on it like Sylvia had taught her. Just when Rhain was close to engulfing his tongue into her mouth, he pulled back and smiled. As serious as she had ever been in her life, she stepped toward him, stood on her tiptoes, grabbed him by the back of his head, and pulled his mouth into hers and began sucking away on his tongue. Fred pulled Rhain's body as tightly against him as he could and liquefied in her warmth.

After a couple minutes of passionate panting and petting, Fred and Rhain, still connected by their tongues, made their way to the couch. With Rhain lying underneath him, Fred began to slide his hand up her dress and rub her thighs.

"Oh," Rhain moaned at his touch. She had never been touched by a man before. It was soft. It was gentle. Is this what she had been missing?

She grabbed his hand and guided him even farther up her thigh, thrashing her tongue in and out of his mouth the entire time. Before she knew it, her hips were grinding wildly against Fred's centerpiece to a well-set table. She was carrying on like an excited little puppy whose master had just walked through the door.

"Rhain," Fred tried to mumble, but Rhain had her tongue buried deep in his throat, and with her hand keeping his head in place, he couldn't manage to pull away. "Rhain, baby, Rhain, wait."

Oblivious to Fred's words, Rhain continued squirming, off beat and tonguing him down. Eventually Fred was able to pull himself away from her. He sat up and began to chuckle as he wiped all of Rhain's slobber from around his mouth.

With a triple somersault and a back flip off the parallel bars of embarrassment, Rhain's landing was a perfect stick as her feet sat planted into a mat of complete humiliation. After the successful completion of such a difficult dismount, Rhain decided, at that moment, that perhaps she'd make a far better gymnast than a writer.

"Oh God, I'm sorry. I'm so sorry," she said as she jumped up off the couch and began to fix her dress. "Oh God." She put her hand over her eyes. "You must think I'm . . . I must look like—"

"Don't worry about it," Fred said as he put his hand up. He looked over at Rhain, who was a nervous wreck and continued chuckling. "It's okay."

Rhain removed her hand from over her eyes and just stood there staring at Fred, who was in hysterics as if this embarrassing situation had fingertips and they were tickling him up under his armpits. Soon her embarrassment and humiliation turned to anger.

"I'm standing here already feeling like a complete idiot and you're laughing?" Rhain said to Fred.

"Excuse me?" he said, still chuckling as he looked up at Rhain. "I don't mean to . . . it's just that—"

"Do you really think you sitting there laughing at me is making me feel any better?"

"I'm sorry," Fred said, trying his best to stop laughing. Once he realized that Rhain was dead serious, that she was truly upset and embarrassed, he was able to take his hand and swat off the laughing bug. But it was a little too late for Rhain, who now had tears in her eyes.

Before she was going to stand there and let that man see her cry like some little kid, she'd rather him see her angry like a grown-ass woman.

"Fuck you!" Rhain yelled before storming into her bedroom and closing the door behind her. She knew that Fred would take that as her dramatic exit, but she was really even more embarrassed now for using the F-word. Sure, she cursed here and there, but the F-word . . .

"Rhain? Rhain?" Fred called as he walked over to her bedroom door. "Please, Rhain, I'm sorry. I didn't know . . . I didn't realize . . ." Words escaped him.

"Where's your smooth talk now?" Rhain asked from behind the closed door as she sat on her bed, arms folded, pouting. "You were talking all that stuff about women being intricate creatures and now you can't even say your own name, huh?" She looped her index finger around the rim of her shoes and removed each shoe, one at a time. She then pulled the stockings off, putting a run in them with her fingernail. "What a waste. And for such a fake ass, nig—" Rhain caught herself from saying the dreaded N-word just before the last syllable was enunciated. The N-word was even worse than the F-word in her book.

Before her mother passed away, Rhain had heard her refer to her father as the N-word more times than she cared to recall. Rhain loved her father more than any child could love their father. Rhain had been Daddy's little girl up until the seventh grade, when he took up a mistress who had two daughters of her own from the marriage she was in when she started the affair with Rhain's father. Eventually Rhain's father left her mother for the woman, who also divorced her husband to be with him. And even though Rhain saw how much his sin of adultery had hurt her mother, her heart couldn't refrain from still loving her father.

After her parents' separation and divorce, Rhain spent every weekend with her father and his new family. At first it took some getting used to. As an only child, Rhain wasn't accustomed to playmates, but the woman's daughters turned out to be really nice. And the woman, who soon became her step-mother, wasn't anything like the one that poor girl, Cinderella, had to endure. So even though Rhain looked forward to her weekend visits with her father, she didn't look forward to that look of be-trayal on her mother's face, or the silent treatment she gave her every Friday once she walked in the house from school, knowing she was going upstairs to pack to go to her father—the enemy. Even on Sundays, upon her return home from her visits with her father, Rhain received the look as well as the silent treatment.

On Sundays, at six P.M. sharp, Rhain's father would drop her off at home. Rhain's mother would be standing in the doorway, arms folded, waiting for her. Her father would smile and wave, but her mother would fold her arms and turn her nose up at him. Every Sunday he smiled and waved knowing that there would be no reciprocity from his former wife. Once Rhain walked into the house, her mother would slam the door closed behind her. Then without saying a word, she'd head up the steps to her bedroom, slamming that door too. Rhain would just stand outside in the hallway for a moment like a puppy whose owner was bitter with it. But the following Monday morning, it was business as usual. Her mother would be her happy, joyous self, loving and caring with all smiles. This was the woman who was Rhain's best friend. This was the way Rhain wanted her mother to be seven days a week.

It wasn't until one day while playing in the backyard with Olivia, the daughter of one of Rhain's mother's girlfriends, that Rhain realized that it wasn't just the Friday afternoons and Sunday evenings that she went off to her father's house when her mother was bitter, but that it was the entire weekend.

"My mommy says your mommy doesn't do anything but lie in the bed all weekend, moping and crying," Olivia said nonchalantly. "She already lost your daddy, and she's afraid she's going to lose you too; then she'll have nobody."

From that day on, Rhain started making up excuses, at least one weekend out of the month, as to why she couldn't go visit her father, and of course, her mother never forced the issue. She took great pleasure in dialing his phone number, telling him that his daughter had something to tell him and then handing Rhain the phone to deliver the bad news.

Pretty soon it became two weekends out of the

month, and then three until Rhain eventually severed her relationship with her father in its entirety, something she regretted after the loss of her mother. But thinking that her mother would make heaven a living hell if she suspected that her daughter had rekindled her relationship with her former husband after her death, Rhain decided against reaching out to her father. As hard as her father tried to reenter her life, Rhain refused him, the same way she was now refusing Fred.

"Go away and stay away," Rhain shouted to Fred. "You can exit the same way you entered, and take your rosebush with you!" Rhain could have sworn she heard a chuckle from the other side of the door. "That does it," she mumbled to herself as she rose up off the bed and flung the door open. Just as she suspected, Fred was on the other side attempting to muffle laughter with his hand. Rhain just shook her head in disgust and stormed by him.

"Rhain, I'm sorry," Fred said, reaching out to grab her by the arm, but he was just a couple inches short of achieving his goal. He proceeded to follow her into the kitchen, where she snatched every single rose out of each vase and glass she had rested them in. "Rhain, wait. I wasn't laughing at you. It's just that you didn't seem like the type—and when you started kissing me and then I couldn't breathe, and then—"

"No need to explain yourself. I just want you to go," Rhain said, snatching up the last bundle of roses. "Take your flowers and go." She threw the roses at him and, once again, attempted to storm off.

To her surprise, Fred grabbed her by both arms, pulled her against him, and proceeded to kiss her even more passionately than they had kissed before.

Rhain tried to tug and fight, but eventually gave in, wrapping her arms around Fred's shoulders and taking in his tongue.

Picking up Rhain by her waist, Fred lifted her up to the countertop, pulling her dress to her waist to allow her to open her legs wide so that he could find a space in her warmth. With her legs wrapped around Fred, ankles crisscrossed, Rhain threw her head back and stared up at the ceiling as Fred began planting kisses all over her neck. Her moaning let Fred know that the slight pressure he was applying with his teeth provided more pleasure than pain.

Fred pulled away from Rhain just long enough to take a look at her, to make sure her face showed the exact same pleasure that her moans indicated. He then took his position between her legs again and his tongue entered her mouth. As Jon B played, the two moved and grooved, making his song "their song." Their huffing, puffing, and panting was just the backup that song needed.

Silently, each in their own minds, they hoped the song would play forever, but once Fred placed his hands on the elastic waistband of Rhain's panties and attempted to pull them off, it was as if the two found themselves in the middle of the dance floor, dancing their hearts away and the DJ pulled the needle off the record.

"Stop!" Rhain said. "No way, uh uh." She pushed Fred away and hopped down off the counter.

"Rhain, what's wrong?" he said, now totally confused. "A minute ago, on the couch, you seemed pissed when I pushed you away, and now you seem pissed that I'm pulling you closer."

"I wasn't pissed because you pushed me away. I

was pissed because you were laughing at me," Rhain said.

"But I wasn't laughing at you."

"It doesn't matter. I just can't," Rhain snapped.

Fred shook his head. "Woman, you're a hard nut to crack."

Taking offense, Rhain replied, "And what's that supposed to mean?"

"It just means that one minute you're all over me, definitely catching me off guard, and when I stop you, you storm off and throw a tantrum like some child," Fred said, throwing his arms up. "Now that I'm giving in to your advances, you push me away. What do you want? What don't you want? I mean, I'm confused here."

Rhain looked at Fred, who was clearly confused in regard to her actions. "I'm sorry, Fred." Rhain sighed. "Having dinner here, at my house, was a mistake. You really should go."

"No, I shouldn't," Fred said, stepping in close to Rhain. "Yeah, I got a little thrown off in there in the living room. I mean, I just didn't peg you as the type of girl who would get down like that on the first date."

"Get down?" Rhain said as if offended.

"Yeah, I mean, it was funny to see that side of you come out of nowhere. That's why I was laughing. It just seemed so out of character for you . . . like you were trying to be something that you weren't. It's not that I wouldn't love for a woman as beautiful as you to jump my bones, but . . ."

As Fred's words fell off, Rhain just waved her hands to quiet him, having heard enough. "Please, say no more. That's enough, Fred. I know where you're coming from, and I'm as embarrassed as shit right now, so can you at least allow a girl to hold on to just an inkling of her dignity and bow out gracefully, please?" Rhain put her head down, fighting back tears. This had been the date from hell.

"Are you kidding?" Fred asked. "No way am I leaving you here alone." He paused as he slowly walked over to Rhain and ran his hand down the side of her face. "To enjoy all of that wonderful-smelling food all by yourself."

Rhain looked up with a smile.

"There's that smile."

Fearing that her gap might be showing, Rhain quickly turned her open mouth smile into a tight one.

"Why do you do that?" Fred asked.

"Do what?" Rhain asked, not having the slightest idea of what he meant.

"Deliberately smile with your mouth closed, as if you're trying to keep it jailed?"

"No reason," Rhain lied. "I guess I don't even realize that I'm doing it."

"I think you do realize it because whenever I make mention of your smile, you hide it. I mean, not that those beautiful, thick, full lips aren't a delight to look at as well."

Rhain interrupted Fred with laughter. "Will you stop it?" she said, pushing him on his chest, glad that the tension between them was now dissolved, but still feeling the need to explain her actions to Fred. Now that he was still standing there, more than likely going to remain for dinner, she just couldn't allow him to think that she was a loose woman, one who had sex with a guy on the first date.

"Fred, if I tell you something, do you promise not to laugh?"

"You're asking me that?" Fred snickered.

"I know, I know, but seriously."

"Seriously, I promise," he assured her.

"I really don't typically act like that on a first date," Rhain confessed. "And it really does matter to me what you think of me. I mean, I'd love to go to your Christmas party."

"Huh?" Fred said, confused.

"Never mind."

"Look, it's okay, Rhain. I don't think any differently of you. You really don't have to explain—"

"But I do." Rhain paused. "I guess I really don't know how to act on a date because this is actually my first date."

Fred waited, thinking there had to be more words for the end of Rhain's sentence, something like the first date at her house or her first date with a man as nice-looking as he was, something else. When he saw that no words were going to follow, Fred spoke. "Are you trying to tell me that you've never been out with a man before?"

"That's what I am telling you."

"If you don't mind me asking, how old are you?"

"Twenty-five."

There was silence.

"This next question may seem kind of personal, and I don't want you to take offense but—"

"No, I haven't been out with a woman either," Rhain said, saving Fred the embarrassment of asking that question. She had been embarrassed enough for the both of them. "I'm not gay. I've just simply never dated before." Again there was silence. "So, I wasn't trying to be a tease or anything, I just . . . I just . . .

I've already embarrassed myself enough tonight, and I knew what all that kissing and rubbing and grinding was leading to, and I didn't want to make a fool out of myself by not knowing what to do," Rhain continued talking very quickly. "I mean, I wanted to; never in my life have I wanted to, but tonight with you, I wanted to and I would have, only I don't—"

"Shhh," Fred said, putting his index finger on Rhain's lips.

Staring at her eyes, he slowly replaced his finger with his lips. Gently, he cupped Rhain's head in the palm of his hands and kissed her as if she were his new bride. "There are some things in life that you don't have to already know how to do," he said as their lips parted. "Some things just come natural." He kissed her again, this time more intensely. "And you seem like a natural."

Before she knew it, as if Fred couldn't have been more right, Rhain's body began to naturally go with the flow of Fred's as the two slid down each other's bodies and became a puddle of chocolate on the kitchen floor.

This time, when Fred went to slide her panties off, Rhain assisted him by lifting her bottom off the kitchen floor. When he then removed her panties and inhaled her scent, Rhain closed her eyes and inhaled, too, wondering if her pussy actually smelled like roses, or if the scent was the actual roses that she had thrown on the kitchen floor that now lay beneath her and Fred.

The sudden wetness and warmth of Fred's tongue penetrating her caused Rhain to jerk her body. Fred placing his hand on her flat stomach was his way of telling her to relax as he continued to fuck her with his tongue. He sucked, poked, and stroked, allowing his saliva to drip down the crack of her ass and soak her inner thighs.

"Oh, Fred, what are you doing?" Rhain asked as she closed her eyes and arched her back, slowly rolling her hips to the beat of Fred's tongue.

"I'm tasting you," Fred said as he made her lose it when he began sucking on her clit the way he had been sucking on her tongue.

"I can't take it! I can't take it no more," Rhain shouted as she pushed Fred's head up.

Fred removed his tongue from the pool of lust between Rhain's legs, and then laid on top of her and plunged his tongue into her mouth. He then used his hands to massage the wetness his tongue had created. Rhain squirmed with every movement of Fred's hand as he wildly stroked and cupped her pussy. It wasn't until the pain had been surpassed with pleasure that Rhain realized that it was no longer Fred's hand and fingers connecting with her private part, but that he had entered her womanhood with his erect manhood.

She wanted to scream like the teenage girl does in horror movies when she's about to be murdered after having sex with her boyfriend, but instead she bit her bottom lip and allowed a groan to rumble deep in her throat.

With her eyes squinting in both pain and pleasure, Rhain laid there as Fred gently moved in and out of her.

"I can't believe you're inside of me," Rhain said as tears formed in her eyes.

"This was meant to be, Rhain," Fred said as he pulled his dick all the way out of her and then slid it back in.

"Ahhh, Fred."

"Rain on me," he said to Rhain as he looked in her eyes and increased the momentum of his strokes. "Rain on me, woman. Do it now. Do it . . ." His words fell off as he continued to increase the momentum of his strokes, on the verge of bursting.

Rhain couldn't believe that her cherry had finally been popped. While most women had had multiple sex partners by the age of twenty-five, and some even had two or three kids, Rhain had never allowed a man to enjoy the warmth of her womanhood. But now, the twenty-five-year-old virgin was no more.

Rhain slowly began rolling her hips. At first she worried if she would be off sync with Fred's strokes, but her body naturally began to move perfectly with Fred's. She had long passed the feeling of pain and wrapped herself up in the feeling of ecstasy. Rhain lay there staring up at the ceiling with a huge smile on her face as she and Fred made love on a bed of roses . . . on Valentine's Day.

Chapter V

Kiss It to Make It Better

It was after midnight and Rhain still found herself on the kitchen floor with Fred. She had no idea how long they had been there or how many times they had made love. All she knew was that all of the sex she could have been having over the years was made up for in one single night

"You okay?" Fred whispered in Rhain's ear as he lay on his back beside her.

"Mmm, hmmm," she answered, lying on her stomach with her chin resting on her crossed arms. Her lips had a smile on them as she picked up one of the roses, closed her eyes, and inhaled the scent.

"I still can't believe you're a virgin," Fred stated.

"Was a virgin," Rhain reminded him.

He sat in deep thought for a moment while he stared up at the ceiling. "Why?"

"Huh?"

"Why?" he repeated. "Why me?"

Rhain chuckled. "What do you mean?"

"I mean, why did you choose me? After all of these years of holding on to your virginity, why did you choose to give it to me?"

Rhain rolled over on her back and thought for a second. "I don't know." She shook her head and looked over to Fred, who returned her gaze. "I really don't know. There was just something about you."

"What was that something?"

"Like I said, Fred, I really don't know."

"There had to be one thing."

After staring at Fred for a moment, Rhain crawled on top of him. "There's not one thing. It's everything."

Fred smiled and lifted his head to kiss her.

"You made me feel so good when you did that one thing." Rhain blushed.

"I did a lot of things to you, sweetheart. Which *one thing* are you referring to?"

"You know." Rhain giggled. "When you went down there." She lowered her eyes down toward her private part.

"Oh, that," Fred said. "What? You want me to do it again?" He started to push her off him so that he could go down on her.

"No," she was quick to say, pushing him back down by his shoulders. "I want to do it to you. I want to make you feel good." Fred had a look of surprise on his face as Rhain began to kiss her way down his body. "But you're going to have to teach me." Rhain cupped Fred's dick into her hands and kissed the tip of it. "Now what? What do I do next?"

"It's simple." Fred lifted his head to look down at Rhain. "You just put it in your mouth." On that note, Rhain wrapped her lips around the tip of his dick and began sucking it. "Now just bob up and down on it." He moaned.

"Like this," Rhain said as she began to bob her head up and down with his dick in her mouth.

"Yeah, baby, just like that," Fred said as he laid his head back down, closed his eyes, and placed his hands on Rhain's head while she continued sucking his dick. "Oooooh."

"Mmm," Rhain moaned as if she was sucking on a lollypop.

"Now massage my balls," Fred instructed her. "Massage my dick with your mouth and my balls with your hands."

Rhain licked and sucked Fred's dick as she rubbed his nut sack gently. Before Rhain knew it, she was into the groove of things, soon switching shit up like a pro. She was massaging his balls with both her hands and her mouth, switching up and blowing Fred's mind. He had gotten his dick sucked before, and plenty of times, but Rhain was making it seem like the first time with the way she was handling it. Most chicks just liked to play around with it, kissing it and licking it. But Rhain was doing all of the above and then some, including nibbling down the side like it was an ear of corn.

"Ewww shit!" Fred jerked as Rhain accidentally let her teeth hit the tip.

"Sorry," she apologized as she proceeded to kiss it to make it better and then inhaled it once again, using pleasure to make Fred forget all about the pain, and that's just what he did as Rhain sucked him off until he exploded into her mouth.

"Oh damn!" Fred said as he came.

After realizing that Fred was cumming, Rhain

pulled off of his dick after some of the warm lava filled her mouth. She embarrassingly began to gag and spit it out. She then looked down sadly as if she had possibly ruined the moment.

"It's okay," Fred panted after jerking off the remainder of his cum into his hand. He then sat up and kissed Rhain on the cheek. "Don't worry about it. Next I'll teach you how to swallow."

Chapter VI

What a Girl Wants

FROM: McKinneyS@rightcorp.net
TO: MyLove69@aol.com
SUBJECT:Thank you

Darling, you really, really shouldn't have . . . but I'm so glad you did. I just happened to be at the receptionist's desk when the delivery man showed up with the lovely bouquet of roses. I had no idea they were going to be for me. And the poem attached was simply Shakespearean. I'm staring up at them now as I type this e-mail. Just looking at them makes me happy.

I don't need to tell you that at first I had my doubts about us, but over these past couple of weeks, I've felt so brand new and appreciated. You truly know what a girl wants and what a girl needs. I just wish it hadn't taken this long.

Love ya

"Hmmm, I see she got the flowers," Rhain said to herself as she read the e-mail from her highest-paying client's wife, Susan McKinney. "I knew flowers to the job would do the trick."

The e-mail had been delivered to Rhain's mailbox Friday evening, and here it was Sunday evening and she was just now getting around to checking her e-mails. From the moment she walked through the door on Friday evening she had started preparing for her date with Fred, and of course, she spent Saturday with Fred too; he never left her apartment until Sunday morning. They managed to make love all day and night, even through Sylvia's knocking on the door, which started after Rhain had to unplug the phone. She didn't answer the door for Sylvia, though. She was afraid Sylvia would see that Fred was still in her apartment. She'd know that he had never left. *What would she think of me?* she thought.

Sunday morning and afternoon were spent recuperating from her weekend with Fred. Rhain slept like a baby. She even managed to use her pillow to smother the knocking on her door, caused by none other than her anxious, nosey neighbor, Sylvia, who was trying to get the details of Rhain's date.

She had every intention of telling Sylvia the fairy-tale-like details of her date with Fred, but it wouldn't be until she could enjoy a few more laps alone in her pool of breathtaking thoughts where the water temperature was just right.

Rhain saved the e-mail into the cyber folder she had created for her client and leaned back in her chair and smiled, pleased that everything she was doing to woo Mrs. McKinney for Mr. McKinney, in order to patch up their relationship, was working smoothly. The flowers, the letters, the e-mails, the poems, the cards, each serving its purpose. Rhain even threw in an extra and picked up an additional bottle of her favorite cologne, Miami Glow, and sent one to Mrs. McKinney with a little note that read, "You don't need this to light up my life."

Rhain got up from her computer and walked over to plug her phone in and turn her cell phone on just in case Fred was trying to call her. She then fell back on her bed and allowed her mind to replay each and every position Fred had managed to fuck her in. The ringing of the phone jerked Rhain out of her thoughts. She sat up and then looked at the caller ID. Sylvia's number showed up. Rhain looked at the clock on her nightstand that sat next to the phone. It was eight P.M. Rhain hadn't even cleaned up from the weekend or gotten herself ready for work the next day. She knew if she picked up that phone, she'd spend the next two hours filling Sylvia in on all the details of her last night as a virgin. She decided to let it go to voice mail, and not ten seconds later, just as she predicted, her cell phone rang. Once again it displayed Sylvia's number, and once again she allowed it to go to her voice mail. Rhain felt a little bad about dodging Sylvia, but she did want to get her house and herself together, and she loved the idea of keeping Miss Sylvia waiting on the edge of her seat. After all, Rhain had waited twenty-five years to lose her virginity; Sylvia could wait a little bit longer to hear about it.

Come Monday morning, Rhain woke up with a bittersweet feeling. A part of her was still swept away from her romantic two-evening date with Fred; another part of her felt somewhat hurt that she hadn't even received as much as a phone call from Fred since he'd left her house in the wee hours of Sunday morning. The only phone calls and voice messages she had received were all from Sylvia, and that stopped once Rhain finally called her back and told her blow by blow all of the details of her date with Fred that she had been dying to hear.

Checking both her caller ID and her cell phone to make sure that she hadn't missed Fred's call while sleeping, she was disappointed to see there were no missed calls. With a deep sigh, Rhain got up and headed to the bathroom. After using the toilet, she walked over to the sink and prepared to brush her teeth. She turned on the water and went to put the toothbrush to her mouth, and then she paused.

Staring at her reflection in the mirror, Rhain could do nothing but smile. *I don't even look the same anymore,* she thought as she turned from side to side to get a good look at her profile. She put the toothbrush down and used both her hands to roam about her body. She started with her neck, then allowed her hands to slide down her breasts and then to her stomach. She then placed her hands on her hips and turned to get a good look at her behind.

"Ass even looks fatter." She giggled.

Rhain liked what she saw. She beamed in the glow she felt she was now subdued in. She put her face closer to the mirror and observed her skin. Rubbing her face, it appeared as though a few of her acne bumps had gone on hiatus. Once again Rhain smiled, a huge smile, a smile so confident that she didn't give a damn about the gap in her teeth. As a matter of fact, on this morning, it seemed darn right sexy. It was sexy enough for Fred anyway.

As the thought of Fred entered her mind, her smile faded. But then she caught herself. "Girl, this is the first man you've let into your life." She pointed at herself in the mirror, imitating words Sylvia would probably say to her. "Don't let him take your smile away, not when it's taken you so long to find something to smile about."

Rhain took a deep breath, straightened her shoulders, and stuck out her chest. "Obviously you've got something men like. Mr. Simmons might have been your first, but he surely won't be your last." And on that note, Rhain proceeded to brush her teeth and put on her clothes she had laid out for work.

As she was putting on her sweater, she heard a rush of sirens outside her bedroom window, which faced the alley. She wanted to be nosey and see what was going on, but she couldn't find out much from fifteen stories above the alley, so she decided to go ahead and get dressed.

After getting dressed, Rhain grabbed her keys and purse and headed for the elevators. She pressed the Down button and waited a moment for the elevator to stop at her floor. When the doors opened, standing inside was a young nice-looking couple. Rhain didn't know them, but she had ridden the elevator with them several times before, never speaking, just politely smiling and wishing the elevator would hurry the fuck up so that she wasn't forced to ever have to make conversation with them. But today was a new day. This was the new Rhain. The old Rhain was a scared little child, never wanting to just branch out and be seen, but

the new Rhain was a grown-ass woman, and everything about her was worth seeing.

"Good morning," Rhain said in a jolly tone as she
stepped in and pushed the lobby button, even
though it was already lit up.

"Good morning," the gentleman said. The lady
remained silent, simply giving Rhain the once-over.

She could feel their stares. To shake them off, she
flung her long, dark brown hair and allowed it to
sway back and forth across the middle of her back.

"I almost didn't recognize you," the gentleman
said. "You're the same lady who's always on the
elevator. It's just your hair is usually up in a bun,
right?"

"Right," Rhain said, turning around with a huge
grin on her face. But once she looked over at the
woman, Evilene, her smile faded and she turned to
stare back at the elevator doors. Once they opened,
she could feel the sense of hurry Miss Thing had in
trying to get off the elevator, so she stepped to the
side and allowed her to brush by her, the gentleman a step behind her.

Before he exited, he turned to Rhain and just
barely whispered, "Well, it looks nice," and winked.

Rhain blushed and smiled and ran her hands
down her hair. She got so caught up in the nice
gentleman's compliment that she forgot to get off
the elevator and the doors closed. She ended up
having to ride the elevator all the way up again
before making it back down to the lobby.

Once Rhain walked out of the apartment building door, she ran smack into Sylvia, who was finishing up her morning jog. She almost trotted right
past Rhain, but then stopped and did a double take
when Rhain smiled and waved at her.

"Rhain, is that you?" Sylvia said as she proceeded to walk small circles around Rhain while looking her up and down. "Your hair." She flung it up with her hand. "And you've got on lipstick: Mary Kay Whipped Berries. Oh my God and brick-colored blush." Sylvia paused for a moment. "You look . . . you look . . . hell, you look the shit, ma," Sylvia said, giving Rhain a high five.

"Thank you, girl." Rhain blushed. "I figured you made me buy all that stuff from you, I might as well start wearing it, huh?"

"Rhain, I knew up under that cute little virgin girl act there was a hoe ready to break out."

"Sylvia, you are a mess," Rhain said. "Look, I gotta go. I'm going to be late for work."

"All right, girl, but do you want me to go get my husband's boxing gloves for you to borrow or do you have your own?"

"What?" Rhain asked, confused.

"Boxing gloves, because you are for certain going to have to fight off Mr. Irving today, and every other man in the office for that matter." Sylvia laughed.

Rhain just shook her head and laughed at her friend as she walked away to get into her car. Sometimes Sylvia reminded Rhain of a white Willona from *Good Times*. As Rhain started up her car, she thought about Sylvia's comment again, chuckled, and then pulled off.

As Rhain drove down Interstate 71, she hummed along to the jazz tune that was playing on the radio. She realized that her radio had been programmed to that light jazz station ever since she had gotten that car. And although she had a nice CD collection at home, it was for show, to fill up the built-in CD holder on her entertainment center. Rhain reached out and put her hand on the dial. She then pulled back. *This is the new Rhain, remember?* she told herself. Try something new. Rhain reached out and turned the radio to 98.9, the home of the *Tom Joyner Morning Show.* Destiny's Child's song from the *Charlie's Angels* soundtrack was playing.

Rhain started out humming it, but after a minute or two, she was singing the words: "All the ladies . . . independent . . . throw your hands up with me." By the time she made it to work, she had sung along with Ne-Yo and Keyshia Cole too. She pulled into the parking lot with ten minutes to spare before it was time to officially clock in. She put her hand on the door handle and opened the door. She stepped one foot out of the car but then paused.

For years, and without fail, Rhain had always been ten minutes early to work. Being ten minutes early became expected of her. Well, she was tired of doing what was expected of her, so with a smile on her face, Rhain lifted her foot back into the car and closed the door. She put the key back into the ignition and turned it just enough for the radio to come on. Feeling really funky and rebellious from her normal self, Rhain turned the station to 107.5, which played R & B and rap, and thanks to Kelis, by the time she got out of the car and headed into her office, she was feeling *Bossy.*

"Good morning, Miss Garrett," Evelyn said. "Miss Garrett?" She stood up from behind the desk. "Oh my God. Look at you. You look, you look . . ."

"Gorgeous," Jim from legal said as he entered the reception area. "Let me help you with your coat," he said.

"Thanks, Jim," Rhain said. *Damn, I must look good,* she thought. *Jim has never noticed me before.*

One time Rhain had missed the last step while going down the stairs and Jim was right behind her and didn't even lift a hand to help her up. "Hey, watch your step," is all that asshole had said.

"Is this a new coat?" Jim said, sliding it off Rhain. He then inhaled. "Smells new."

"Yes, it is," she replied. "Well, it's been in my closet since last year; this is just my first time wearing it."

Rhain normally wore her full-length leather coat. It covered her entire body, which she preferred. But today, she felt bold enough to let some leg show, which is why she pulled that black, leather calve-length skirt out from the back of her closet. The tight-fitting ribbed turtleneck she had planned on taking back to Lerner New York complemented the skirt wonderfully.

"Okay, are you Miss Garrett or are you her twin?" Evelyn joked.

"I am she." Rhain smiled as she started to walk away. "In the flesh." She threw a little twitch in her ass for Jim to catch, and then made her way to her desk.

Rhain sat down at her desk and turned on her computer. While it powered up, she checked her voice mail. Once her computer was up and running, instead of checking her company e-mails, she logged on to her AOL account and checked to see if Fred had sent her an e-mail. He hadn't. Rhain was trying to be strong, but the fact that she hadn't heard from Fred since their date, the date on which she'd given up her virginity, she was feeling a little hurt.

"It's only been one day, going on two," she told

herself. "Give it some time. Besides, as Sylvia would say, I wouldn't want him to be a bugaboo."

"Rhain, is that you?" Mr. Irving called from his office. Rhain deliberately ignored him, pretending not to hear him so that he would use the intercom, like she preferred him to. "Rhain," he repeated, now through the intercom.

"Yes, Mr. Irving," Rhain answered.

"Can you come into my office for a moment?"

"Sure."

"Thank you, sweetheart."

Rhain sucked her teeth at the sound of him calling her sweetheart.

"It's Miss Garrett," Rhain said as she walked through her boss's office. His back was to her as he looked through a file on his credenza.

"Huh?" he said, turning around.

"It's Miss Garrett or Rhain, not sweetheart," Rhain said with a painted-on smile. "Now what was it you needed?"

Speechless, Mr. Irving scanned Rhain from head to toe. After swallowing and putting his eyes back into his head, he was finally able to speak.

"Uh, Miss Garrett, I uh, just wanted to let you know that Mrs. Irving loved the Valentine's Day gift."

"Good, I'm glad she liked it so well."

Rhain stood there waiting for Mr. Irving to say something else, but he didn't. He just sat there staring at her. Finally, he stood up.

"Miss Garrett, I uh, hope you don't mind me saying, but you look . . . you look good."

"Thank you, Mr. Irving," Rhain said. "Now if there won't be anything else."

Subconsciously, Mr. Irving licked his lips. He

couldn't help it. Rhain stood there looking like the last supper and he was starving. After a moment of silence, Rhain assumed that Mr. Irving didn't need anything else, so she turned to exit his office.

"Uh, wait," Mr. Irving said as he stood up from behind his desk.

Rhain's mouth dropped wide open, and she covered it with her hand. She tried not to laugh and she succeeded, but she was smiling hard . . . but it was not as hard as Mr. Irving's dick. It was bulging from his pants, fighting to get out.

Oh my goodness, Rhain thought. She couldn't believe all of that meat her boss was packing. But what she couldn't believe more was the tingle she was starting to feel between her legs. *Down girl,* she told her kitty cat. She didn't know what was going on. Perhaps Fred had ignited a flame inside of her that couldn't be put out. Before Rhain realized it, she was licking her lips too.

"Look, Rhain, Miss Garrett, uh," Mr. Irving said as he stood up and went to close his office door. He stood in front of the door, staring at Rhain. He followed her eyes down to what they were admiring, and out of embarrassment, he immediately took his hands and covered himself like he had been butt naked, and then walked back over to his desk and sat down. "I'm sorry, Miss Garrett. That's just something I don't have any control over. You just caught me off guard."

"Caught you off guard?" Rhain questioned. "You asked me to come in here."

"No, I mean you caught me off guard by looking like that."

Rhain looked down at herself. "I can't help the way I look, Mr. Irving."

"Yes, I know. I know. But you look good. You look real good and I just wanted you to know."

This was the most humble Rhain ever remembered Mr. Irving being. Normally he was too sexy for his shirt, figuring he was the one who should be making women drool instead of the other way around.

"Didn't mean to catch you off guard with my new look, Mr. Irving," Rhain apologized.

"Oh, no need to apologize," Mr. Irving said, standing again, but then looking down at his hard-on and quickly sitting down again. "Damn it!" he said, wishing the damn thing would go down.

Rhain had seen Mr. Irving flirt with every pair of legs in sight, but she had never seen him so taken by any of them before. She was flattered.

"Look, Mr. Irving, it's okay," Rhain said, walking over toward him. "It really is."

He put his head down in the palm of his hands. "I'm just so embarrassed."

"Don't be." Rhain put her hand on his shoulder.

He looked down at her hand resting gently on his shoulder. He closed his eyes and slowly placed his hand on top of hers.

Rhain took a deep breath and just stood there, allowing her boss to stroke her fingers with his own. He opened his eyes and looked up at her for approval. She didn't want to give it to him one way or the other, so she just closed her eyes and hoped that he would stop touching her, or that it would stop feeling so good—whichever came first. But neither happened. He kept touching her and it kept feeling good, especially when he lifted her hand and placed her fingers into his mouth and began sucking her fingers.

"Ooooh," she moaned as she stood in front of

him panting like a puppy trying to keep up with the big dogs.

He inhaled her fingers one by one like they were covered in chocolate. With her fingers still in his mouth, he stood up. After a couple more licks, he interlocked his fingers with hers and dropped them down. Rhain opened her eyes only to be staring into her boss's. He released her hands and then slowly walked behind her. She looked straight ahead as she felt his dick poking her ass. The next thing she felt was his hands cupping her ass through her leather skirt. Then his heavy breath hit her neck before his lips did.

"Ohhh, uhhh, oooh," she breathed deeply as his hands made their way around to her front and up to her breasts.

He stood there fondling her breasts as he kissed her neck. While he kissed her neck, he allowed his hands to roam down to the sides of her skirt and he slowly lifted it up to her waist. Holding her skirt up with his left hand, he took his right hand and stuck it down her panties, causing her to moan when his fingers slid past her clit and into her pussy. Instantaneously, Rhain began rocking back and forth on his fingers. Her rocking and moaning made Mr. Irving's dick grow even harder. Rhain felt like it was poking at her ass as Mr. Irving began pumping himself against her.

"You're so wet. Is that why your mama named you Rhain? So you could just pour down all over a brotha? Gotdamn, girl," Mr. Irving said as he finger fucked Rhain until she rained down on his fingers.

Feeling her wetness, he couldn't take it anymore. He turned Rhain around and pushed her panties and stockings down. He pushed his phone out of the way and then sat Rhain up on his desk. He removed her shoes and then pulled her stockings and panties off. Rhain watched him unbuckle his belt and pull his huge Mandingo out. Her eyes almost bulged as big as the balls that had been in his pants. It looked like a huge hairy monster coming at her, no, *cuming* at her, as precum dripped from the tip of it.

Mr. Irving spread Rhain's legs open by her inner thighs and his erect dick dove directly into her wetness.

"Jesus!" she shouted as he worked the middle.

Once she got past the sharp pain of his opening her up to fit him in, she was able to get into the groove of things. It felt bigger than Fred's and it curved slightly upward, which took some getting used to. But once she did, she had Mr. Irving by his nice and tight ass cheeks, pushing him in and out of her.

"Fuck me," she softly moaned. *Did I say that?* she asked herself.

"I am fucking you. Damn, I'm fucking you," Mr. Irving said, pronouncing a syllable with each stroke. "And I'm about to cum . . . I'm . . . a . . . bout . . . to . . . cummmmmm," Mr. Irving said as he banged Rhain's pussy at full speed until he nutted inside her.

By this time she was biting down on his shoulder through his shirt, still grinding his dick, as she was only seconds from her own climax. In order to speed her up, Mr. Irving coached her on.

"That's right, Rhain, get that dick. Get that dick, baby. Cum on it. Cum on it."

"Yes, yes, yes!" she panted as she started to cum.

"Shhh," he said as he put his hand over Rhain's mouth. "Shhh."

She continued her muffled screams as she fucked his dick wildly until she juiced.

She took deep, heavy breaths as she came down off of her high. Mr. Irving pulled out of her and tucked himself into his underwear and pulled up his pants. He stood in front of Rhain with a gloating look after seeing how pleased his lover was. It was at that moment that reality set in for Rhain.

Oh my goodness. I just screwed my boss. Her head fell back as she thought to herself, *What have I done?* She immediately hopped off the desk and started putting her panties, hose, and shoes back on.

"Mr. Irving?" they heard a voice and knocking outside the door. The voice was almost a whisper, but when Mr. Irving didn't respond, the voice was louder and sounded a little upset. "Mr. Irving!" She knocked again. After this went on a couple of times, the doorknob to Mr. Irving's office turned and slowly the door opened. Standing in the doorway was Evelyn.

By the time Evelyn opened the door, Rhain had just managed to slip her last shoe on.

"Evelyn!" Rhain said, out of breath. "Hi, we were uh, just in the middle of . . ." Rhain couldn't even think of a lie quick enough, but finally one came. "Dictation."

Evelyn, in a huff, walked over to Rhain, and in a loud whisper said, "Leave out the-*tation*; it was more like just *dic-*."

"What?" Rhain said with a confused look.

"Look, I know what you two were in the middle of," Evelyn said. "For Christ's sake, the entire office does." She then turned to Mr. Irving. "Somehow you accidentally pushed the page system button. We heard everything. And I do mean everything."

While Rhain stood frozen stiff, Mr. Irving walked over to the phone and turned the page button off. He then collapsed in his chair like he could just die.

"Oh no," Rhain said.

"Oh yes . . . or more like yes, yes, yes," Evelyn imitated. She then looked over at Mr. Irving with rage in her eyes. "Son of a bitch," she spat before storming out of the office.

Rhain's eyes began to fill with tears. Before Mr. Irving could see them fall from her eyes, she fled the scene.

"Rhain, wait!" Mr. Irving called, but she had already grabbed her purse and had run out of the office, leaving her coat and all.

By the time Rhain burst out of the office building doors, her eyes were pouring with tears. She could barely see clearly enough to find her car key. Once she got into the car, she sat there for a second, allowing the entire horrible scene to repeat in her mind. She then began wailing. Once she was able to calm herself down, she put the key into the ignition and started the car. The radio was still locked in to 107.5, and playing on the radio was a song called "Promiscuous Girl." Rhain immediately turned off the radio and began crying again.

She needed to get it together. She had to get it together. She was a big girl now, so she'd better start acting like it. But if this was what being a big girl was all about, she'd rather go back to being a big baby again.

Rhain pulled out of the parking lot and just drove. She had no particular destination in mind; she just wanted to drive, drive far away. As she drove, she thought about how drastically her life had changed. In the last three days, she had gone from being a virgin to now having two sex partners. She felt disgusting, dirty. She wanted to take everything back, but it was too late. She had to face reality, and unfortunately, the reality was the fact that she had given up her virginity to a practical stranger—a man who she'd probably never hear from again—and that she had then turned around and slept with her boss. Not only had she slept with her boss, but every employee at the company heard her having sex with her boss over the paging system.

Cringing at the thought of everything in her recent past, Rhain decided to focus on now, the present. And right now she had some decisions to make. She had no idea what her future held, but she did know that it didn't include Heigan National Insurance. No way could she continue working there. Maybe today's incident was just more of an incentive to quit that dead-end job and step out on faith and pursue her writing career full-time.

With just a mustard seed of hope, Rhain turned her car around and headed back to her office. When she pulled back into the parking lot, she took a deep breath, and with her head held high, she made her way back into the building. She passed Evelyn and a few other whispering employees, still holding her head up high. Had she planned on staying employed there, she would have had her head between her legs. But as far as Rhain was concerned, she never had to see those fuckers again, so what did she care what they thought about her?

When Rhain showed up back at work, she had every intention of quitting her job in order to take the risk of being self-employed. Ironically enough, when she arrived back at her desk, she was greeted by a pink slip and a breakdown of her severance package and her COBRA health insurance plan. Rhain's initial instinct was to be pissed. *How dare they get rid of me when I was about to quit,* she thought. But then a huge smile covered her face as she knew this was nothing more than confirmation that it was finally time that she move forward with her lifelong dream. Not only would she use her severance package to live off of, but she would file unemployment for what it was worth, and when that ran out, she'd pull money out of her 401k, if need be. But her hopes were that she could get the word out so strong about Rhain's Originals to the point that business would pour in from across the country. Hopefully money would start rolling in so quickly that she wouldn't even need the full six months of unemployment that she was entitled to.

I'll never have to worry about getting hit on by a boss, sleeping with a boss, or even having a boss for that matter, Rhain thought. *I'll be my own damn boss.* And even more so, she wouldn't have to deal with other people. She could crawl right back into her old shell if she wanted to; besides, Rhain never wanted to go back to that place where grown people left one another sticky notes like "please clean out the microwave after you use it."

She'd definitely miss the feeling of security that direct deposit provided for her, but at the same time, Rhain had always been confident of her writing skills. She had made a fairly decent secondary income; now she was really going to put her skills to the test by becoming a full-time ghostwriter, and seemingly she'd have more time on her hands than ever—maybe she could even give birth to that novel.

Rhain was startled out of her thoughts by Mr. Irving walking up to her desk. She jumped.

"I'm sorry, Miss Garrett. I didn't mean to frighten you," Mr. Irving said.

"Oh, Mr. Irving," Rhain said with her head down, not able to look him in the eyes. "That's okay."

He watched as she looked down at the paperwork that he had left on her desk. "I'm sorry about that." He pointed to the pink slip and the severance package.

"Oh, don't worry about it."

"That's what I had called you into my office to tell you about this morning, but—"

"Wait a minute," Rhain snapped as a fire brewed inside the pit of her stomach. "You mean, you were going to give me my walking papers this morning, before you . . . before we . . . ?"

"Well, yes, you didn't think we prepared that package in just the last hour, do you?"

"So you fucked me knowing damn well you were about to let me go?" Rhain said, getting loud, not giving a flying fuck about saying the F-word.

"Those weren't my intentions, Rhain," he said, looking around to see if anyone was listening. "And hold it down."

"I will not hold it down," Rhain yelled as tears formed in her eyes.

"Look, I'm so sorry, Rhain. I am so sorry," he said, putting his hands on each of her arms to comfort her. Rhain took a deep breath and looked away. "As you can see in the package, I had them throw in an extra six weeks, just to show you how much I hate to see you go, and it's not just you. Evelyn and Kenya going to get packages, as are a few other employees over the next few weeks. Who knows, we'll all probably be out of work by the end of the year with the way things are looking."

"Yeah, but it looks like the old pussy is getting the ax first, huh?" Rhain said sarcastically. "Can't get rid of the new pussy just yet; you've still got a chance with them."

"That's not fair, Rhain," Mr. Irving said in his defense. "I had no idea you and I were going to . . . you know."

Rhain just stared at Mr. Irving and then dropped her head and shook it left to right in defeat. "Look, it doesn't matter anymore. It's been nice working for you." Rhain proceeded to gather her belongings, which wasn't much.

"I really am sorry," Mr. Irving said as he proceeded to help Rhain pack up her things. He got her a box that some office supplies had come in and he helped her place her things inside.

"Looks like this is everything," Rhain said as she stared down into the box on her desk.

"You gonna be okay?"

"Yeah." Rhain nodded. She looked around and opened a couple more drawers just to make sure. "I guess this is good-bye, Mr. Irving."

"Please, call me Jeff." He smiled.

"Good-bye," Rhain said.

"Uh, look, Rhain," Jeff said. "If you're not busy later on tonight—"

Before he could finish his sentence, Rhain's handprint was embedded on his face.

"What the hell was that for?" he said, holding his face after Rhain's powerful slap.

"Not only do you fuck me before you send me packing," Rhain raged, "but to add insult to injury, you try to fuck me after you lay me off too? MEN!" Rhain said as she picked up her box and stormed off, leaving Jeff standing there rubbing his cheek, mumbling obscenities toward her.

She grabbed her coat from the closet and walked out to her car, throwing her box in the backseat. She then got in the driver's seat and turned on the car. She turned on her radio and changed the dial from the R & B hip-hop station back to her smooth jazz. Perhaps a change was in order, but definitely a change for the better and not the worse.

I can't be a virgin again, but I'm not about to become some slut bucket, Rhain thought to herself. *The old me was boring and afraid to take risks, and the so-called new me was maybe too much of a risk-taker, but the newer me is going to show 'em both how to do it by living out my dream.*

Rhain gunned the engine and then sharply peeled out of the parking lot, leaving the old Rhain behind; but little did she know, living out her dream could be, in all actuality, a nightmare.

Chapter VII

When It Rains, It Pours

Rhain parked her car in her assigned parking space. With her purse on her arm, she grabbed the box from her backseat and headed toward her apartment building doors. After that, everything else became a quick blur.

"That's her," someone yelled. Then out of no-where, cops began to swarm around Rhain.

"Rhain Garrett?" an officer asked her

"Ye . . . yeah, yes," Rhain said nervously as she stared down the barrel of the officer's gun. "I'm Rhain Garrett, but what's going—"

Rhain's words were cut off by an officer coming up behind her and jerking her by the arm. The box fell from her arms, and the next thing she knew, she was becoming intimate with the pavement. The officer slammed her to the ground and put his knee in her back while another officer handcuffed her arms behind her back.

"Get up," yelled the officer who had initially snatched her up. He pulled her to her feet and pushed her over to his squad car and threw her into the backseat.

From that point on, it was as if someone had hit a mute button. The officer stood at the backseat with the door open, and his foot rested on the door base. Rhain saw his lips moving, but she couldn't make out anything as his words dragged on while he read her her rights.

He got in Rhain's face and looked to be yelling, but Rhain had no idea what he was yelling about as she just stared at him like a retard.

"Do you hear me?" The officer's words finally registered. "Do you understand these rights as they have been read to you?"

Rhain nodded her head yes because she figured that's what he wanted to hear, and she didn't want to make him any angrier than he already seemed to be. The officer slammed the door closed and then walked around to the driver's side and got into the car. He turned on his lights and sirens and then drove off.

The city buildings seemed to go by in a haze as the cruiser drove her down to police headquarters. Once they arrived, Rhain was hauled into the station, catching a glimpse of a couple of cameramen from the local news stations. After her fingerprints and mug shots were taken, Rhain was stripped down and a cavity search was performed on her. She was then thrown in a holding cell, where she waited for about an hour before an officer came to get her.

"Garrett," the officer yelled as he unlocked her holding cell. "Come with me."

The male officer removed Rhain from the holding cell. With her hands cuffed in front of her and her ankles shackled, she was led toward one of the two interrogation rooms. As Rhain passed the first interrogation room, she looked through the glass on the door and saw a familiar face.

"Sylvia!" she began shouting. Rhain became emotional at just the sight of a familiar face. She had felt so alone, so afraid, like someone had lifted her out of the world she knew and placed her somewhere so foreign and far away. "Sylvia! Sylvia!"

Upon hearing her name called, Sylvia looked up toward the door. Her eyes locked with Rhain's momentarily, but only for a second as the officer quickly continued to pull Rhain to the interrogation room right next to Sylvia's.

"Please, that's my neighbor, that's my friend," Rhain pleaded with the officer, trying to plant her feet into the ground so that he couldn't move her. But her one hundred and forty-three pounds were no match for the officer's two hundred and fifteen. "Let me talk to her, please. Just let me talk to her. She's my friend."

"Call her when you get your one phone call." The officer snickered.

This angered Rhain as he overpowered her and managed to get her completely inside the interrogation room. He pushed her down into one of the chairs that sat around the table that was in the middle of the room.

"Why am I here?" Rhain yelled out. "What do you want from me?"

"Calm down, Miss Garrett," a detective said as he entered the room. "You can go, Officer Rankins," he said to the officer who had escorted Rhain to the room. "I can handle it from here."

"You sure, Detective Somore?" Officer Rankins asked. "She's a firecracker."

"Trust me," Detective Somore said as he sat down in the chair across from Rhain, "I've dealt with tougher broads than this one." On that note, the other officer exited the room, leaving Detective Somore alone to question Rhain.

"Miss Garrett, I'm Detective Somore," he said as he rested his arms on the table and folded his hands.

"Please, Detective, no pleasantries," Rhain cried. "Why am I here and when can I go home?"

"Miss Garrett, I think you know exactly why you are here."

"Since when is screwing your boss during business hours a crime?"

"Huh?" Detective Somore asked with a puzzled look on his face. "Miss Garrett, you have been arrested for the murder of your girlfriend's husband."

"Whoa, what?" Rhain said, her mind completely blown away. "My girlfriend's husband? But I don't even have any friends."

"Miss Garrett, you murdered Frederick McKinney. We have circumstantial evidence and we have motive. So why don't you save us both some time and just confess?"

"Frederick McKinney? I don't even know any gotdamn Frederick McKinney. And like I said, I don't have any friends, so he's certainly not any husband of one of my girlfriends."

"I thought I just heard you tell Officer Rankins that the woman in the next room was your friend."

Rhain thought for a moment about Sylvia. "Well, uh, yeah, well, actually, she's my neighbor."

"Don't you consider your neighbor a friend?"

"Well, yeah, but I certainly didn't kill her husband. Besides, her husband's name is George."

"It's not her husband we're talking about, and besides, when I say *girlfriend*, I don't mean a female friend, Miss Garrett. I'm talking about your girlfriend *girlfriend*." The detective raised an eyebrow.

Catching on to what the detective was trying to say, Rhain was appalled at his accusation. "Okay, you are just sick," Rhain said with a disgusted look on her face. "I'm not into girls, so I know you've got the wrong person."

"Not into girls, huh?" the detective said as he took out a notepad and began flipping through it. "So you and your friend, pardon me, your neighbor— Sylvia, I believe her name is—never shared a passionate moment together in your apartment, namely, the kitchen?"

"What? Are you kidding me? Sylvia and I never . . ." Rhain's words faded off as she remembered that night in her kitchen when she and Sylvia tongue-kissed.

"Is it all coming back to you now?"

"Detective, honestly, it wasn't anything like that," Rhain assured him. "Sylvia and I aren't a couple or anything like that. She was just teaching me how to kiss. It was the night of my first date with Fred, my first date in my life, period."

"So you do know Frederick McKinney?"

"No, this was Fred—Fred Simmons."

Detective Somore took a deep breath, looked over to the one-way mirror, and nodded. A couple seconds later another detective entered the room.

"Miss Garrett, this is my partner, Detective Hughes," Detective Somore said.

What does this asshole want me to say? Rhain thought. *Oh, hi, Detective Hughes, pleased to meet you?*

Rhain sat silently as Detective Hughes sat down next to his partner and handed him a folder. Detective Somore opened the folder and pulled out some pictures and slid them in front of Rhain.

"Like I said previously, so you do know Frederick Simmons McKinney the third?" Detective Somore said as he tapped his finger on one of the pictures.

Rhain looked down at the photos and began to cry. "Oh my God!" she yelled. "Oh my God." The two detectives looked at each other, then back at Rhain's reactions. "Fred, oh my God. That's Fred. That's Fred Simmons. What happened to him?" Rhain asked the detectives. "Who did this? What happened? How'd he die?"

"His throat was cut and then he was stuffed behind a Dumpster in the alley behind your apartment building," Detective Somore answered.

"The sirens," Rhain said as she thought about the sirens she had heard earlier that morning from her bedroom window. "That's what all those sirens were about this morning."

"So you were there?" Detective Hughes said in an insinuating tone.

"Yes, I mean no," Rhain said, catching herself. "I was at home. I heard the sirens, but I wasn't there at the scene . . . with his body." Rhain tried to look down at the pictures again, but she couldn't. She turned away and began gagging, sick to her stomach.

"Miss Garrett," Detective Somore said, "Detective Hughes and I are going to get you some water. We'll be right back."

The two detectives got up and exited the room, closing the door behind them.

"Did you see her reaction when we showed her the photos of Mr. McKinney's dead body?" Detective Hughes asked Detective Somore as they walked to the watercooler. "Appeared as though she had seen the dead body for the first time."

"Yeah, and if that was her first time seeing his dead body, that only means one thing." The two detectives looked at each other. "She's not the one who killed him and left him there like that."

"But if she's not the one who killed him, then who is?"

"I don't know," Detective Hughes said as he removed a paper cup from the cup dispenser. "But let's not go clearing her too soon. Just because she might not be the one who killed him and dumped his body there doesn't mean that she doesn't know who did."

"Yeah, and it doesn't mean that she didn't have anything to do with it either."

Detective Somore took a deep breath. "You got a change of clothes in your locker, Detective?" Detective Somore asked his partner.

"Yeah, why?"

"Because it looks like it's going to be a long night. I got enough unsolved murders cases; I don't need to go adding any more to the pile. This one's fresh. Our chances are greater of getting this case resolved. We need to find out who killed Frederick Simmons McKinney the third. Somehow Miss Garrett is connected to all of this, and I'm not going to sleep until I find out how."

Detective Somore filled the cup with water, and

then he and his partner returned to the interrogation room to continue questioning Rhain.

"Here you are," Detective Somore said, handing Rhain her cup of water.

"Thank you," she said, taking a sip and then setting the cup down on the table.

"Okay, Miss Garrett, back to Mr. McKinney," Detective Somore said, sitting down. Detective Hughes took the chair next to him. "How did you meet his wife?"

Once again, Rhain felt as though her head was about to explode. Her heart sank into her stomach. "Wife?" Rhain said.

"Yes, Mrs. McKinney," Detective Hughes chimed in. "Susan McKinney."

"Don't deny knowing her, Miss Garrett," Detective Somore said in a stern voice. "We've confiscated your computer, and we've seen all of the e-mails you've sent her. We've even found receipts from flowers and gifts that you've sent her."

"Oh no, oh no," Rhain said. She started to get dizzy and weak. This was all like one big nightmare. "Susan McKinney—Fred's wife? He has a wife?"

"You lied to us, Miss Garrett," Detective Somore said to Rhain. "You told us that you didn't know the victim or his wife, and now you're saying that you know both? People only lie when they are trying to hide something. What are you trying to hide, Miss Garrett?"

"Or should we say who are you trying to protect?" Detective Hughes asked.

"Nothing, no one." Rhain tried to assure them. "Please, it's not what you think."

"Then why did you lie?" Detective Somore huffed.

"I didn't lie," Rhain stated. "I honestly didn't know who you were talking about. When I met

Fred—Frederick—he introduced himself to me as Fred Simmons. I had no idea that that wasn't his real name or that he had a wife."

"So are you trying to tell us that you just happened to have met the husband, by coincidence, of Susan McKinney, the woman you were sleeping with?" Detective Hughes asked.

"Sleeping with?" Rhain said. "I wasn't sleeping with Susan. I've never met her before in my life. I've only contacted her on the computer and through letters and stuff. Her husband hired me to send her those e-mails and gifts and things."

"So Fred hired you?"

"Yes, no, I guess, I don't know," Rhain said, getting confused. "If Fred was her husband, then I guess he was the one who hired me."

"So you did know Susan's husband, then, and you did know that he had a wife?" Detective Somore said, successfully confusing the shit out of Rhain.

"Yes, I mean no, I mean . . ." Rhain was stuck. She didn't know what to say. Nothing she said seemed to matter. This was all some big twisted joke, and she was the punch line. Now all she had to do was figure out who in the hell was the comedian. Because the shit wasn't funny.

Chapter VIII

In Cold Blood

After Rhain explained to the two detectives how she had been hired via e-mail to pretend to be someone she had only corresponded with via e-mail, in order for him to patch things up with his wife by sending her love poems, letters, e-mails, flowers, and so on, she was hoping they would believe her and let her go. But that was the furthest thing from what happened.

The truth gets you nowhere, Rhain thought as she sat in her cell. *I might as well have just made up a bunch of lies. Maybe I'd be out of here by now.*

"Garrett, you've got a visitor," a female guard hollered into Rhain's cell.

Rhain quickly made her way down from the top bunk and followed the guard to the visiting room.

"Sylvia!" Rhain said as she raced over to the phone and picked it up so that she could communicate with Sylvia through the glass. "Sylvia." Rhain began to cry. "Oh God, Sylvia, you are my friend. You are my friend." Rhain couldn't control her tears. "My only friend."

"Rhain, honey," Sylvia said once she picked up the phone to talk. "It's okay. It's okay."

"No, it's not, Sylvia. It's awful in here," Rhain said as she wiped her tears away.

"I know. But you can get through this. It's not that bad. It's never as bad as it seems."

"Easy for you to say. I'm in here and you're out there." Sylvia couldn't respond to that. Rhain was right. "Frederick's dead, Sylvia, but I guess you know that," Rhain said after gaining her composure.

"Yeah," Sylvia said, shaking her head. "I know that."

"I saw them questioning you yesterday when they arrested me." Rhain paused for a moment. "You told them about the kiss—our kiss."

"I know. They were questioning me about all kinds of things, Rhain. I was scared. They have this way of asking questions that gets everything twisted. I had to tell them the truth, but of course, they have a way of twisting the truth as well."

"I know, Sylvia. It's okay. Trust me, my mind is still in knots." Rhain rubbed her forehead. "What else did you tell them?"

Sylvia shrugged her shoulders. "I don't know . . . the truth."

Not comfortable with Sylvia's response, Rhain took her shovel and dug a little deeper. "The truth . . . like what truth?"

"Come on, Rhain, I don't know. Just the truth." Sylvia dodged answering the question. "I mean, come on, Rhain, I'm on your side. I know there has to be a reason why you did what you did."

Rhain's eyes filled with tears, and she felt the sharp pain from the knife in her back. "Why I did what I did? So what are you saying here? You . . . you think I . . . Sylvia, you think I killed him? Do you think I'm the one who killed Fred?"

Sylvia leaned in close to the glass and whispered into the receiver. "Rhain, like I told the police when they were looking into an alibi for you, I called and I knocked. I didn't hear from you for two days, Rhain. What am I supposed to think?"

"It's not what you're supposed to think, Sylvia," Rhain yelled. "It's what you're supposed to know." Rhain stood up and started pounding the glass with the phone. "I didn't do it!" she yelled at the top of her lungs. "I didn't do it! I don't care what you or the police think. I didn't do it, damn it! I didn't do it!" Rhain was going nuts, still beating the phone against the glass.

Scared to death, and shocked at seeing the soft-spoken Rhain, the Rhain she knew, completely lose it and flip the script, Sylvia jumped up from her chair and backed up.

"I didn't do it!" Rhain continued yelling as several guards rushed her and carried her away. She cried, kicked, screamed, and wailed all the way to solitary confinement. "I didn't do it!" Rhain knew in her heart that she didn't do it. But could she convince the rest of the world of that?

Rhain had no idea how long she had been in solitary confinement. She sat on the ground and rubbed the huge knot that was on the left side of her forehead, compliments of the billy club one of the officers had slugged her upside her head with during her fit after Sylvia's visit.

"Damn, this joint smells like a fish pond with three-day-old dead carp in it," one of the two female officers who entered Rhain's cell joked.

Rhain was oblivious to the fact that she had urinated on herself, or how long she had been wading in it.

"She must be on the rag or something. Get this bitch cleaned up," the other officer said as they each took Rhain by the arm and led her to the shower.

Alone in the shower, as the two female officers stood off to the side and guarded her while she showered, Rhain let the water run down her face and blend with her tears. *All I want to do is wake up from this nightmare*, she cried to herself. *That's all I want to do.*

"Come on out of there," one of the officers yelled, throwing her a towel. "You ain't at the fucking spa."

After Rhain got out of the shower, she got dressed and was escorted back to the interrogation room.

"Oh no," she said, once she entered the room and saw Detective Somore and Detective Hughes in there waiting for her.

"Miss Garrett, we're glad to see you again too," Detective Somore said as Rhain sat down in the chair. "Oh, Officer," Detective Somore said to the officer who had brought her into the room, "I think you can remove those handcuffs."

Rhain looked at Detective Somore to make sure he was serious. He nodded to the officer to confirm his order, and the officer removed Rhain's cuffs and then exited the room. This was the first break he had given her since she'd encountered him. She sensed some relief in the forecast, but after hours and hours of straight interrogation, Rhain's initial assumption proved to be wrong.

"Explain all of these e-mails and letters and poems to Susan, Miss Garrett, if she wasn't having a lesbian affair with you," Detective Somore said, slamming the pile of e-mails they had printed off of the computer in front of her.

Exhausted, Rhain could barely keep her head up. "I've explained it to you over and over," Rhain cried. "I was hired to send her those things. If you've managed to retrieve all of those e-mails, how come you can't find the one asking me to do these things?"

"I know coming out of the closet is embarrassing, Miss Garrett, but imagine how embarrassing this has all been for Mrs. McKinney," Detective Hughes stated. He then pulled out a copy of the *Columbus Dispatch* and laid it down in front of Rhain.

"What's this?" she said as she picked up the paper. She saw a picture of some woman who was fairly attractive. The name underneath the photo was that of Susan McKinney. Next to that picture was Rhain's mug shot with her name underneath the photo. But it was the headlines that had Rhain grabbing her aching belly. "'Woman arrested for killing her lesbian lover's husband,'" Rhain read the headlines. "I can't believe this is happening." Things had gone from bad to worse, to being just completely fucked up. "'Wife says she had an affair with Rhain Garrett, who later, out of jealousy, murdered her husband.'"

"See," Detective Hughes said, taking the paper

back from Rhain. "Mrs. McKinney came out of the closet. How hard do you think this is for her?"

"Mrs. McKinney is a liar!" Rhain shouted, slamming her fist down on the table. "I've never met that woman in my life."

"But you've sent her flowers and cologne," Detective Somore said. He pulled out a small card from the folder in front of him and began reading it, "'You don't need this to light up my life.'" He then threw the card over to Rhain. "Looks like your handwriting to me."

"That's because it is," Rhain said.

"So you admit that you sent this to your lover?" Detective Somore asked.

"Yes," Rhain said, tired and drained. "No, I mean, I sent it to Mrs. McKinney, but . . ." Rhain couldn't even finish speaking. She began trembling and just broke down in tears. "I keep telling you, it was her husband I was sleeping with, not her. I didn't even know her."

"Now tell us again why Mr. McKinney was even at your house," Detective Somore said, taking out his pad so that he could compare what Rhain was saying with his notes of what she had already told him.

"I can't . . . I can't remember anymore," Rhain cried as she collapsed onto the table. "I didn't do it."

"Yes, you did, Miss Garrett, just admit it," Detective Somore said to Rhain, feeling no sympathy. After all, Rhain was starting to cave in just like they wanted her to. "Mr. McKinney found out about you and his wife and he came over to confront you, didn't he? Once you saw what a nice-looking man he was, you figured, 'What the hell,' and went for him too. Or he looked at you and saw a nice-looking woman and figured, 'What the hell, if my wife is fucking her, so will I.' You two got into an argument. It started in the living room maybe. You two ended up in the bedroom, or the kitchen maybe—where you keep the knives . . ."

As Detective Somore continued to talk, Rhain began to visualize everything he was saying in her head. Pretty soon, the truth as she thought it had happened—her date with Fred—began to take the form of what Detective Somore was describing. *I did drink a lot of that tequila,* Rhain told herself. *Maybe I drank too much. I remember him being inside of me. We drank, we made love. We drank. We made love. I think.* Rhain buried her face in her hands and began rocking, trying to remember every detail of her weekend with Fred, but now there were so many blanks that she couldn't remember. All she could visualize now was what the detectives were telling her what happened.

"The next thing you knew," Detective Somore continued, "Mr. McKinney had you down on the kitchen floor and raped you. You were a virgin; no way did you give yourself to a man you had only met one time before, in a bar, no less. You're not that type of girl."

"You're right," Rhain said before she even knew what she was saying. "You're right. I wouldn't have done that." Rhain began to cry. "I'm not that type of girl."

Detective Hughes nodded at his partner, giving him the signal to keep going because they almost had her pushed just to where they wanted her, over the edge.

"He raped you. Not only that, but he was the husband of your lover, the woman who wouldn't leave her husband to be with you. You had to kill him, Rhain. You had to."

"Yes, I had to," she admitted. "I had to."

"And you stayed in all weekend, not knowing what to do with his body," Detective Somore said. "That's why when your friend—your neighbor—Sylvia tried calling you and coming over to your place, you couldn't answer the phone or let her in. You didn't know what to say to her over the phone, and if she came over, you were afraid she would see Fred."

"I was afraid Sylvia would see that Fred was still in my apartment. She'd know that he had never left. What would she think of me?" Rhain talked in a daze.

"After you killed Mr. McKinney, you cleaned up the apartment."

"I cleaned my apartment after Fred was gone," Rhain said, still talking in a daze.

"Somehow you managed to get his body down to that alley; wrapped him up in something maybe, and dragged him down the back stairs. Then you stuffed him behind the Dumpster. You called Sylvia later that night. You wanted to tell her what you had done, but you were afraid, so you just made up some story about Mr. McKinney spending the weekend with you."

"I called Sylvia." Tears began to pour down Rhain's face. "Oh God, everything you are saying I did. Oh my God. I killed Fred! I killed Fred!"

It had been fourteen hours since Rhain had been taken into the interrogation room, but she had finally told the detectives what they wanted to hear, that she had killed Frederick Simmons McKinney the third in cold blood.

Chapter IX

A Friend of Mine

"Garrett!" the guard called out as she distributed mail to the inmates who were gathered around hoping and praying that at least one of their family members or friends had thought enough of them to spend thirty-nine cents to mail them a letter. They didn't even care if the pages inside of the envelope were blank, or better yet, if the envelope itself was vacant. Just the concept of being thought of was enough. "Garrett!" the guard repeated.

"I'll accept it for her," a girl with long, thick jail-house braids down her back replied from the crowd.

The guard looked her up and down, allowing her eyes to stop at the midnight brown eyes of the six-foot-one-inch tall, could-have-been-a-WNBA basketball star. The guard twisted up her mug and looked at the girl like she stank and said, "Bitch, this ain't the fuckin' Oscars. What you talkin' about, you'll accept it for her?" The other inmates chuckled; some because it was slightly humorous to them, others because they were trying to befriend the smart-mouthed guard who hated her job at the prison and the women it housed even more. And rightfully so. This particular guard had been spat on, had piss and feces thrown at her, had been attacked, had been called names, and had been threatened over the five years of her employment. But the high she got from being in charge of another human being was worth all of the negative fringe benefits of the job.

"Here, take it," the guard said, handing it to the girl. "But next time tell Miss Langston Hughes to get her lazy ass out of her cell and come get her own mail." Once again, a few of the inmates chuckled at the guard's reference of Rhain to Langston Hughes. For the last year, Rhain had been writing letters and poems and making cards for other inmates just like she used to do when she was a free woman. Of course the pay wasn't nearly as good; nothing more than a Twinkie, postage, a book or something, but considering no one on the outside was putting any money on her books, she had to do something to make a little change in that place. So if she had to become part of the prison system, so did her dream—Rhain's Originals.

"Thanks," the girl said, snatching the letter from the guard, rolling her eyes and then walking away. "That bitch knows Rhain ain't got a lick of mail in the eighteen months she's been here," she mumbled under her breath as she headed back to the cell that she shared with Rhain.

When the woman arrived at their cell, Rhain was sitting Indian style on her top bunk doing her favorite pastime, writing in her journal.

"Hey, girl," Rhain's cellmate said, entering the cell with the letter behind her back.

Rhain tore her eyes away from her journal and looked up at her. "Oh hey, mama. What's up?"

"Got something for you," she said, pulling her hand from behind.

"What?" Rhain closed her journal and hopped down off the bunk, eyeballing the envelope the entire time.

"This!" She flashed the envelope like it was a shiny new nickel and she was a six-year-old little girl who had just found it lying on the sidewalk

"What is it?" Rhain said, extending her hand in slow motion to receive it.

"Mail, for you."

Rhain took the letter and stared at it momentarily. First she stared at her name on it. *Yes, it's really mine*, she thought. Next, she allowed her eyes to wander to the return address. Once she saw who the sender was, she retreated back to her top bunk. She laid down on her back and held the envelope up in front of her where she continued to stare at it before opening it.

"So, who's it from?" her celly asked, but Rhain was still zoned out as she stared at the letter. "Forget you, then." She smacked her lips, picked up her copy of *Sola*, a novel about a female assassin, by Dakota Knight, and got as comfortable as possible on her bottom bunk and started to read. By now, Rhain had ripped open the envelope and was reading as well:

Dear Rhain,
I know it's been a while since I've written you. Who am I kidding? This is my first time writing you

since you've been incarcerated. I just didn't know what to say, which is also why I never came back to visit you again after that first time.

Rhain paused from reading the letter as she thought about that day Sylvia had come to visit her in jail. She recalled the look of shock on Sylvia's face when she began ranting and raving like a lunatic. For the first time ever, her neighbor had seen an entirely different side of her—a side that, if one didn't know any better, might indicated the actions of a wild woman capable of murder. With that thought, Rhain came to the conclusion that maybe she shouldn't have reacted the way she did. But it was far too late for woulda, coulda, and shoulda. She found her place in the letter where she had left off and continued reading:

Although I haven't written or visited you, that doesn't mean that I haven't thought about you. I think about you constantly. My husband thinks I'm crazy, not that he didn't before; but now he does more than ever when sometimes I'm lying in bed thinking about some crazy conversation we've had and I just burst out laughing. You were so crazy, girl. I always thought of you as a homely and boring little thing, but now that I look back at it, you were, in your own way, indeed, a-one-of-a-kind trip . . . just what you've claimed to be—an original. I appreciate that about you so much more now.

The truth is, Rhain, I've always admired you. You never got caught up in the world and its crazy definitions of excitement and fun. You just lived in this private little world of your own, and I feel privileged that I'm one of the very few people, if there were ever any others, that you shared your world with.

Guess what? I'm saved now. I know you're crack-ing up; as foul as my mouth was and impure as my thoughts were. But you know I didn't have many friends around here. And although you never consid-ered yourself as having many friends either and always referred to me as your neighbor, you were my friend, Rhain. And once you were removed from my life, there seemed to be only one other friend to seek out, and that friend was Jesus.

Not to end this letter on a sour note, but I know you're only months away from being put to death. It was an article in today's newspaper that reminded me of such and prompted me to write this letter. But I just couldn't live with myself if I didn't at least make an effort to make it so that even after you leave this earth I can see you again.

A puzzled look crossed Rhain's face as she read that last line in the letter. *Okay, I'm tempted to agree with your husband, Sylvia; you are crazy.* Rhain laughed to herself and then continued to read the letter:

I know that you probably think that I'm crazy too. But what I'm trying to say is that now that I've given my life to Christ and believe that Jesus Christ died on that cross for me for the remission of my sins, I have the comfort of knowing that no matter what happens to me on this earth, I have a promise of eter-nal life with the father. In heaven is where I can see you again, Rhain, but first you have to believe in the same. Acts 2:21 of the Holy Bible says, "And it shall come to pass that whosoever shall call on the name of the Lord shall be saved."

Call upon Him, Rhain, for He is the only one who will not forsake you. I did. Man did. But He won't.

Call upon Him and believe what I said. But don't just take my word for it. Seek the word. Pick up the Bible, everything I'm telling you is there. So if you don't believe me, believe God, for He is not a liar and He is a fulfiller of all promises.

I love you, Rhain, and I'll see you in heaven . . . if you believe.

Love, Sylvia

Rhain had no idea that she was crying until the wet tears dripped into her ears and tingled them. She rested the letter down on her chest and stared up at the ceiling as if this God that Sylvia had talked about in her letter was going to appear. While staring up, she thought about all of the advice Sylvia had ever given her, most of which had panned out to be credible and of good mind. *Why would she steer me wrong now?* Rhain thought to herself, but just to be on the safe side, Rhain felt that some sort of confirmation was needed.

Rhain jumped out of her bed and headed out of the cell. As she walked through the prison, she ignored all of the hellos, catcalls, and foul remarks other inmates made toward her. She was on a mission and fully capable of blocking them out, which she did. She finally made her way to the prison library, where she walked up to one of the inmates who worked in the library.

"What do you need?" the girl asked Rhain when she looked up from the desk she was sitting at after feeling the presence of Rhain standing over her.

"I'm looking for a book in particular that I'm hoping you can help me find," Rhain spoke.

"Okay, I'll try," the woman said, rising from her seat. "And what book would that be?"

"A book about a friend of mine," Rhain replied.

"A friend of yours?" the woman said, almost in a chuckle of disbelief. "What is the title of the book that this so-called friend of yours is in?"

With a huge smile on her face, Rhain answered, "The Bible."

Chapter X

"Gotta Get Off on Your Own, Girl"

"Mmm, ohhh, uhhh, ahhh." Rhain moaned as she stroked her clit up and down expeditiously, as if masturbating was going out of style. But surrounded by nothing but women, if she wanted to please her sexual desires, she had no other choice but to finger herself unless she decided to hook up with another woman.

One might think that the last thing a girl on death row would be thinking about was sex, but two years after being convicted of the murder of Fred, Rhain's body still had needs, and she had promised herself that before she bumped uglies with another woman, she'd continue masturbating. Besides, she remembered reading something about homosexuality in the Bible and how it was a sin.

"Oooh, oooh, oooh," her cellmate said as she climaxed, twirking herself off in the lower bunk as she listened to Rhain moan and groan and rub her wetness. "Oh, my goodness." Her roommate huffed and puffed. "Is that what Al B. Sure meant by 'Gotta Get Off on Your Own, Girl'?"

Rhain burst out laughing at her cellmate's little funny. "Damn you, Pricilla, you fucked up my nut," Rhain said, sucking her teeth.

"Sorry," Pricilla laughed. "But I got mine."

"And you know that was probably going to be my last nut until I walk the green mile tomorrow," Rhain said in an attempt to find humor in the fact that the next day, at midnight, she would be put to death for the murder of Frederick Simmons Mc-Kinney the Third. She pulled her hand out of her pants and rested it on her stomach. She stared up at the ceiling and let out a deep sigh.

"You all right up there?" Pricilla asked, knowing that this being Rhain's last day on Earth had to be fucking with her head, even though she was trying to pretend like it wasn't.

"Yeah, as all right as I'm going to be," Rhain replied. There was a brief moment of silence until Pricilla spoke.

"Feel like braiding my hair?" she asked Rhain.

"It's already braided."

"Yeah, but they need to be redone. I washed it today with the braids in it. Just take each braid out one at a time and redo it for me. Come on. You know nobody can braid this long-ass shit like you do, and seeing how your ass ain't go'n be here to braid it no more . . ."

"Fuck you, Prissy." Rhain chuckled. "Have you no heart?"

"Oh, girl, you know what I'm trying to say."

"I know, boo," Rhain said, hopping down from her top bunk. "Come on, I'll do it."

"Cool," Pricilla said, getting up out of her bed to get her comb and brush. "But wash your hands first." She made a face as if she smelled a bad odor.

"You got your nerve," Rhain said as she walked over to the sink and washed her hands. Pricilla followed suit.

Rhain sat down on Pricilla's bed and opened her legs. Pricilla found her spot between her cellmate's legs and sat down with her back to Rhain. The girls chit-chatted for a while, and before they knew it, Rhain had already rebraided over half of Pricilla's hair.

While Rhain continued to finish off a couple more braids, Pricilla pondered over a question she had been wanting to ask Rhain. Since Rhain would be put to death the next day, she figured now was just as good a time as any, and pretty much the last time she would be able to. "Do you regret doing it?" Pricilla asked Rhain. "I mean, now that you have to die for doing it, do you regret killing that man?"

"You know what?" Rhain said as she thought for a minute before continuing. "I don't even remember doing it, let alone regret doing it. I don't even remember telling the cops I did it or writing that damn confession. I guess the whole situation was just so awful that I just blocked it all out."

"Yeah, well, I remember slicing up my stepfather and my moms," Pricilla said, "and I don't regret it, not one bit. That bastard would probably still be fucking me if I hadn't done something about it. And my moms, that bitch got it for not stopping his ass. I know she knew he was fucking me. I know she knew. For a long time I kept having this vision in my head; I just kept seeing her one day opening my bedroom door while he was fucking me, and then closing it. I mean, the bitch didn't call 911, come back in there with a butcher knife and cut his fucking throat or nothing. She just let it go on and on just so he could keep paying bills because her stupid ass never finished school and she was too illiterate to go out and get a job so that she could take care of her damn self. So that bitch deserved to die too."

Rhain took in Pricilla's harsh words. "You's a cold-blooded bitch," Rhain said as she finished the last braid of Pricilla's hair.

"That's what happens when society doesn't protect children. We protect ourselves—by any means necessary. Little girls like me who nobody cares about grow up to be just what you said, cold-blooded bitches."

Even despite the harsh words Pricilla tried to hide her feelings behind, Rhain knew that deep down inside, she was nothing but that same scared and hurt little girl who used to get molested by her stepfather. Rhain felt sorry for her. "Well, if I had been your mother, I would have protected you," Rhain said with a smile in an attempt to comfort her cellmate.

Pricilla turned around and faced Rhain. "I know you would have." She smiled back. "You're a good girl," Pricilla said, reaching up to touch Rhain's face. "And you would have been a good mother too. Just the kind of mother a girl like me needed. And I would have been a good little girl too. Then maybe things would have turned out different for us."

As Rhain sat there staring at Pricilla while she rubbed her face, the soft, gentle touch felt so good to her. Rhain closed her eyes and took in Pricilla's touch. It would be the last touch she'd ever receive from another human being, besides when they strapped her down to lethally inject her. And it felt good to Pricilla to be touching someone as sweet and as caring as Rhain. Stroking Rhain's face with one hand, Pricilla placed her other hand on Rhain's knee and allowed it to slowly travel up her leg and then down inside her pants. There Pricilla sat between Rhain's legs, stroking her face with one hand while stroking her pussy with the other hand.

At first, Rhain moaned in ecstasy, but when she opened her eyes and they focused in on Pricilla and she realized that it was another woman making her feel so good, she pushed Pricilla away and tried to get up. *What would Jesus do?* she asked herself.

"Don't," Pricilla said softly. "Don't push me away, Rhain." She was almost pleading. "Let me make you feel good."

"Pricilla, I can't," she said, shaking her head. Rhain tried to smile to let her know that it wasn't personal; she just didn't get down like that.

"Please, Rhain," Pricilla said, managing to put her hand back down Rhain's pants and massage her throbbing clit. "I owe you. After all, I did fuck up your last nut. Let me pay you back."

Before Rhain could reply, Pricilla leaned her head on Rhain's chest and rested it there and focused on plunging her fingers in and out of Rhain's waterfall. Just like lots of people struggling with their spiritual walk, Rhain was overcome by her flesh. She'd have to repent later.

"Oh, Pricilla," Rhain moaned as she rubbed her hand down Pricilla's freshly done braids and began pumping her hips back and forth, fucking her fingers.

Pricilla looked over her shoulder to make sure the coast was clear; then she began French-kissing

Rhain, pushing her down on her bed while still massaging her moistness.

"Pull the cover over us," Rhain whispered.

Pricilla did as she was told, staying on top of Rhain. When she pulled the cover over them, she wormed her way down to Rhain's pussy, pulling down Rhain's pants. After sliding Rhain's pants off, she buried her face in Rhain's pussy and began fucking her with her tongue. She licked and sucked Rhain's clit while fingering her.

"Oh, Rhain, you taste so good, baby," Pricilla said. "You taste so good."

Pricilla removed her own pants while she continued eating Rhain out. Once her pants were off, she laid her body on top of Rhain's and began grinding her hairy pussy on Rhain's.

"I'm going to miss you," Pricilla said to Rhain as tears filled her eyes.

"I'm going to miss you too, girl," Rhain said as her eyes filled with tears at just the thought of knowing her life would soon come to an end.

Pricilla then proceeded to kiss Rhain and press her coochie against Rhain's. She then reached her hands down and separated Rhain's pussy lips and pressed her clit against Rhain's thick clit. Pressing herself firmly against Rhain, she began pumping her and Rhain began pumping her back, keeping up nicely with her rhythm.

"Oh, Rhain," Pricilla moaned.

"Mmm," Rhain hummed.

"You got the bomb-ass pussy, Rhain. Just like I knew you would. Does it feel good to you?" Pricilla said as she stared down at Rhain, grinding her hard. "Huh? Does it?"

"Yes," Rhain said in an inaudible moan.

"Does it, baby? Does it feel good? Let me hear you say it. Say it louder."

"Yes, yes, yes," Rhain mumbled in a groan.

Pricilla covered Rhain's mouth with her own and fucked her wildly as the two women came in ecstasy. Together the two women cried.

When the two of them heard footsteps coming, Rhain quickly retrieved her pants and climbed out of Pricilla's bed and into her own. Pricilla put her pants back on and pulled the covers over her just before the guard showed up at their cell.

"You have a visitor," the guard spoke.

"Who?" Pricilla asked.

"You, Garrett," the guard said, looking up at Rhain. "Let's go."

Rhain climbed out of her bed and gave Pricilla a puzzled look, wondering who on earth could be coming to visit her.

Maybe it's my father, Rhain thought as she was led out of her cell and to the visiting room. *Wouldn't that be about a blimp? My father coming to see me after all these years?*

Once Rhain arrived in the visiting room and the guard pointed her toward the strange woman sitting at the table waiting for her, she knew that the visitor wasn't her father.

"Rhain Garrett?" the woman stood up and asked once Rhain approached the table. She then extended her hand toward Rhain.

"Yes," Rhain said, trying to figure out who the woman was. As Rhain held out her arm to shake the woman's hand, it dawned on her just exactly who the woman was. Her hair was different than it was the day the detectives had shown Rhain the picture of her in the newspaper, but it was her all right.

"I'm Susan, Susan McKinney," the woman said, then took her seat. Rhain just stood there trippin' as the woman signaled for her to sit down as well, which she did. "I begged them to allow me to see you. I know you're wondering why I'm here, so I'll get right to it. I know you didn't kill my husband, Miss Garrett, and I know you didn't because . . ." She paused and used her index finger to signal Rhain to lean in closer to her. When Rhain leaned in, Susan pressed her lips against Rhain's ear and whispered, "Because I did." Susan then pulled back and looked at Rhain with a devilish grin.

Rhain just sat there stunned with a confused look on her face as Susan explained herself. "I found your business card in the son of a bitch's coat pocket," Susan stated. "At first I thought to myself, hell, maybe this is business. But then when I flipped the card over and saw your home phone number handwritten on the back of it, I knew it was anything but business. After all, your business number was printed on the front of the card, so if it was business, he wouldn't have needed your home number, right?" Susan asked, continuing without waiting for Rhain to reply. "So I visited your Web site, and I was pretty intrigued by that little ghostwriting business of yours. I figured it must have been your creativeness that attracted Frederick to you in the first place, so I decided to be a little creative myself. That's when I came up with the idea to manipulate you into pursuing me. Of course I had to hire you to do it. And God knows I hated coming off of that fifteen hundred dollars, but I figured that was much cheaper than a hit man." She chuckled. "I followed him that night to your apartment. All of those weekends away on business—I knew that son of a bitch was lying. Then he'd come home to me complaining about sleeping in strange beds all over the country. Fucker was sleeping in pussy is what he was doing."

Once Rhain was finally able to get a grasp of the reality she was now plagued with, she spoke. "But, I . . . I didn't know Fred was married."

"Fred? You called him Fred? Humph," she said, shrugging her shoulders. "You two got close quick, huh? Do you always get so close to other women's husbands?" Susan was now becoming visibly angry.

"I swear to you, I really didn't know that—"

Susan cut her off. "Sure, that's what they all say."

"But—"

"Look, I guess what you knew then and what you didn't know then doesn't matter. All that matters is what you know now, and that's the fact that you fucked my husband, so it was only fair turnabout that I fucked you." A horrible cackle came from Susan's mouth. "And boy did I fuck you. I guess the saying is right: Revenge is best served cold—cold blooded. I mean, what woman wouldn't love to see both her cheating husband and his whore of a mistress dead?" Susan said. "Looks like with Frederick's death, though, I was able to kill two birds with one stone."

Tears filled Rhain's eyes. She couldn't believe what she was hearing. She was going to be put to death for a murder that she didn't commit. No wonder she didn't remember killing Fred; she hadn't killed him. All of those consecutive hours of being interrogated by the detectives had made her delusional. The story they planted in her head was what she believed to be true, but yet here the truth was slapping her dead across the face.

"Anyway," Susan said, standing up with a sigh as

if Rhain had wasted enough of her time. "I hope you enjoyed sex with my husband while you could. I always did when he was at home fucking me and not whores like you. Nevertheless, the way ol' Frederick boy could beat up a pussy, I know it was good for you. As a matter of fact"—she leaned down in Rhain's face—"wasn't his dick just to die for?" Susan began laughing hysterically at her little pun as she began walking away toward the exit. Before she made her exit, she turned to Rhain and shouted, "See you in hell."

With a huge knot in her throat, Rhain just sat there. She couldn't move. She couldn't say anything. Hell, she could barely breathe.

"Visit's over. Come on, Garrett, let's go," the guard said as they walked over and stood behind Rhain. Still Rhain couldn't move. "Garrett, let's go," the guard said louder.

After several repetitive deep, heavy breaths, Rhain's chest began going up and down as the roaring tears tried to fight their way out. Finally they succeeded.

"Nooooooooo!" Rhain began to yell. "Noooooooooo!"

The next thing Rhain knew, she was flailing her arms and screaming. The last thing she knew was that she had been clubbed over the head by the guard. Lights out.

Chapter XI
Déjà Vu

With a guard on each side of her and the chaplain a couple steps behind her with Bible in tow, Rhain took the last steps she would ever take. Her life flashed before her eyes. For so many years she had just lived—but never lived it up. It wasn't until those last couple of days, before she was hauled off to jail, that she had decided to let her inhibitions go. If only she had done so a long time ago. If only she had taken Sylvia's advice and had just lived like the young vibrant woman she was. But now it was too late.

"This is it, Garrett," one of the guards said as they approached a closed door.

Rhain stopped and stared at the closed door; she knew that her final fate was on the other side. She swallowed hard. Tears filled her eyes as she began to tremble. The chaplain placed his hand on her

shoulder. She turned and looked at him as a tear
rolled down her cheek.

"Your Lord and Savior Jesus Christ awaits you
with open arms, but only if you believe that He died
for the remission of your sins. He loves you, no
matter what, for He knows that even sinners have
souls."

Rhain turned around and took a deep breath.
One guard opened the door, and they led her
inside. Once inside the room, Rhain looked around
in complete terror. It was then that she wished she
had listened to her public defender and filed an
appeal.

The room's walls were painted white and the
floor was white tile. And in the middle of the room
sat a stool with a rope dangling over it that was
hanging from the ceiling.

"What . . . what . . . what's that rope for?" Rhain
asked nervously as she tried to jerk away from the
guards. "What the hell is going on? Is this some
kind of joke?"

"Miss Rhain Garrett," a man in a white coat
walked up to her and stated, "you are sentenced to
die by hanging."

"No!" Rhain shouted. "No! No! Noooooooo-
oooo!" Rhain yelled as the guards restrained her
and walked her over to the rope. "Oh God, no!
This can't be happening."

"The Lord is my shepherd, I shall not want,"
Rhain heard the chaplain praying as the guards
lifted Rhain to the stool and placed the rope around
her neck.

"Noooo," she yelled as she felt the rope burn her
neck as it tightened around her. "Noooo!"

The next thing Rhain knew, the stool was suddenly removed from underneath her. Her neck snapped and her feet dangled three feet from the ground.

"Noooooo," Rhain heard herself yell as she frantically rose up in bed from her sleep. Immediately she put her hands around her throat. "It was only a dream," she said, relieved, as she breathed heavily. "It was all just a bad dream." Rhain looked down at her pajama top, which was clinging to her with wetness from the cold sweat she had awakened out of. "Yes, just a dream. I still have my sanity, and I still have my job—for now anyway." Rhain took a huge deep breath of relief.

Rhain got out of her bed and headed to the bathroom to take a shower. After getting out of the shower and changing into some fresh pajamas, she returned to her bed. At first she was afraid to close her eyes for fear that once she drifted off to sleep, she would have another nightmare. But she soon convinced herself that lightning wouldn't strike twice and she fell back to sleep.

"Jesus!" Rhain said, grabbing her heart upon the ringing of the phone that had brought her out of sleep. After another ring, Rhain answered the phone. "Hello," Rhain said into the receiver.

"Are you wet?" the voice on the other end said.

"Excuse me?" Rhain questioned with a weird look on her face.

"I said, are you wet?" the voice repeated. "Your name is Rhain, isn't it? Rhain, wet, Rhain, wet . . . get it?" Rhain didn't reply. "I suppose that isn't such a good opening line for my first phone call to you, huh?"

By then, the voice registered in Rhain's head and she knew just who the caller was.

"Fred," Rhain said, making sure she said his name in a statement form and not as a question. She wanted him to know that she knew exactly who he was, that she didn't just go around giving her number out to men in bars.

"Miss Garrett." He laughed. "I guess I better keep my day job. Comedy's not my thing, huh?"

"Uh, no, it's not," Rhain agreed with a slight chuckle.

"So, how's your day?"

Rhain looked over at the clock. It was already two o'clock in the afternoon. It took her so long to get to sleep after tossing and turning that she didn't realize how late it was. "It's a day. I can't complain. How's yours?"

"Aaah, so-so." There was a moment of silence. "So . . ."

"So, how about that drink? You agreed that we could get together again sometime like we did in Carlos'."

Rhain sat on the phone in silence. She definitely knew what Beyonce was singing about with that "Déjà vu" song. And if Rhain was going to experience déjà vu, it damn sure wasn't going to be anything from that lifelike nightmare she had had.

"I'm sorry, Fred, but I'm going to have to renege on my word," Rhain said. "It wouldn't be fair for me to lead you on and make you think that you have a chance with me. You see, I'm in love with somebody." Rhain smiled as those words crossed her lips.

"In love?" Fred questioned. "Well, this person you're in love with . . . he's one lucky man."

"It's not a man," Rhain declared.

"Oh." Fred sounded shocked. "Then this person you're in love with . . . he's . . . rather, she's a lucky woman."

Rhain chuckled. "It's not a she either."

"Oh, okay, well, I'm not into bestiality or anything like that."

Rhain burst out laughing. "No, silly, it's not a dog or anything like that either."

Curious to know who was coming between him and his drink with the woman he thought might be the girl of his dreams, Fred continued to inquire. "Well, who are you in love with?"

"Myself," Rhain said with a huge smile on her face before hanging up the phone. "I'm in love with myself." And she truly was.

For the first time in her life, Rhain truly felt content in her skin. She was happy with the person God had designed her to be. If God wanted her to have a gap between her teeth and acne all over her face, then so be it. Those were external things that could be fixed. What mattered was what was inside, and that was a talented, decent, and genuine person. Inside of Rhain was a gift from God that was bursting at the seams to get out, and she was no longer going to keep it concealed in any form. It was time to step out on a limb called *faith*, because the limb is where the fruit is anyway.

After hanging up the phone with Fred, Rhain walked over to her computer and logged on. She then began typing up her resignation letter that she planned on turning in to her boss on Monday. Perhaps she'd never know the true meaning behind the dream she had, but she did get one thing out of it—something reality had failed to give her all of these years—and that was inspiration. Now she and her words no longer had to hide behind other people. And that included her well-paying client, Carrington69. She couldn't type fast enough the e-mail she sent him notifying him that she was no longer available to continue with his project.

As Rhain created a new document in order to write what she knew in her heart was going to be a bestseller, she stated, "Finally, I've got something of my own to write about! No more ghostwriting for me."

THE END

About the Author

Joy, a native of Columbus, Ohio, after thirteen years of being a paralegal in the insurance industry, finally divorced her career and married her mistress and her passion, writing.

In the year 2000 she formed her own publishing company, END OF THE RAINBOW. Her sole purpose with END OF THE RAINBOW was to introduce, to all those she encountered, the quality of sharing her grandmother had instilled in her. This domino reaction would incite those with a passion in life to envision and manifest it, and those unaware of their passion, to unearth it. Joy shares what she has learned in the literary industry by conducting a workshop titled **Self-Publishing: The Basics You Need to Get Started**. In this informative workshop, Joy touches on everything from copyrighting and bar coding to ISBNs and economical printing on demand.

In 2004 Joy branched off into the business of literary consulting, in which she provides one-on-one consulting, and literary services such as ghostwriting, professional read-throughs, and so on. Her clients consist of first-time authors, national bestselling authors, and entertainers. Joy has been able to present a couple of clients' manuscripts to a publisher and land book deals for them.

Joy has come a long way since the debut of her first title, **Please Tell Me If the Grass Is Greener.** Since then she has published a diary of poems titled **World on My Shoulders;** she has collaborated on the publication of an erotica anthology titled

Twilight Moods, in which her contribution is titled **"Daydreaming at Night";** and she was also featured in **The Game: Short Stories about the Life**, in which her contribution is titled **"Popped Cherry."**

Joy has also written a children's work titled **The Secret Olivia Told Me,** which will be published in Spring 2007 by Just Us Books under the name E. N. Joy. Joy self-published her first full-length novel, titled **The Root of All Evil,** which was eventually picked up by a major publishing house and rereleased. In addition, they signed Joy to do two other novels, her *Essence* magazine best-seller, **If I Ruled the World,** and **When Souls Mate** (the sequel to **The Root of All Evil**). They also signed Joy to a novella deal titled **An All Night Man,** in which Joy's contribution is titled **"Just Wanna Love Ya."** Joy's triumphant street novel **Dollar Bill** is also an *Essence* magazine best-seller.

In another of her works, Joy was able to shine with two of the brightest stars in the literary field, Nikki Turner and Kashamba Williams, in the anthology **Girls from Da Hood 2,** in which Joy's contribution is titled **"Wanna B."** In 2007 her short story titled **"BEYATCH!!!"** will appear in **Street Chronicles, Volume 2 . . . The Girls in the Game Edition** and her short story titled **"Life of Sin"** will appear in an Urban Erotic anthology presented by Noire. She also has a short story titled **"Behind Every Good Woman,"** which will be published in 2007, in an anthology titled **Summer Breeze.** Her full-length novels **Mama, I'm in Love (. . . with a gangsta)** and **WET** are 2006 and 2007 releases.

Not forsaking her love of poetry, Joy published several of her poems in 2006 in a book of poems titled **Traces of Love**. "I plan to turn my focus back to poetry one day soon," Joy says. "I still write poetry and have another diary of poems, titled **Flower in My Hair,** waiting in the wings. But lately my spirit has been moving in another direction." Needless to say, Joy will no longer be penning street lit, erotica, or adult fiction after the release of the above-mentioned forthcoming titles. Joy, under the name E. N. Joy, is the editor of, as well as a contributing author to, the anthology titled **Even Sinners Have Souls**, which features the literary industry's most dominant and prolific authors in the urban street lit arena as well as urban erotica/romance, where they will take a break from penning their norm to publish a work that gives God total glory. **Even Sinners Have Souls** is more than just a book; it's a movement and a phenomenon. It's a ministry. Joy is currently working on a Christian fiction piece titled **Me, Myself and Him** that will debut under Urban Christian in the fall of 2008 under the name E. N. Joy. In this novel, a woman struggles in her walk with God because she's trying to hold on to the love of a not-so-God-fearing mate. She realizes the difficulty of trying to live in the word while walking in the world. Finding herself trying to please man and God, she encounters the tough issues of reality. Of course this novel pushes the envelope of Christian fiction, but it wouldn't be Joy's true literary style if she didn't do this. "I have matured both as a; writer and spiritually. My walk in life has changed, therefore my writing has changed; I just hope that the dedicated following of readers I've been so blessed to have earned will decide to take this spiritual journey in the written word with me as I shift from writing any more Joy books and Joylynn M. Jossel books to pen what God has called me to do."

Joy continued by saying, "When God called me, I had to be obedient and say, 'Yes, Lord. No more street fiction; no more erotica.' Giving up writing under those names and what they stood for is like giving up the old me, which I don't mind at all. My intent is not to switch up to a different audience completely. Hopefully I won't lose the readers I already have, but instead, gain the readers I don't have. I know I might have to give up a few of my readers that I've worked so hard over the years to earn . . . but my soul still says YES!"

You can visit JOY at www.JoylynnJossel.com